"I thought you were on special assignment with... what's his name again?"

"Cullen Archer," Mei said with a sigh as she slipped past Chief Catherine Tanner.

"So what's wrong? Why aren't you two nosing around the nightclub where that courier was killed?"

Mei shook her head. "I don't know." Swallowing hard, she muttered, "No...I do know. It has to do with my family. Cullen—ah, he said to call him that—wants to start our investigation at my father's gallery."

Catherine frowned. "Surely Interpol doesn't think—I mean, *you* don't suspect your father in any way?"

"No," Mei shot back quickly. "But...you know my relationship with my folks. I can't march into my father's office acting like the cop they never wanted me to be."

"A cop is what you are, Mei Lu," Catherine said with no softness in her tone. "It's the career you chose. You took an oath to uphold the law, which transcends all other loyalties." Catherine paused. "Tell Archer straight out about your concerns."

Mei Lu nodded dutifully. It wasn't what she'd hoped for. She'd really wanted Catherine to take her off the case—not just because of her father but because Cullen Archer made her feel more a woman and less a cop.

Dear Reader,

It's always exciting to be asked to participate in a continuity within the Harlequin Superromance line. It means individual authors have an opportunity to work closely with fellow writers to develop a group of loosely connected stories. WOMEN IN BLUE is one of these.

My story, like the other five in this continuity, is first and foremost a love story about two people whose lives are enriched after their paths cross. Mei Lu Ling is a Houston cop attached to the White Collar Crimes division. Her family owns and operates a prestigious import and export firm dealing in high-end Asian art. She left the family business, electing instead to become a police officer. She went through the training academy with five other women; they formed close ties. The five friends understood Mei's problems with her family and helped her cope with an ever-widening estrangement. So it came as a blow when an unforeseen situation (described in the first book of the series) caused the women to pull away from one another.

Suddenly the police chief (one of the original six "women in blue") assigns Mei Lu to special duty as a Chinese-language translator for Cullen Archer. He's an insurance investigator working with Interpol to break up a smuggling ring that's moving national treasures out of China. Mei Lu is drawn to Cullen, but she initially has doubts that center on his ex-wife. Mei is also drawn to his adorable twins. Cullen, meanwhile, tries not to suspect Mei's father or her brother of being involved. Throughout the story, events conspire to bring them together—and keep them apart.

I hope readers will want to read about all the individual struggles faced by these six friends, the WOMEN IN BLUE.

Roz Denny Fox

I love hearing from readers. You can reach me at P.O. Box 17480-101, Tucson, AZ 85731 or via my Web site, www.korynna.com/RozFox

She Walks the Line
Roz Denny Fox

HARLEQUIN®

TORONTO • NEW YORK • LONDON
AMSTERDAM • PARIS • SYDNEY • HAMBURG
STOCKHOLM • ATHENS • TOKYO • MILAN • MADRID
PRAGUE • WARSAW • BUDAPEST • AUCKLAND

ISBN 0-373-71254-5

SHE WALKS THE LINE

www.eHarlequin.com

Printed in U.S.A.

To the other five authors of WOMEN IN BLUE:
Kay David, Sherry Lewis, Linda Style, Anna Adams and
K.N. Casper—it's been a treat to work with you. Likewise,
my appreciation to our individual editors. This continuity
has been made more cohesive thanks to your extra effort.

Books by Roz Denny Fox

HARLEQUIN SUPERROMANCE

CHAPTER ONE

MEI LU LING SHRUGGED into her shoulder holster and slid it into place. She took a moment to reflect on last Friday's ceremony, which allowed her to walk into Houston PD headquarters a full-fledged lieutenant. Only two of her four best friends from the academy, a twenty-six-week class that now seemed a distant memory, had attended her ceremony, even though Mei had invited them all.

She'd noticed Crista Santiago at the back of the room, and Risa Taylor had popped in long enough to see Catherine Tanner, the chief, do the honors. Mei was happy her new department captain had had a court commitment, and that Catherine had volunteered to replace him. It also pleased her that two of her friends had been able to slip away from their duties. Especially Risa, considering everything she'd undergone not long ago at the hands of the internal review board. Risa and Crista were the only members of their once close-knit group who knew what it was like to struggle up the department ladder without family support. And none of Mei's family would have put in an appearance if their lives depended on it.

But, at thirty-one, after more than six years as a cop, Mei had no regrets. She was content with her life and a career solving white-collar crime in the city where she was born and raised.

Stepping back to scrutinize her full image in the bedroom mirror, Mei rechecked her dark hair, twisted into a knot at the nape of her neck. When she'd entered the academy she'd been advised to cut her waist-length hair, and she had. She'd worn a pixie cut until after leaving street patrol, because the dregs of society fought dirty, and a woman couldn't afford to have hair a perpetrator could grab. Now, though, she worked more with "civilized" crooks.

The thought of any crook being civilized prompted an involuntary smile as she donned her trim navy jacket. Satisfied that she looked okay Mei detoured through the kitchen on her way out in order to bid her dog goodbye. He was a mixed-breed shelter rescue she'd named Foo Manchu—mostly to irritate her mother. Aun Ling disliked anything that poked fun at things Chinese. She detested her son, Stephen's, Foo Fighter tapes. Aun collected jade and porcelain figurines of Chinese Fu dogs. Mei had always loved the collection, and as a kid had spent hours dusting it. Perhaps another reason she'd chosen the name Foo.

She checked his automatic pet feeder to make sure there was enough kibble in case her day ran late, then headed outside into a beautiful March morning. At the curb, she unlocked and climbed into an aging subcompact, a sorry-looking vehicle Mei Lu prayed would last until she could find time to test-drive and buy a new model.

Her home—half of a duplex that sat two blocks off Bellaire Boulevard in a slightly seedy part of town—and her automobile were major blights on her life, as far as her affluent parents were concerned. They lived in an upscale area known for rambling homes built on huge lots. Mei preferred her eclectic neighborhood, insisting that her street was as safe as any in the city.

A fifty-minute battle through heavy traffic brought her to the police department parking garage downtown. She walked into the office early, out of habit. Few of her colleagues in her new unit were at their desks yet. Propped in the middle of hers sat a message from Chief Tanner, requesting Mei's presence upstairs.

Mei let her mind run through cases she'd closed or passed on before leaving her old group, but she couldn't think of one that would necessitate an urgent audience with the chief. She remained apprehensive, however, as she folded the note and hurried from the room.

It was well-known that women on the force had to take extra care to dot every *i* and cross every *t*. More so than a man working a similar case. Police departments had long been bastions of good-old-boy philosophies, so it helped that Mei and the four other women had entered the academy at a time when Catherine Tanner served as an instructor. She'd helped them avoid the pitfalls she'd had to navigate herself. Nevertheless, Mei was again reminded of Risa's recent problems with Internal Affairs. She'd been accused of shooting her partner, which had sparked a messy investigation that had affected all their jobs. As a result, their trust in one another had shattered. Mei, Crista, Lucy Montalvo and Abby Carlton had temporarily stopped meeting for any reason. Heck, who was she kidding? The friends were still wary and scattered. Risa's problem had caused seemingly irreparable damage to their friendship. They'd all become a lot more hesitant about confiding in peers. As well, Risa's ordeal had left Mei Lu feeling extra worried about a summons of the type that crinkled in her pocket as she was shown into the chief's office by Annette Hayworth, Catherine's personal assistant.

Mei's qualms tripled when Catherine, lacking her normal smile, rose from her desk and shut the door. Lately, everyone had sensed a greater-than-usual tension in their chief. Since Catherine made such a point of closing the door, Mei assumed this call was personal and, therefore, serious.

More uncertain than she'd ever been around the woman she considered friend and mentor, Mei hovered at the entrance. Rather than take a seat automatically, she blurted, "Has someone lodged a complaint against my promotion already?"

"What? No. Nothing of the sort." The chief returned to her desk and motioned Mei into a chair opposite. The diamond chips in Catherine's wedding band sparkled in the morning sun streaming through a side window. Although she'd been widowed for almost a year, the ring was one of Chief Tanner's few feminine accessories. She was broad-shouldered but slender and her six-foot height in regulation pumps intimidated many people. Although not as a rule Mei Lu…

Mei sank into the straight-backed chair, only slightly reassured by the denial.

"I called you here to discuss a new case that's come to my attention," Catherine said. She picked up a yellow legal pad and thumbed back two or three pages.

"Ah. Another pillar in our community suspected of corporate crime?" Mei finally smiled. She loved digging into puzzles that, when all was said and done, amounted to fraud, embezzlement or elaborate con games. A degree in Business Administration, plus having served three years in her father's Hong Kong office, gave her an advantage over others in her department. Mei's background allowed her to navigate elite cocktail parties where careful listening sometimes exposed corporate wrongdoing. Many of her male colleagues stood out like sore thumbs at such events.

"This case is unusual," Catherine continued. "It appears we have a new ring of smugglers here. Asian artifacts," she said. "Rare pieces, I'm told."

Mei's stomach tightened. Her father, Michael Ling, and her brother, Stephen, bought and sold high-end Asian art. Ling Limited dealt in expensive, often one-of-a-kind, authentic Chinese works, many of them antique. Surely Catherine didn't suspect Mei's family of anything unethical?

"I received a call from a Brett Davis at Interpol. Cullen Archer, a patron in the Houston art world, is their local contact. Actually Archer is a notable private insurance investigator. I'm told he's scrupulous and has a history of producing results for our foreign counterparts when it comes to tracking stolen paintings and such."

"I'm happy to serve in any way I can," Mei said, bowing her head. "But if Mr. Archer is so effective, how can I possibly augment his work?"

"I'm assigning you for several reasons, not the least of which is your dedication to the investigative process. I trust you implicitly and this case is classified, Mei Lu. The missing pieces are from Beijing museums. High-ranking officials stand to lose their jobs if the items aren't located." Catherine tore off a sheet of paper and wrote in bold, broad strokes. "This is Mr. Archer's home address. He's expecting you within the hour."

"Is this more than a one-time consultation?" Rising, Mei Lu accepted the address. She felt marginally better for having heard the chief's glowing words of praise.

"All I really know is that Archer needs a note deciphered. It's written in Chinese. I'll let your captain know I have you on special assignment. We'll leave the length of time open-ended until I hear back from you or Archer."

With her composure restored, Mei pocketed the paper

and strode briskly from the office. Her last stop before leaving the station was to sign out one of the new stun guns she'd qualified on last week.

In her car, she consulted a map. The address lay within what locals called the Memorial area—elegant, older estates that screamed inherited wealth. Mei didn't know why that surprised her. Private insurance investigators were well paid—usually ten percent of the insured value. On an item insured for a million, his cut would be a hundred grand so it stood to reason that he'd be an art patron. She hadn't expected Mr. Archer to live this close to where she'd grown up, though. Her parents' home was in a newer gated community. Mei Lu envisioned having to jump through all manner of security hoops to gain entry to Archer's house.

When she found the proper coordinates and turned down a tree-lined drive, she discovered the majority of estates boasted perimeter wrought-iron fences equipped with electronic surveillance devices that allowed visitors to address someone inside via a speakerphone.

Mei pulled up to Archer's gate and pressed the bell. A woman identifying herself as Freda answered. "Is this the home of Mr. Cullen Archer? If so, he's expecting Lieutenant Ling."

The woman's response was raspy and garbled. What she repeated sounded like *Lieutenant Lu*. Mei assumed the woman had confused her middle and surnames which was common enough. Rather than correct her, Mei shouted, "Yes." Like magic, the big gates swung inward on well-oiled hinges.

The house, partially hidden from the street, came into view as Mei rounded a gentle curve. She liked it immediately. It was a two-story rambling structure, the upper floors supported by stucco arches—not pillars, but wide arches forming a covered walkway that in a few months would offer shelter from the hot summer sun. The arches were repeated on a building connected to the main home by a breezeway dripping with vines. As Mei drove past a colorful bed of spring annuals, she saw a six-car garage. A similar extension directly opposite the garage was probably quarters for a housekeeper, or house manager, as many were now called.

The parklike grounds were immaculate, she noticed, worrying what the owners would think if they glanced out the tall windows and saw the wreck driven by one of Houston's finest. Her Toyota clearly needed washing—as well as some body work, courtesy of a recent hit-and-run on her street.

Mei didn't know if it was the opulence facing her, but something made her flip down her sunshade and check her makeup in the mirror. She wore only a smudge of shadow to accent her dark eyes, but now extracted a tube of peach gloss and swept it lightly across her lips before gathering her notebook and small square purse, which thankfully matched her tan pumps. Mei loved suits and had been happy to leave uniforms behind after her rotation on street patrol. The March weather was still pleasant enough for suits.

Vowing not to let the Archers intimidate her, no matter how old their money, Mei slid from her car. Even at that, she dragged in a deep breath as she approached the imposing nine-foot-tall, carved wooden doors.

The bell she pressed sounded muffled by distance. No surprise there. What she didn't expect was to have the door yanked open by a freckle-faced, red-haired woman probably in her mid-fifties. Racing back and forth behind the harried-looking woman was a gap-toothed boy in bathing trunks, dripping water all over the marble entry. A second child, this one a pigtailed girl, also in swim wear, screeched in a high-pitched voice, "Freda, shut the door! Mopsy's gonna escape!"

The woman grabbed Mei's elbow and jerked her inside just as the boy chortled triumphantly and dropped a brightly colored bathing towel over a huge white rabbit. The girl fell to her knees and scooped up the squirming bundle, forcing Mei to leap aside once again. The children looked almost alike, except that the boy had short-cropped hair and the girl had soaking wet braids that stuck out at odd angles.

"Phew!" The adult—the housekeeper from what Mei could deduce—scraped wisps of hair off a perspiring forehead. "I'm not even going to ask which of you rascals opened that rabbit's cage *this* time. You have ten seconds to put her back before I have a chat with you-know-who." The woman rolled her eyes elaborately to the left, and the children, faces decidedly guilty, ran up a wide curving staircase amid protests and giggles.

Mei watched their progress. She saw first one, then two long white ears and a twitching pink nose peek out from under the towel both children fought to carry.

"Excuse our chaos," Freda murmured. "Follow me please, Lieutenant. I'll take you to Mr. Archer. He's in his office and said to show you right in."

The woman dashed off, deftly avoiding a pile of little olive-green men Mei identified as toy soldiers. As she walked, Freda pushed aside a doll carriage and then a big red fire engine. Mei picked her way through various rooms and hallways, noting as she did how incongruous the toys were among well-lit, clearly locked cases containing Samurai swords. On a wall, she spied at least two Renoirs. Scattered among overturned toys were pedestals on which stood Chinese vases that appeared to be the real thing.

In Mei's childhood home, as she and her brother were growing up, neither would've been allowed to leave toys within sight of guests. She and Stephen had had a room designated for play. Even there, her mother expected order at all times.

Because the man she'd come to see was on the phone when Freda opened his office door, Mei had a chance to assess him.

Cullen Archer glanced up and rose politely while attempting to end his call. "Cloris, I'll fax you a list of the people we invited to the Villareal showing last year, okay?"

Freda's gesture toward Mei Lu appeared to suffice as an introduction. Archer acknowledged her presence with a nod. But then Mei Lu felt abandoned by the housekeeper, who left her standing awkwardly in front of a total stranger.

And when she took a second look at Cullen Archer, Mei suffered a little punch to her stomach. Not easily rocked by a man's looks, she found it odd that her heart beat noticeably harder. Granted, he was tall, rangy and casually but expensively dressed. An abundance of black hair glinted silver at his temples.

He was distinguished, yes. But Mei had expected a much older man. Even after seeing the children, she'd presumed her host had grandchildren visiting. These homes typically belonged to Houston's long-established residents.

Clearly, the western-cut shirt Archer wore didn't come off any rack. Nor did his gray slacks, one leg of which had caught on the upper edge of rich-looking, hand-tooled cowboy boots. It wasn't until he stepped around his desk and pulled out a chair he obviously intended for her that Mei drew near enough to glimpse his eyes. They were indecently long-lashed and a shade lighter than his slacks. She felt pierced through as his gaze ran the length of her body, and in a more leisurely manner cruised up to her lips, where his incredible eyes lingered.

Mei flushed, wondering if in her haste she hadn't put her lip gloss on straight. Reluctantly, she dropped into the chair, discreetly tugging down the navy skirt that slid up to mid-thigh. Clutching her purse atop her notebook, she sat statue-straight instead of letting her shoulders touch the brown leather chair back.

ONCE HIS GUEST had taken a seat, Cullen circled behind his desk again, all the while attempting to wind down his call. "Listen, Cloris, I know you've had a hard time corralling the committee members for a meeting. I'll find an hour to discuss the glitch in the program this week. Right now I have a scheduled appointment."

Cullen turned then and stared squarely at said appointment. Heat crawled up his spine. He didn't know what he'd thought a Houston police lieutenant would look like. Not, he decided, like the woman seated across from him as still and regal as a princess. For a fleeting moment, he wondered what it had taken her to reach a lieutenant's rank.

He'd expected from the name Mei Lu that she'd be Asian. The police chief, whom he'd never personally met, had assured him the lieutenant fluently spoke and read Chinese. Cullen had just never imagined his interpreter would be so slender, so tall or so attractive. Standing, she'd barely had to look up to meet his eyes, and he was a solid six feet. Her sleek hair was imprisoned in a knot a millimeter or so above a starched shirt collar; Cullen's fingers itched to loosen the bonds holding the shiny black mass. Or maybe it was her blouse with its severe front tucks and pointy collar that made him feel an uncharacteristic desire to muss her up a little. More than a little, he realized, then deliberately turned and paced as far from her as the phone cord allowed. It'd been a long time since he'd been attacked by such immediate lust.

Stretched to the end of his tether, Cullen wheeled again and noticed that the woman—the lieutenant—had beautiful skin. A pale saffron. As she'd taken the chair he pulled out, Cullen had detected a faint hint of sandalwood mixed with something sweet. He found the scent a pleasing combination. Too pleasing.

"Cloris. I have to go. I'm keeping my guest waiting. Yes, I'll call Robert and Caroline. We'll coordinate for Tuesday, I promise."

Absently dropping the receiver in its cradle, Cullen drew a hand through his thick hair. "Sorry about the wait. May I offer you a beverage before we begin? I believe we have coffee, tea, or bottled water in various flavors."

"Thank you, but no." Mei wanted to get down to business. The intense way this man studied her left her feeling at a disadvantage.

"I hope you don't mind if I pour myself a cup of coffee. That was this year's chairwoman of an art showing we're trying to put together. Cloris Gaston has a way of talking on and on without taking a breath. I find I need some caffeine."

Mei relaxed a little. "In that case, I'll have a cup of tea."

Cullen rounded the desk and strode toward a corner of the room Mei now saw held a coffeepot, microwave and minibar. He'd just set two cups on a tray when one of the children Mei had seen earlier, the girl, tore into the room, sobbing loudly. Cullen stepped out from behind the counter and swung the child up in a tangle of bare arms and legs.

Mei noticed that the child's bathing suit was wetter now than it had been before. A damp stain spread across the front of Cullen's shirt and dripped down his gray slacks when he abruptly sat, placing the girl on his lap.

Mei tensed, expecting a severe reprisal.

"These look like real tears," Cullen said after a cursory assessment. Taking out a snowy handkerchief, he dabbed the girl's tear-streaked cheeks.

Nodding, the child managed to sob out, "Bobby punched a hole in my sea horse float. He was playing monster, but I told him I didn't wanna play. He wouldn't quit even when Freda told him to stop, Daddy. Bobby knows I hate it when he makes monster noises. I slipped on the pool steps and fell and cut my knee."

Mei watched Cullen inspect the injury. The tender manner in which the big man ministered to his child impressed her. If she or Stephen had ever interrupted her father when he was holding a meeting, they'd have spent a full day in their rooms contemplating their grievous infraction of the house rules. It wasn't that she and Stephen weren't loved; it was more that all things in the Ling home had an order. The adults' privacy held the highest priority.

Mei listened as the girl Archer introduced as his daughter, Belinda, begged her father to punish the offensive Bobby. Cullen didn't barter, which also impressed Mei. He washed her cut at a sink behind the bar, dressed her knee and gave his daughter a hug. After which, he advised her to go back and settle her differences with her brother.

"Belinda and Bobby are twins," Cullen remarked to Mei. He filled a tea ball, which he placed in a flowered cup, then poured hot water into a small metal teapot. He set the cup and pot on his desk. "By and large they're great kids for eight-year-olds," he said, returning for his pottery mug. "Belinda, though, is the original drama queen. I suspect sometimes she only wants to check out my guests. If she'd really come to complain about her brother, he'd have flown in right behind her to defend himself." Grinning, Cullen sat down again opposite his guest. "Do you have children?" he inquired suddenly.

She shook her head, but her hand quivered pouring her water. "I'm not married," she murmured, casting her eyes down as she dunked the infusion ball. The aroma of jasmine enveloped her, instantly settling her jumpy stomach. She managed to gain a firm grip on the cup's handle.

"I didn't mean to embarrass you by getting personal. I'm divorced with kids, and I've found that having children in common is often an icebreaker." Cullen had seen the tinge of red creep up her neck. "I...uh, I've wasted enough of your time, not to mention taxpayer money. Shall we get straight to it?"

Mei nodded, replacing her cup without ever tasting the fragrant tea. She was afraid her unsteady hands would make her appear too flighty for a law officer. Normally, she wasn't giddy around men, a fact her friends teased her about unmercifully. One by one, Mei had watched those same women fall in love. Risa, Lucy, Crista, and the latest, Abby, who'd twice given up her career to follow Thomas Riley. This time to North Carolina. The women had spoken over the weekend, Abby had sounded happy with her move, and Mei hoped she was.

Mei didn't exactly *envy* Abby or the others. Rather, she was confused by the changes that had come over all her friends with the entry of lovers into their lives. Lately, she'd felt less connected to them. Mei tried, but she didn't understand how the women all juggled love and their police careers. Because of that, she sometimes felt as if she stood outside their old circle, looking in.

Cullen regained Mei Lu's wandering attention by pulling a manila file folder from his drawer and flipping it open. "I assume your chief briefed you."

"Not really. She said you needed me to translate… something. Some document having to do with artifacts smuggled out of Beijing?"

Separating a glossy eight-by-ten photograph from papers in the file, Archer slid it silently across the desk.

Mei leaned forward to see better, and also to avoid a glare from the window. When a picture of a glazed earthenware warrior painted in exquisite detail came into focus, an involuntary gasp escaped her lips. "The Heavenly King," she breathed, running a fingertip over the colorful statue. "Tang Dynasty, 709. Excavated in 1981 from the tomb of An Pu in Henan province."

"Right on all counts." Cullen was admittedly floored by the woman's knowledge. "A member of the Houston Art Buyers' Guild received this photo in the mail, accompanied by a typed memo—in English—asking if he might know of a buyer for the piece. The memo also said he'd be contacted within the week by a courier who would supposedly bring him the statue to authenticate. No courier came, so the dealer, suspicious anyway, sent the packet to Interpol. To an agent who, with my help, had recovered a stolen carving for him last year."

"Then no one's seen this statue?" Mei dropped the photo on the desk.

"No. But a second, smaller print turned up, along with this note, in a belly band worn by a man dressed in old-style Chinese garb. His body's gone unclaimed in the morgue. Interpol was combing U.S. newspapers and chanced on a small article from Houston. It described how police, stopping to investigate a disturbance in the parking lot of an Asian nightclub, scattered a group of men. Someone in that group apparently shot our guy. I've viewed the body and the evidence. I think he's probably the courier."

"May I see the note? I assume it's what needs translating?"

Cullen hesitated, although he wasn't sure why. "I spent time in Guangzhou last year, tracking a forged silk tapestry. I had to work from police notes jotted in Chinese. I'm moderately familiar with what's called grass Chinese. Very informal scribbling. Shorthand, if you will. This appears to be a formal letter, Lieutenant Lu."

Mei's head shot up. "Lieutenant Ling. Lu is my middle name. My surname is Ling."

Cullen held tight to the letter. "You wouldn't be related to Michael?" Even as he asked, Cullen wanted her to deny the connection. But then, he hadn't expected a police translator to be so familiar with Chinese art.

Mei deliberately took her first sip of tea. "Michael Ling is my father," she said eventually. "Stephen, my brother, also works in the family business. For a time, I headed our Hong Kong office." Setting her cup back in its saucer, she pried the note out from under Archer's hand.

He wanted to snatch the page back, but realized too late that she'd begun to explain what the note said. And he needed to focus on her soft voice.

"It's a simple introduction of the bearer, named Wang Xi, to an unnamed cousin of the person who wrote this. The cousin is being asked to see to Wang Xi's comfort during his brief stay in Houston. He's asked to…to…help Wang Xi knock on the right doors. Complying will remove one debt from the cousin's book." Chewing her lower lip, Mei sat back to mull over what she'd read.

Across the desk, Cullen steepled his fingers. "What book?" he asked abruptly.

Mei shrugged. Even if she'd been inclined to fill Cullen Archer in about the book the writer referred to, she doubted he'd understand. Such books weren't real, but figurative. In traditional and extended Asian families—including aunts, uncles, cousins and dear friends—it wasn't uncommon for heads of households to keep unwritten lists of debts, which weren't always paid monetarily. Favors often sufficed as payment. But that was difficult to explain to non-Chinese.

"Who do you think has the Heavenly King now?" she asked. "Are you quite sure your art-dealer friend didn't end up with the statue?"

"Why would he notify Interpol?" Cullen asked curtly.

"To make himself appear innocent? To turn questions elsewhere after the courier—if that's who Wang Xi was—ended up dead in a parking lot."

"That might fly, except that a month ago, after undergoing a quadruple heart bypass, this particular dealer liquidated his business."

Mei picked up her cup and, while she and Cullen Archer studied each other across his broad desk, drained it.

Archer drummed his fingers on the folder of notes pertaining to the case. "Why Houston? Why not San Francisco or New York City, which certainly have far greater numbers of serious Asian art collectors."

"I'm afraid I have no theory about that, Mr. Archer." He'd begun probing her once she'd revealed her connection to Ling Limited, and she didn't like it one bit. Her father's behavior was always ethical, business or life. In fact,

Michael Ling was honest to a fault. Mei Lu had seen him draw up a check for fifty cents for a mail-order customer who'd miscalculated the state tax.

She kept her eyes trained on tea leaves that had filtered from the ball to settle in the bottom of her cup. Her mother made a practice of reading the leaves.

Just when Mei was sure the man who faced her with a scowl would finally tell her what was on his mind, his twins burst into the room. They were freshly scrubbed and now dressed in shorts and bright colored T-shirts. Belinda wore pink, her shining curls swept up into a ponytail held in place by a pink flowered scrunchie. Bobby's clothes were more sedate—dark-brown shorts and a plain olive shirt. Both children wore sandals. Each dashed shy glances at Mei Lu even as they pounced on their father.

"Freda says come to lunch. She sent us to ask if the lady police person is going to eat with us." Bobby's voice rose above his sister's. It was he, not Belinda, who turned to Mei, demanding bluntly, "If you're a cop, where's your uniform and badge? And where's your cop car?"

Mei smiled. "I used to wear a uniform, Bobby. I drove a patrol car, too. Now I work in a different department. I'm sorry if you're disappointed."

Bobby didn't look so much crestfallen as suspicious. "All the policemen I've ever seen carry guns."

His sister wiggled her way to the foreground, managing to put herself center stage. "I told Bobby policewomen are diff'rent from policemen. I bet you take bad guys out with kicks and stuff like Charlie's Angels in a movie Mom let us rent."

Mei honestly didn't know how to answer the child. And she certainly didn't want to admit she carried a Taser.

Fortunately, the children's father came to her rescue and exclaimed, "Enough. Quit bugging Lieutenant Ling. Go tell Freda we're almost finished here. Tell her to give me five minutes, then I'll join you kids for lunch on the terrace."

The children thundered out with a chorus of *yippees* and *yays*. Mei saw that Cullen's eyes followed both of them indulgently and lovingly.

Turning again to his guest, he said, "I apologize for my children's interruption. I've noted your translation. Thank you for your assistance. I believe that concludes our business, Lieutenant." He stood, clearly dismissing her.

Despite her curiosity, Mei rose as well. She'd love to know what was contained in the other pages stacked in the folder Archer had shut. She also wondered vaguely about the whereabouts of the twins' mother. Did Cullen have his kids all the time? It didn't matter—although, he'd begun to ask about *her* life. Regardless, Mei sensed that her host had clammed up as soon as he'd learned about her relationship to Michael Ling and Ling Limited.

She extended her right hand, shifting the almost-empty cup she still held. Fumbling, Archer barely brushed her knuckles with his fingers.

"I understand your children are waiting for you," she said. "In a way, I'm sorry we don't have longer to discuss this case. Puzzles of this nature intrigue me."

"I appreciate your willingness to drop your work and interpret for me. However, I haven't got time to fill you in on the mostly boring details I've gathered to date."

Mei Lu pasted on a false smile, and reached beneath his arm to set her cup solidly back in its saucer. "There's a Chinese proverb my father's fond of. 'Never talk business before the third cup of tea.' I'm generally too impatient to practice it, myself."

"I'm afraid you've lost me." Cullen wore a similar forced smile.

"Loosely translated it means, accept the first cup of tea in friendship when it's offered. But if you aren't offered another, it's time to leave."

Mei Lu turned then and left the room. She avoided various toys still scattered in the hallway, thinking what a waste this was of her first morning as a lieutenant. At the entry, she found herself glancing back at Archer's office and again caught her breath as she looked at the man who'd stepped into the hall. Presumably he wanted to ensure she *did* leave his home—without filching one of his expensive vases. Mei was overwhelmed by the feeling that it was just as well she wasn't going to be faced with seeing this jarringly handsome but patently distrustful man a second time. Still, Cullen Archer caused butterflies in her stomach.

His twins dashed out from where they'd been playing under the curved stairs. "Bye, policewoman," Belinda called, waving madly. "Come again when you can stay and have lunch with us."

"I'll shut the door so I can make sure Mopsy doesn't sneak out," Bobby Archer declared, sounding adult and clearly not echoing his sister's generous sentiment.

Mei Lu recognized in the boy's eyes a coolness very similar to what she'd seen in his dad's. Maybe Bobby resented the divorce and felt the need to protect his mother's interests. She hurried out, wondering if the boy had perceived her fleeting attention. But that was impossible—wasn't it?

She sensed movement at Archer's office window and knew he'd gone back to monitor her departure. To Mei Lu's relief her car started without a hitch. The last thing she needed now was the humiliation of being stuck in his driveway.

CHAPTER TWO

AFTER RETURNING TO THE PRECINCT, Mei plunged straight into writing an official report on her meeting. Chewing thoughtfully on the end of her pen, she tore up her first draft, and began again in her small, neat penmanship. What had she learned about the smuggling ring? Nothing useful. But Catherine was a stickler for reports. Comprehensive ones. Mei decided she should also include a few personal impressions such as the fact that Cullen Archer apparently liked playing the lone cowboy.

Most cops hated filing reports more than any other part of their job. Especially the men. Mei didn't understand their objections, or their propensity for delay. She felt that writing a report while the information was still fresh—instead of bitching about it—would make their lives less stressful. But then, some cops thrived on stress.

Coffee, doughnuts and stress. And, in some cases, cigarettes.

"Well, well. I thought the chief said we wouldn't have the pleasure of the China doll's company today."

Mei gnashed her teeth before looking up, knowing she'd find Captain Sheldon Murdock behind that booming observation. And talk about cigarette odor—his suits always reeked. Even now the smell preceded him into her cubicle. Still, that might be the least offensive thing about the captain, who was the only negative aspect of her promotion. Her former commander had been decent and respectful of his staff.

"Good day, Captain. As you see, I'm definitely here now." Discreetly, Mei Lu slid a blank sheet of paper over what she'd written. Shel Murdock was a blabbermouth. It was widely known that he expended a lot of effort attempting to pick up information from underlings—information he fed to higher-ups as his own. This was a practice the previous chief had encouraged, but Mei knew Catherine deplored it, as did most younger cops. Filched evidence often contained half-truths and gave rise to rumors, which fueled distrust among peers, who should be able to rely on one another without hesitation.

"What's that you're hiding, sweet thang?" Murdock drawled, propping his wide butt on Mei Lu's desk. He leaned closer, actually trying to tug away the sheet covering her report.

Mei anchored it with her elbow. She stared coolly up into Murdock's eyes. "Sir, please call me Lieutenant Ling or just plain Lieutenant. I've worked hard to achieve my rank."

"Oooh, guys, listen to her. Chilly Lilly!" The captain slid off Mei's desk and made a mocking gesture with his hand.

"Better back off, Cap'n," muttered the sergeant. "She's one of the chief's special chicks. Call her anything you want at O'Malley's when we're having a beer after work. In-house or at official sites she's Lieutenant Ling. Remember how fast Jake Haslett got busted back to patrol for a little teasing he did."

"Yeah, yeah." Murdock hitched up his pants. "So, Lew…tenant," he said, drawing it out. "Since you're here, does that mean I can assign you cases in our regular rotation?"

"After I finish this report and deliver it upstairs to the

chief as she requested. Then I'll be ready to take the next
case that comes in." She emphasized *next* to let Captain
Murdock know she didn't want him shoving all the crappy,
already-worked-to-death cases off on her like someone
across the hall had tried when she first joined the white-
collar crimes division. Mei was wiser now.

"Cap'n, you'd better ask old Iron Pants, er…Chief Tanner, before you assign the lieutenant. I took her call this
morning. The chief said to consider Ling on special assignment until further notice." Sergeant Chuck Marshall stood
and handed Murdock a sheaf of messages. He indicated
one, presumably Catherine's.

Silence fell over the office. Only the department clerk
kept typing. Her earphones were in place.

"Look, guys," Mei said, rapping her pen sharply on her
desk. She resented that this byplay was still happening at
this stage of her career. She especially resented what wasn't
a slip of Marshall's tongue. Usually she fired back at anyone who tacked rude monikers on Catherine. Today,
though, Mei simply wanted to get on with her task. "I've
worked with most of you in the past," she said evenly.
"Nothing's changed except that I've received a promotion.
I didn't stand on that dais alone on Friday. Yet I don't hear
you giving Lieutenant Herrera a hard time."

A few people, those who were good cops, returned to
work. Others didn't hide their animosity. Murdock hesitated a fraction longer, then stomped into his office and
slammed the door.

Ignoring the men who continued to glare, Mei calmly
gathered up her notes. It was time to find a more secure corner in which to finish her report. Mei didn't consider her
leaving a retreat by any means; she was just being practi-
cal, since Catherine had stressed the importance of the case.

The truth in this department was that no matter how progressive a spin public relations put on hiring practices, subtle harassment of females still existed, and tended to flare up following a transfer or a promotion.

Catherine worked hard to crack down on gender or racial bias. But she couldn't cover all bases, and even she had her hands full. Some city official or other was constantly running to local reporters with allegations of internal police corruption.

An investigator from Mei's previous unit looked up as she passed his door. He jumped up, calling her. "Mei Lu. Do you have a minute? I just received notice that Judge Burkholder authorized an appeal in David St. John's case. Since you presented our evidence at the original trial and phase two will probably fall to me, I'd like to pick your brain if I may."

Mei skidded to a halt. "You're kidding! Someone granted St. John's appeal? He's guilty as sin. He bilked more than thirty senior citizens out of their life savings. What are the grounds for granting him another hearing?"

Her fellow investigator stood aside, then followed her to his desk where the St. John file lay open. "Same old stupid technicality, Mei. David engaged a new attorney, who claims the arresting officer brought him in, booked him and stood him in a lineup, all before giving St. John access to counsel."

"The officer nabbed him coming out of the victim's bank. He had her cash on him. Three former victims, *and* Mrs. Baxter, picked him out of that lineup." Mei sat down and thumbed through the folder. "Don't tell me we're going to have to let that creep walk on this one, Patrick. I couldn't prove it but I strongly suspect he's pulled his scam in other cities. This problem is spreading nationwide."

Pat Wilkinson spun a second chair around and sat beside Mei. "I've got no doubt that you're right. Even though St. John only drew an eighteen-month sentence, I want the bastard to serve every second. Guys who prey on old folks or kids are at the bottom of the food chain. My grandpa lost his savings in a similar scheme last year in L.A." He shook his head. "I never thought Gramps would trust a stranger with his bank information. I guess the elderly are prime targets for fast-talking con men and women."

"Sure. They see their savings dwindling. The con artists are often normal-looking people who come across as trustworthy. They all promise to double or triple whatever money the victim has put away. Of course, the victims want to leave something for their children."

"According to your notes, you recommended not putting any of these victims on the stand unless absolutely necessary."

"Right. Because in general they can be easily rattled by slick opposing counsel. Defense attorneys tend to question their failing eyesight or faulty hearing. Last year I did months of legwork and had a female con dead to rights. Her lawyer shredded our case. Her transactions were all verbal. She claimed she never said what the victims claimed they heard. But with this St. John guy—Mrs. Baxter might make a good witness."

Mei and Patrick retraced her early work through every twist and turn. It was quitting time before he seemed satisfied that he'd gleaned enough information about the case to let her go.

She ended up dashing off a passable report on the artifact smuggling, and ran it upstairs moments before Catherine's assistant left for the day. The chief's office was closed and dark. "I'm glad I caught you, Annette," Mei said breathlessly. "Can you put this report envelope on Chief

Tanner's desk? I wouldn't ask, but she impressed on me earlier that she wants to keep this information confidential."

"Oh, Lieutenant Ling. Chief Tanner tried to reach you before she left. No one in your department knew where you were."

"Sorry, I should've told Captain Murdock I was next door consulting with Pat Wilkinson on an old case. Did the chief need something specific? Should I bother her at home or try her cell?"

"No. She's attending a city council meeting tonight. She only wants to be called in extreme emergencies," Annette said.

"I'd never contact her after hours without authorization," Mei stated firmly. People at the precinct already thought she, Risa, Crista and Lucy had undue access to Catherine. The last thing Mei wanted was for another rumor to start. Not that Annette would talk out of turn... "I won't be going straight home, either," she added. "I plan to work out for a while at the Shao-Lin Martial Arts Studio. Chief Tanner has the number. Could you add that information to your note? In case she comes back after her meeting and wants to reach me after reading this report."

Annette nodded. Mei waited to make sure the woman did place the envelope on Catherine's desk. Call her paranoid, but early in her career she'd had an important report inexplicably disappear. She swore she'd turned it in, and the man responsible for handing it over to a superior was just as insistent that she'd done nothing of the sort. Since then Mei had tracked the progress of her reports.

Forty-five minutes later, having donned a loose-fitting shirt and pants to work out in, Mei was in the process of closing her locker when Crista Santiago bounded into the dressing room. Crista always did everything with a limitless energy that Mei envied. Mei was tired of avoiding her old friends. Words had flown and meanings were misconstrued after Risa was wrongly accused of shooting and killing her partner. Some of the once-close group of women had felt a need to pull back for the sake of their own fledgling careers, and hard feelings still existed. So many times she and Crista had talked about working out together again. Thinking tonight was as good a chance as any, Mei Lu shot her friend a welcoming smile.

"Qué pasa?" Crista said, unable to sidestep Mei Lu.

Mei shrugged. "Nothing's happening in my life—how about yours? Are you upset, Crista? Or annoyed? Those are the only times I've heard you revert to Spanish."

"Could be Alex's influence," she said, referring to her fiancé, a man she'd met when she'd investigated the drive-by shooting of his daughter. "Or it could be the fact that I had a double homicide last night on the east side, and I'm beat. Two teens vying for top spot in their gang. So senseless," the dark-eyed woman said as she pulled on a T-shirt and sweatpants. "But I think you're holding back, Mei. Right before I left the station I heard whispers that you tangled with Captain Murdock." Crista lowered her voice. "Can you talk about it?"

Mei lifted an eyebrow. "Wow, news does travel at the speed of light. I wouldn't say we tangled, exactly. You know Murdock and his cutesy names. I merely informed him I'd rather he called me Lieutenant or Lieutenant Ling."

Crista whistled through her teeth. "Just watch your back, okay? I hear Murdock blocked another woman's request to join his staff. It's no secret that he favors the likes of Eddie Fontanero. I avoid Sergeant Creepo at all costs."

"I've heard the rumors. But those incidents were a few years ago. Before Catherine was made chief."

"Yeah, I know. Still…" Crista let the word trail off as she tugged on wristbands and started warming up. "Hey, does Catherine seem on edge to you?"

Mei paused in her own stretches. "How so?" She considered their morning meeting. "I saw her today. I get the feeling she's exceptionally busy."

Crista flung her arms from side to side. "Thursday, she and I passed in the parking garage. Cathy seemed…I don't know…unusually distracted. She almost always has time for small talk, and she didn't. Know what I mean?"

Mei nodded. "Yes, but I didn't see anything unusual I could point to."

"Me, neither," Crista murmured as the women walked into the main gym and rolled out mats. "Not until Alex brought some articles in the paper to my attention. I have to agree with him that someone's gunning for Cathy. Maybe someone outside the department. Alex believes it's pressures coming from in-house. Maybe corrupt cops."

Mei faced Crista out on the main studio floor. "Want a partner?" At her friend's surprised nod, the two women bowed, as was customary in the martial art of Wing Chun. As was also Mei's habit when any of her friends brought up their significant others, she abruptly fell silent.

If Crista thought that odd, she didn't comment. Because as soon as Crista faced an opponent, her mind and body focused totally on winning her match. Which she generally did handily, especially when Mei Lu was her partner. Early on in the women's relationship, the fact that Mei was notably inept when it came to martial arts—a skill everyone seemed to assume should be hers by birthright—had turned out to be a source of levity at the academy.

At a young age, Mei did attend wushu–kung fu classes

with Stephen. She soon fell behind her more dedicated sibling, and Grand Master Chin had advised Mei to seek a new pursuit. By her third day at the academy, she wished she'd applied herself more back then. Mei would be eternally grateful to Crista for taking her under her wing. Committed to her sport, and good at it, Crista offered Mei after-hours sessions that paid off. She'd improved, and had actually moved on to intermediate level, a matter of pride for both women. Mei would settle for solid competence. Crista had her sights set on attaining her master's level.

This afternoon, Crista landed a punch Mei should have easily blocked. After the third time Crista had to help Mei off the floor, it became apparent that Mei's attention kept wandering to a children's class going on in another part of the vast gym.

"Something's up with you. Even at your worst, you never just handed me a match." Bending, Crista picked up and uncapped a bottle of water. "You know one of those kids over there?"

"Huh? Oh, no." Flushing, Mei grabbed a small towel and blotted sweat from her neck. "Sorry, I can't seem to concentrate."

"That's evident." Crista recapped her bottle. "Are you leveling with me about El Capitan Weasel?"

Mei Lu grinned. "I wouldn't assign Murdock that much importance." She reached for her own water and splashed some on her face. "My mind must be stalled on a new case I went out on today. There were these really cute, precocious kids."

"Corporate criminals getting younger every day, are they?" Crista teased.

"The twins have nothing to do with the case. Their father is connected to…to…Interpol."

Crista snorted. "Lucky you. At least, in your work, nobody dies."

"Someone did, though," Mei blurted out. Then she winced. "I shouldn't have said that, Crista. The case is classified. I should just put it out of my mind. As far as I know, my part in the matter began and ended today after I translated a letter."

"Oh." Crista's eyebrows became a slash over the bridge of her nose. "Hey, what's this? A chink in Mei Lu's armor? Am I hearing personal interest in...a man? *'The man from Interpol,'*" she singsonged.

Mei dropped her water bottle and hurriedly grabbed it before too much could puddle on the mat. Her heart raced again at the indirect mention of Cullen Archer. And that disturbed Mei. "Honestly, Crista. Ever since you fell in love, you see romance around every corner. I said a man *died.*"

"Okay, okay. You're so touchy. Dead guys are right up my alley. You want to skip this session and talk about your case?"

Mei gathered her few belongings. "I'm really no match for you tonight. And I honestly can't discuss the case. Catherine assigned it a high level of confidentiality. I think I'll go on home and let you maim Sergeant Denholm. I see him looking around the room, spoiling for blood. He reminds me of that guy at the academy you had to shut up. What was his name?"

"Schwartz. Bernie Schwartz. I'm in no mood to take on Denholm. Sure you wouldn't rather go for coffee—or tea? Sometimes it helps to unload on an impartial listener. I hope you know I'd never repeat anything you tell me off the record."

"I know, Crista. But this really isn't my case to talk about. Can I have a rain check on the tea and call you for a rematch?"

Crista grinned cheekily. "Sure. Although, I don't want you going soft in your cushy new job."

"Next week, then? Same time?" Mei said as they both headed back to the dressing room, passing Sergeant Denholm, a man more than a little flabby around the middle.

"Hey, Ling. I saw how you let Santiago whip your butt. I'll gladly show you how a man cuts that hot tamale down to size."

"You know, Denholm, I was on my way out," Crista said. "But you've been pushing for a slaughter."

Spinning, Mei turned back, too. "I'll referee, just to keep you honest, Sarge."

His grin faltered, and he tried to backpedal. The women closed ranks and, because others had heard his bragging, he ended up going along.

It did Mei's heart good to see Crista flatten the big-mouth in three out of three tries. "You know what?" she said, calling to her friend who'd barely broken a sweat. "I changed my mind about having tea. Come on, Crista. My treat."

"I probably shouldn't have been so rough on him," Crista lamented later as the friends trudged down the street toward a coffeehouse in the next block.

"Why not? He's been asking for it. Now maybe he'll shut the heck up."

"If only. More like now every macho jerk in Denholm's squad will want a piece of me, when we both know the number one rule in Wing Chun is to not let an attacker provoke you."

Mei pulled open the door to the coffeehouse. "Quit beating up on yourself. Denholm claims he wants to learn the Wing Chun system of kung fu. Tonight was another step in his training. At least, that's what you told me all those times you bounced me off the carpet."

"That's different. I like you, Mei Lu."

Mei, who got into line first, glanced around and pulled a face at Crista. "Thanks—I think." The women burst out laughing and jostled each other, still smothering giggles as they placed their orders. The revelry broke whatever tension had gripped them earlier. By the time they picked up their orders and found a table in the corner, Denholm's plight and Mei's case were taboo subjects. The two old friends chatted about inconsequential things. Harmless gossip. Half an hour later, they parted, still in high spirits.

On the drive home, Mei reflected on how much she missed the nights the five, or sometimes six, would meet for coffee, drinks or dinner. The first crack in their bond occurred when Catherine became chief. They all understood that her job brought with it weighty new responsibilities. Nevertheless, she'd been the first to pull back. Relaxed as she felt now, Mei hated recalling the next fracture that occurred, after Risa had been accused of killing her partner. Mei shuddered, and the warmth of the evening fled. The whole mess rushed to the forefront of her mind.

Maybe the situation would've gone differently if the friends had been more experienced in their individual fields. Instead, after working the required street patrol, they'd barely been settled into their new jobs—Mei in Corporate Crime Investigation, Risa in Sex Crimes, Lucy in Missing Persons. Crista was in Homicide, but with a different unit. Abby had worked part-time with the crisis intervention team.

At the first catastrophes their friendship had collapsed. Mei hadn't known what to do—hadn't known what to say—to comfort Risa. She recalled a phone conversation that had ended badly. Even after IA cleared Risa, one thing led to another and it was as if their earlier friendship ceased to exist. Some blamed it on falling in love. Grady Wilson had backed Risa, and their relationship had deepened. Jackson Davis had come into Lucy's life at the very point when everything was so confused. Mei felt both men were exactly what her friends needed.

Mei hadn't been as willing to admit that Alex Del Rio was good for Crista. Of course, she'd always felt more like a sister than friend to Crista. Abby, who'd already been in and out of love, suggested Mei might be jealous of Crista's happiness. Mei Lu had given it serious thought, but honestly believed jealousy wasn't part of her reaction. Truly, Mei had never met such a dark and brooding man as Alex. She'd been concerned for Crista. Alex was...intense. And he'd been married before, but his wife died of a brain aneurism a couple of years ago.

Looking back, Mei had no idea why his having been married was a sticking point. After all, they were of an age where many of their contemporaries were divorced and some had children. She was probably the oddball.

But boy, talk about intense. Thomas Riley, the former Delta Force officer Abby Carlton had fallen for, could be another poster boy for intensity. Still, as Catherine once said, every one of the men was sinfully good-looking. "Hot" was how she'd put it.

As Mei parked in front of her duplex just after six, she actually paused to wonder if Catherine would attach that label to Cullen Archer. *Hot.* In Mei's opinion, it certainly fit. Flustered, she grabbed her purse, notebook and keys, and flew into the house. Thankfully Foo's effusive greeting steered her priorities in another direction.

"Yes, I'm glad to see you, too, mutt." Shedding her suit coat, Mei locked up her weapon, then hung her jacket in the closet. The next thing she did was find one of Foo's squeaky toys to toss across the room. It was a nightly ritual. His ambling gait on stubby legs too short for his big feet never failed to make Mei laugh. The shelter had said no one there wanted to venture a guess as to the breeds in his background. Built low to the ground like a basset, his soft fur, perky terrier ears and pug-like face expelled him from that breed. To say nothing of his waving plume of a tail. But he almost smiled, and Mei had loved that about him from the minute she set eyes on him. Life held enough sorrow; she liked surrounding herself with bright colors and silly offbeat objects that always lifted her spirits.

She changed into jeans and a T-shirt, and took Foo out into her compact backyard so he could chase a ball around. She supposed her propensity for lots of color and things her parents would call junk came from having lived amid such order all her life. The Ling home could grace the pages of *Architectural Digest* or *House Beautiful.* On the high-ceilinged, ice-toned walls hung rich brocade tapestries that provided splashes of color. However, her mother rarely spoke of their beauty; rather, she added up their monetary value. Mei and Stephen had grown up in a veritable museum. Stephen, Mei's elder by two years, had slipped easily into the family habit of collecting for the sake of owning. Once close, the siblings had a clash of principles the last year Mei spent in Hong Kong at the family business. Leaving the firm had been heart-wrenching, one of the hardest decisions she'd ever made. But it'd been for the best. She'd found her true niche in police work.

She heard her phone ring. Aware that Catherine's meeting might let out around seven o'clock, Mei raced inside to scoop up the receiver before her answering machine kicked in. "Hello," she said, still out of breath.

"Lieutenant?" a male voice inquired. A vaguely familiar one, too, but Mei couldn't quite place it.

"Yes," she said more hesitantly. Her home phone number was unlisted, as were most officers'.

"You sound like I caught you running a marathon or something. This is Cullen Archer."

"Mr. Archer?" Mei found it even harder to breathe normally. "I haven't been home long. You caught me playing with my dog."

"Ah. Well, I'm down at the Port of Houston." He rattled off a dock number, and Mei automatically stored the information. "We have a second corpse. A second dead courier, I'm betting."

Mei's thundering heart nearly stopped beating. "Oh, no! How? Why? Did you call Homicide?"

"They contacted me," he said. "There's a second photograph and another note in Chinese. If I might interrupt your play, I'd like you to come and have a look. I'll see that security lets you drive straight in."

Mei bit her lower lip.

"Well?" he demanded impatiently.

"Of course. I already turned my report in to the chief, though. I'd assumed you wouldn't require my services again."

"You thought wrong. Do I need to call your chief first?"

Mei realized she was squeezing Foo's ball out of shape. She tossed it lightly across the kitchen and closed the back door after the dog streaked in and dived after the blue ball. "I'm more than half an hour away. Shall I meet you at the morgue, instead?" She hadn't applied to Homicide because she'd never gotten used to the smell of death. The morgue, while sterile, gave her the creeps, too. She had huge respect and great empathy for what Crista and Risa did.

Her caller spoke to someone out of Mei's hearing. He came back almost immediately. "The team says we'll be here at least another hour trying to figure how the courier and his assailant breached security. Get here as fast as you can, okay?"

Mei pulled the phone away from her ear and frowned at it. "Yes, sir," she said in a syrupy sweet voice. "Am I to report to you, then? I don't know your rank. Or does Interpol naturally take precedence in local investigations, kind of like the FBI?" She heard Archer clear his throat several times.

"Please come, Lieutenant. I have extensive experience in tracking down international art thieves and next to none when it comes to murder."

She bent a little. "On that score we're even. If you don't mind, I'd rather leave that particular aspect of the case in the very capable hands of our homicide squad. But I'll head out right away. I admit I'm curious about the photo and this note. See you in about forty-five minutes." She hung up, debating only a moment as to whether she ought to change back into the suit she'd worn earlier, or go as she was. Vetoing the suit, deciding it would take too long, she did pluck her revolver from its locked box and secured it under her belt at the back of her jeans. To heck with packing a Taser. The docks were spooky at night. She felt more secure with an equalizer.

Mei grabbed a cherry-red blazer to throw on over her white T-shirt. Red might not be appropriate attire for a murder investigation in progress, but it gave her confidence. And to face Archer and a dead man, Mei Lu needed all the confidence she could muster.

"Sorry, Foo. I'm abandoning you again."

The dog sank to his belly and put his chin on his ball, gazing up at her with soulful eyes.

"All right, come on, then. But I'll have to leave you in the car."

He didn't appear to care. The little dog loved riding in cars. Mei kept a water bowl and bottled water in her vehicle because most of her trips with the dog were impromptu, whether for strolls in the park or quick visits to the grocery store.

Her Toyota choked and sputtered, but the engine finally turned over. Mei patted the dash and gave thanks to the car gods. Once she got under way she never worried about breaking down. That was her father's everlasting concern. So many times Michael Ling had tried to buy Mei a new car. She appreciated that, but repeatedly pointed out that she wanted to succeed or fail in this job on her own.

Aun Ling had plainly never understood her daughter. Of course, Mei's mother had gone from a huge Chinese household in a manufacturing sector of mainland China to a strange land where her arranged husband worked night and day, especially when Mei and Stephen were little. If Mei had rightly deciphered the Wong family history, her mother's once prominent family had, like many others in China, fallen on hard times. While Aun rarely brought up her girlhood, she let slip enough things for Mei to know the Wongs had enjoyed great wealth and prestige.

Aun courted no American friends. She derived immense pleasure from her home, and from entertaining her husband's Asian associates and their wives. Aun also felt duty-bound to arrange suitable marriages for her children. Stephen was more important, because as Aun said often, a woman's purpose on earth was to produce a male heir to carry on the family name. Mei never was quite sure how her mother viewed her position, and she'd adroitly sidestepped Aun's attempts to have her meet the sons of visitors from Hong Kong or, later, mainland China. Mei would have liked a closer relationship with her mother. They always seemed to be at odds, and Mei sincerely regretted that.

She found a parking space shortly after passing Security, having easily identified the proper dock from the gaggle of police cars parked nearby. Mei checked her purse to make sure she had her shield and saw it gleam in the nearly spent sun. She poured Foo's water, lowered her windows a few inches to give him air, and slid from the car. She surveyed the scene as she locked her doors and pocketed her keys.

Mei Lu spotted Cullen Archer almost at once. He exuded a powerful presence even among seasoned men in uniform and those identifiable detectives who always wore rumpled suits. Archer stood casually, his artist's hands bracketing narrow hips. *When had she noticed his well-shaped hands?* More to the point, *why* would she notice—especially since he stood next to what had to be the courier's body now zipped into a body bag and tagged for delivery to the morgue?

Shaking off an edgy feeling Mei dragged in a lungful of fishy air. Shoulders back, she strode straight up to the man who'd requested her presence.

She knew two of the detectives, having been introduced to them by Risa. Mei didn't expect to see Risa here, as she worked sex crimes, but the departments' cases too often overlapped. Mei flopped open her holder and flashed her shiny new lieutenant's shield. Archer grasped her elbow and pulled her aside, into a circle of light cast by an overhead dock flood that had just come on.

He extracted a plastic sleeve holding a photo and a second one displaying a handwritten note on thick, badly creased paper. "I hope you can see these well enough. The detective in charge wants them preserved to dust for prints at the crime lab. Let's hope they find some. I told him there were none on the last set. This fellow is dressed almost identically to the previous courier. Dark, loose-fitting

Mandarin-style shirt and pajama-like pants. As well as these items, his belly band contained a modest amount of cash, so if he carried the actual artifact, his killer obviously wasn't interested in the cash. Oh, and he had the stub of a bus ticket to Houston."

"From where?"

"Seattle."

"Hmm. Not a place he'd attract attention, given their vast Asian community." Mei studied the photo for a few seconds. "The earthenware vase is from the tomb of Lou Rui, unearthed in Shanxi province. So it isn't part of the same collection as the warrior being peddled by the first courier."

"No, but both are on a list of objects that disappeared from a government-operated Beijing museum several months ago. No one can or will say exactly when."

"No," she murmured. "That's not the Chinese way." Mei didn't need to be told that both would be priceless to a serious collector, however. Or to a dealer—like her father. With dread forming in her stomach, she slid the picture under the letter and began reading aloud, until Archer's cell rang. Not only did she deduce it was Catherine on the line, but following his side of the conversation, she realized he wanted her assignment extended so she could help with this case.

"Thanks, Chief," he was saying. "Lieutenant Ling's ties to Houston's Asian neighborhood may be of value to me in unraveling this puzzle. I took the liberty of inviting her here to see this latest victim firsthand. Would you like a word with her?"

Mei reached for the phone with a less than steady hand. "This is Mei Lu, Chief. Yes. Yes." She sighed. "No. I'm fine. It does make sense. Oh—but if I'm to be assigned to

Mr. Archer starting tonight, you'll need to notify Captain Murdock." She listened while a weary-sounding Catherine told her to consider the captain informed. Mei barely acknowledged the chief's standard closing statement to take care and to keep her updated.

Cullen accepted the phone she shut and handed back. "You don't seem pleased with this assignment, Lieutenant."

"It's been a tiring day. In any event," she added briskly, "this note could be a carbon copy of the one you have in your home file. Except that this courier's name is Jung Lee." Mei passed him both plastic sleeves. "I could hardly help overhearing what you said to Chief Tanner. Really, Mr. Archer, I don't know what ties you think I have to Houston's Asian community. I assure you they're far fewer than you seem to believe."

"I don't know, Lieutenant. For starters, there's your knowledge in this field. You've obviously been well-trained."

Mei recoiled visibly, automatically clenching her hands at her sides. Was it her imagination or had Archer worn a faintly suggestive smile? "As you say, sir," she said levelly, "I've studied Chinese history and Dynasty art. If this is all you need from me tonight, I've got a long drive home."

"Certainly. Let's meet at my office tomorrow morning. Say, seven sharp? I like getting a jump on the day. And I promise to make you a pot of tea that holds more than one cup," he said, showing he'd remembered her parting shot at their last meeting. "Come ready to help me work out an investigative plan. We'll follow that with a visit to your father's gallery. His expertise may exceed yours."

Mei gave a short nod, then excused herself to return to her car. By the time she coaxed the cantankerous Toyota into starting, she saw that her nemesis had been swallowed by the evening fog setting in over the harbor.

As she drove off, she couldn't help wondering about one question in particular. Did Archer have an ulterior motive for suggesting they visit her father?

CHAPTER THREE

MEI LU RETAINED just enough of her traditional Chinese up-bringing to feel shame mixed with her worry over Cullen's subtle implication that Ling Limited and her father might somehow be involved in this smuggling case. Saving face wasn't merely a passing fancy in her culture, but something ingrained in children from birth. While it was true that her father was far more westernized than his wife, in some ways he was wholly Chinese. Daughters had no right to be involved in the interrogation of a parent.

Foo whined and snuggled his head against her as she drove home. He was perceptive enough to know when his mistress was upset.

"Sometimes I wish you could talk," she said, reaching down to rub his ears at a stoplight. "By the very nature of Ling Limited's dealings, it's reasonable that Archer might consider it a gallery of interest."

The dog emitted a little bark, licking her hand before she eased her car from behind the vehicle stopped in front of her. Mei felt foolish confiding her concerns to a dog. For a fleeting moment, as she approached an exit that would take her to a street near Risa's, Mei considered swinging by to ask her advice. Risa had street savvy and access to information on Houston's criminal underbelly. Her friends on the force worked a cross section of undercover assignments. As part of her job, Risa dealt with snitches and could probably fill her in…. Mei hesitated for many reasons, including the fact that she no longer felt comfortable just dropping in now that Risa was living with Grady.

Mei was sure of one thing: smuggling rings didn't appear overnight. Especially rings attempting to peddle the items she'd seen in those photographs found on the dead couriers. Illegal exportation of national treasures and artifacts carried hefty fines and stiff jail terms. Early Dynasty pieces ranked right up there with ivory, or trying to peddle endangered wild animals, either alive or for pelts. This was serious business.

When she'd worked at the Hong Kong firm, a clerk had been approached to find a buyer for a rare ivory hairpin topped by an intricate solid-gold phoenix set with ruby eyes. Ling's dedicated clerk had detained the man after she'd pressed a hidden buzzer connected directly to the local police department. They came at once and hauled the would-be seller off to jail.

Mei later found out the poor man legitimately owned the piece. Or rather, his great-grandmother did. The old woman had fallen ill and he, like a dutiful grandson, had been sent to secure money to pay for her care.

The woman died while authorities fought over whether the government had the right to confiscate her property without restitution of any sort because the item was deemed a national treasure. Mei and her clerk felt horrible, and so sorry for the family. Stephen, who'd been away at the time, said Mei had handled the man incorrectly. Her brother told her next time to buy the piece to put in his private collection. He bought estate pieces in China's rural areas and insisted that if word of her actions got out, it'd cause good citizens to be angry at the government—and to feel leery of working with gallery buyers in the future.

But her dad had personally trained the clerk. Mei was positive he'd never approve of the way Stephen chose to ignore the rules. She hadn't discussed the incident with her father, yet it remained an issue between her and Stephen.

A second question nagged her as she drove past the ramp that led to Risa's. Since her father was also a kind, loyal man, could he—would he overlook a flaw in a friend or fellow dealer?

Until she had that answer, she wouldn't seek advice from Risa or anyone else. Meaning Cullen Archer, as well. If he thought she'd automatically throw open the doors to Ling Limited and allow him to interrogate her dad, he needed to think again.

At home, she brewed sweet mint tea in a black earthenware pot of the kind preferred by Chinese all over the world. A methodical investigator, Mei pulled out a chair at her kitchen table and opened her notebook. She made two lists. One contained what she knew about the case thus far. The other was a series of questions. She stopped the question list at the end of page four. On the fact side, she had only three things. The priceless items in the photographs were missing from museums in China. Houston, Texas, was being canvassed for possible buyers. Two couriers had ended up in the morgue.

Dropping her face in her hands, Mei massaged throbbing temples with her thumbs. Not even her favorite nighttime tea soothed her unrest—unrest that stemmed from the first question on her list. Why Houston? Why her city? She knew about collectors who'd pay small fortunes for the privilege of including any of those rare items in their private hoards. Not one lived in Houston.

She took a slug of cold tea, made a face and rose to go dump the contents of the pot. At her feet, her dozing dog stirred. "Come on, mutt. It's late. I don't have any answers, so I may as well go to bed. I'll need a good night's sleep to cross swords with Archer tomorrow."

The dog yawned and staggered to his feet. He trotted at her heels after she flipped off the light. Strangely, in spite of his short legs, he beat her to the bed. Laughing, Mei played hide-and-seek with him by rolling him up in her spread and letting him find his way out. Having spent too many years of her life in solitary pursuits, she couldn't thank Abby Carlton enough for recommending that she get a pet after moving out on her own.

Suddenly lamenting the departure of her good-hearted friend, Mei flopped down on the bed and reached for her private directory and the phone. She assumed all members of her former circle had gotten a postcard last week with Abby's new address and phone number. It wasn't until Mei started to punch in the area code that she realized what time it was in Houston, and how much later that made it in North Carolina. Returning her phone book to the drawer, she jotted down a note, reminding her to try calling Abby tomorrow night.

Finally, as his mistress folded back the spread and gave every appearance of heading to bed herself, Foo took that as his cue playtime was over. He curled up in his usual spot at the foot of her bed. His dark, liquid eyes were closing as Mei shed her clothes and pulled a nightgown over her head.

Her nightly routine was simple. Clean her face, brush her hair and teeth. Adjust the window-mounted air conditioner and turn off the light. It took barely fifteen minutes. Then she lay in bed watching the play of a streetlight across her ceiling as her curtain fluttered in the breeze created by her window unit.

She remembered how Crista had poked fun at her over

her man from Interpol. Rolling onto her stomach, Mei settled in, wishing she had time to do some investigative work on Archer. Although, Catherine said he came with excellent credentials...

Mmm. He came with a good physique, too, Mei mused. Cullen, who'd also changed clothes between their morning and evening encounters, had switched to snug black jeans, a black windbreaker and white sneakers. He looked as if he'd been called out to the murder site from a more relaxed activity. The sneakers had grass stains on the toes. Maybe he'd been playing tag with the twins in his massive yard. She sincerely doubted that his grass stains resulted from anything as plebeian as mowing his lawn. She drifted off to sleep smothering a laugh.

A STRIDENT AND IRRITATING ALARM brought Mei awake seven hours later. She rarely slept late enough for it to ring, and therefore had trouble finding the shut-off button. Yawning as she climbed out of bed, she couldn't believe how well or deeply she'd slept. Generally, starting a new case left her sleepless.

Foo hadn't budged all night either. At the alarm, his head had emerged from under his blanket, then he'd hidden again until the noise abated. Now he bounded out and zoomed straight for the door.

Mei drew on a robe and hurriedly unlocked the door leading from her bedroom to her minuscule back patio. The brick was chilly on her bare feet. She saw the day was going to be overcast, and decided to wear a pantsuit instead of a skirt.

What she liked best about Houston was that there were so few gloomy days. The fall storms that blew in from the gulf she considered more dramatic than depressing. Those storms brought thunder, lightning, and dumped a lot of rain, but blew through fast. Frequently the sun reappeared directly afterward. Today looked bleak, and matched her feelings about meeting Archer again.

"Foo, hurry up." Mei spotted him sniffing around the bottom of the oak barrel that held a mimosa tree she'd bought the first month after moving in.

Mei could hear her neighbors on the other side of the solid wood fence. The Shigiharas were an elderly Japanese couple who spent a good part of every day puttering in their backyard. Mei loved going over there just to see what wonderful new things they'd done. They had a waterfall, a pond filled with koi, and lush bonsai trees displayed to perfection amid a plethora of bright flowers. To add to her gardening acumen, Mrs. Shigihara was a fabulous cook. The old couple liked having a police officer and her dog living next door, and Mitzi Shigihara was forever bringing over lovely wok concoctions or melt-in-your-mouth tempura dishes for Mei to try. In turn, Mei watered their yard and kept an eye on their duplex whenever they flew east to visit their son. She had to be careful not to rave about or even mention the Shigiharas to her folks. Well, not to her mother, anyway. Aun, like many from mainland China, had never forgiven the Japanese invasion. So Mei's neighbors were another contentious issue.

Mei thought her Japanese neighbors' culture as rich and interesting as her own. But she had to remind herself that she lived in a different era from that of her mother. Her dad, because he was American-born and because he'd traveled extensively, had more tolerance.

Later, as Mei sat in traffic on her way to Cullen's, she wondered once again what might possess a cosmopolitan man like her dad to virtually buy a bride steeped in the old ways. An arranged marriage—an exchange facilitated by a Dingzhou matchmaker—meant, to Mei's belief, anyway, that Michael Ling had bought himself a bride.

Why she chose to brood over it today, she didn't know. Unless it had to do with Cullen's insistence that they kick off the morning's investigation by visiting her father. What did Cullen hope to accomplish?

Did he know her father's history? Michael Ling's parents had met in Washington, D.C. Her grandfather taught Asian dialects to American interpreters, and his future wife, an American-born Chinese woman, had been in his class.

Mei knew little else except that they'd split their time between the U.S. and Hong Kong until they'd perished in a typhoon. Stephen remembered them vaguely, he said. Mei had no recollection at all. To her they were faces in an album. When their only son, her dad, was in his teens, they'd opened Ling Limited in Hong Kong, adding branches over the years, which her dad inherited on their deaths. They'd had one, much younger daughter. She and Michael remained close.

Mei's Aunt Tam had married a military pilot from Houston. The childless couple maintained a residence in the city, but mostly traveled. Mei had never asked, but now she supposed it was her aunt's interest in Houston that had prompted her grandfather to open a gallery here.

As a child, she hadn't questioned why so few Asian students attended her school. In the last few years their number had grown exponentially. New Asian businesses were springing up along Bellaire Boulevard, Mei reflected as she identified herself through the speakerphone at the gate hiding Cullen Archer's home.

Freda answered. This time, though, when Mei entered the house, the toys were gone, the floors gleamed and the housekeeper looked less harried.

"I'm here for an early meeting with Mr. Archer."

Freda cast a glance up the stairs. "Mr. Cullen's already in his office. Please talk softly for a while. Then I might get some housework done before the cyclones wake up. It's not like them to sleep late when they're visiting their dad."

"The children are visiting their father?"

"Well, I suppose *visiting* is the wrong word. Cullen and Jana have joint custody. The twins live with her in Austin during the school year. They spend summers here, and some holidays—and any time their mother flies to Dallas or Kansas City for shopping, or otherwise goes globe-trotting." The woman uttered a disgusted snort. Then, as if she realized she'd overstepped her bounds, she rearranged her features and hurried down the hall toward Cullen's office, leaving Mei to follow.

Freda thrust open Cullen's office door and announced Mei Lu. Just as on the previous day, she then made herself scarce.

"You're prompt," Cullen said. "I like that in an associate."

Mei unbuttoned the single button on her jacket and sat in the same chair she'd occupied yesterday. His casual use of the word *associate* didn't escape her. She sincerely doubted it held the same meaning for him as it did for her, and decided to test the waters now. "I see you have a photocopy machine." She avoided looking directly at him as she kept her gaze on the notebook she flipped open. "Since we'll be splitting tasks, wouldn't it be wise if we started with the same facts?"

Raising her eyes a little at a time, Mei added, "I'm sure you see the logic of giving me all the evidence you have up to this point."

She'd quite clearly caught Cullen off guard. He said nothing, then coughed, then rapidly clicked his ballpoint pen—a habit Mei had noticed whenever he seemed deep in thought. As if on cue, Freda breezed into the office bearing a tray filled with steaming dishes. A pot of tea. A small carafe of coffee. On the tray, as well, was a variety of breakfast items. Fluffy scrambled eggs. Buttered homemade breads. Sausage patties and crispy bacon. And an assortment of cold fruit. Freda set the large tray in the center of Cullen's desk. From an apron pocket she produced silverware wrapped in blue linen napkins.

"Scoot your chair right on up here, dear," she told Mei Lu. "Eat while it's hot. The plates are still warm. You'll find two under the meat platter." Beaming into Mei's surprised face, the housekeeper, who seemed to do everything at a dead run, turned and vanished.

Cullen passed one plate and a silver service to Mei. "Correct me if I guessed wrong. But I'm reasonably sure that you haven't had breakfast."

Mei attempted to hide a telltale expression.

Cullen had sharp eyes. "That's what I figured. Last night after I got home from the morgue and told Freda what time to expect you, she pointed out that you wouldn't have time for breakfast." He shrugged. "I mistakenly assumed you lived with your parents. I have no idea why I thought that. Thirty-something women rarely live at home. Dig in." He motioned toward the eggs with his fork.

Mei complied, but hadn't managed to halt one eyebrow from spiking toward her hairline.

"What? You think it's rude of me to bring up a lady's age?" Cullen filched a piece of bacon off the meat platter, grinning as he bit into it.

"I'm only questioning how you know my age. And why."

"For the record, I'm thirty-six." Cullen saved his scowl

for the small amount Mei put on her plate. "Interpol assembles dossiers on everyone involved in one of their cases."

"So, I can request your dossier? I mean, if we're going to work together and you have mine. Isn't turnabout fair play?"

He paused to sample his coffee. "I'll request one for you. How's the tea? I've heard tea-drinkers are fussier than coffee slobs. As a rule, we're happy with anything that's not total sludge."

Mei peered into the pot, poured tea into her cup, then tasted it while Cullen watched. "Lapsang," she announced, pleased. Lapsang didn't usually come from a bag.

"I'm glad you like it. After you left yesterday, and before the call from Homicide, I discovered we were out of tea. I stopped at the market on my way home. I have to admit their selection boggled my mind."

"Thank you for your consideration, but there's no need to feed me at our meetings. I'm quite used to hitting the ground running. We're not here to socialize, but to lay out a plan for finding the people trafficking in stolen treasures. Or worse. Although the dead couriers are Homicide's problem."

Cullen knew he'd been put in his place. "Normally I don't work with a partner. Tracking lost or stolen art is usually a solitary pursuit. So forgive me if I'm unfamiliar with partnership protocol. I felt…hoped things would go more smoothly if we got along."

Ah, they were finally getting somewhere. Mei set her plate back on the tray and poured herself more tea. She leaned back, studying him over the rim of the cup. "That's where we differ, Mr. Archer. I always work with a team initially. But once all the team members understand the scope of the situation we're investigating, we go our separate ways, touching base once a week to update the others on our progress."

"I think we should start by using first names. Call me Cullen. Do you prefer Mei or Mei Lu?"

She waffled a bit, having had this same discussion with Captain Murdock yesterday. And the way her name sounded as it fell musically from this man's lips took her mind off the matter at hand. "In any investigation undertaken by our department, staff would call me Lieutenant. Last night you didn't tell me whether you have a rank at Interpol. If so, I think that would be the most professional approach. I admit I'm surprised to find an agent of theirs living in Houston."

"I'm a civilian on a list of private insurance investigators that all insurance companies can access. They call someone on the list whenever an insured item is stolen or goes missing. If I'm tied up on another case or decline their offer, they go to the next name. As to living here—" he waved a hand airily "—that's a result of my great-grandfather's toil and a bit of luck. Matt Archer was a wildcatter who hit black gold. His wife, Sophia, sheltered their newly acquired fortune in land, cattle and fine art. His son, my grandfather, was something of an entrepreneur. My father, who was ambassador to Indonesia for many years, helped develop an art-exchange program. When Mom died, he married a woman from Djakarta. Never had a desire to come back here." He paused.

Mei murmured for him to continue.

"I attended university in England. After graduation, you might say I fell into a job with a prominent gallery in Paris, as a broker of European art. I saw high-end paintings ship but fail to reach their destinations, and I wanted to know where such pieces went. It turns out I had a knack for getting them back. As a matter of course, I attracted the attention of our insurers, like Lloyd's of London. I soon discovered they paid better for what I'd been doing for a pittance. At times my path crossed Interpol's. Art recovery became an ongoing passion, one I was able to continue even after I moved home to manage my grandfather's estate following his death. Now you have most of what's in my dossier," he said wryly.

Maybe most, but not all. Mei thought he'd neatly skirted the facts surrounding both his marriage and divorce. "You certainly have an interesting, eclectic background. You're no doubt aware that the extent of my investigative experience is local, or in some cases tracking leads into bordering states. I look forward to learning how you hunt criminals and question potential witnesses in other countries."

Cullen glanced over her head and made no comment, but waited for Freda to enter and collect the tray from his desk.

"Sorry to interrupt," she said. "I wanted to give you a heads-up about the children beginning to stir. It seems that no matter how hard I try to keep them from invading your office when you're working, they manage to finagle their way around me."

"That's fine, Freda. Belinda, especially, needs to start her day with hugs."

The woman asked if either of them needed anything else; when both Cullen and Mei said they were fine, Freda cleared the desk and left in a rattle of dishes.

"Your children are lucky you're so easygoing," Mei Lu remarked in the ensuing silence.

"Yes. Well, kids lose enough stability when parents part ways."

"From the little I saw of them, they seem remarkably happy and well-adjusted."

Cullen shifted in his chair, acting almost flustered by the compliment. Mei wondered if fatherhood was an area the coolly competent Mr. Archer had reservations about. If so, she'd find that hard to believe.

Cullen rearranged his features quickly. "Two of the homicide detectives last night were also present when the first courier was found. To date they've turned up no leads. Both men said trying to get information out of witnesses near the nightclub parking lot was like hitting a brick wall. Witnesses either don't speak English or pretend they don't. I hate to say this in front of another of Houston's finest, but I felt solving these murders isn't a high priority."

Mei returned her teacup to its saucer. "Do you consider the officers derelict in duty, or have they truly exhausted every lead?"

"I wasn't at the first site initially. I joined the case several days later. I can't fault how the team swept the dock for clues last night. They were thorough. I saw one officer walk along the row of parked cars and take down the license numbers of two that still had warm engines. He planned to pay the owners visits this morning to see if they saw or heard anything significant."

"It sounds to me as if they plan to work the case."

Cullen let out a breath. "You're right. I'm just a man who likes speedy results. It's difficult to accept that if people saw a man killed before their eyes, they'd stonewall the cops."

"Sometimes cops are the last ones witnesses want to speak with."

"I know. But I'm sure you know that in the past our police department—or I should qualify and say *some* cops in the city have been as underhanded as the crooks."

Mei stiffened automatically. It was an accusation of long standing, one she'd heard Catherine gripe about often enough. "On a force our size, there are bound to be a few bad apples." Mei found herself quoting the chief. "Chief

Tanner cleaned house after she came on board. She out-right fired officers proven to be on the take. She repri-manded and demoted others."

"Hey, I'm not accusing your chief. I occasionally run into the city manager at community events, and he says she's tough. Yet murder is on the rise."

"And Homicide is a division that's spread thin. I have a good friend who works in the Chicano section. That's an-other area of the city where witnesses clam up and sud-denly become deaf and blind. I'll be glad to ask Crista for some tips on how she interrogates. She has a high degree of success."

Cullen opened his folder and turned to a new page in his notebook. "All right. That would be good. I'd like us to go around to the nightclub and talk to people who might've seen our first courier before he was killed. How many dialects are you conversant in?"

"I'm fluent in Mandarin and passable in Cantonese."

"That's great. I told you I spent some time trying to work a case in Guangdong province. I took a crash course in Cantonese. The taped kind, of course. I learned little and retained less. Luckily, I found that the Asians I came in contact with were very tolerant of my frequent goofs."

Mei laughed. "Our language is one of the more difficult. So few foreigners make an effort, and they were probably pleased you did." The knot in her stomach loosened a bit as they talked. She'd been so sure the first thing out of Cul-len's mouth would have to do with her father.

"They understood my pathetic attempts far more easily than I was able to decipher what they said. Maybe I have a bad ear, but many of the words sound alike to me."

"It's not you at all. Chinese is a tonal language. Words have different pitch patterns, but none of the emotional rise and fall you get in English or other European languages." Changing the subject, she said, "I'll be happy to go poke around the nightclub after it opens today. Just give me a list of people the homicide crew interviewed. If nothing else, the bartender may be able to provide some other leads. Is the bar open all day, or only nights? Where is it located?"

Cullen absently read off the address. "Doug Whitsell said they open at noon." He glanced up and narrowed his eyes as he watched Mei jotting it down in her notebook. "Listen, I don't want you going into that part of town alone. Not even in daylight. It's too dangerous."

At first Mei thought he was teasing. But the minute she stopped writing and looked up, she realized he was dead serious. "Cullen." His name rolled easily off her tongue. Too easily. "The address you gave me is two blocks north of the market where I do my grocery shopping."

"Impossible. I've been there, remember. This area is run down. According to the lead investigator, it's a high-crime neighborhood."

Mei pursed her lips. "Honestly! Now you sound exactly like my parents."

He seemed taken aback by her vehemence. "Let's forget the nightclub for a moment and discuss your parents. Your father, anyway."

Mei tried to control her nerves. It was clear that Cullen intended to say more. But his office door banged open and two excited children came thundering in, shouting and trying to see who could gain their father's attention first.

"Daddy, Daddy." The twins ran past Mei's chair. Instead of grappling a white rabbit as they had on her previous visit, they were now in a tug-of-war over a portable phone.

"It's Mom!" Belinda screeched loudest, but her brother succeeded in wresting the instrument out of his sister's hands.

"She's calling from way far away," Bobby declared importantly. "Freda said Bangkok."

"Yes, and Freda said Mom wants to talk to you before Bobby and me get to say a word." Cullen's daughter slipped anxiously between the desk and her father's chair and somehow managed to drape herself over his arm. "Hi, police lady!"

Bobby, too, said hello, and Mei smiled at them both.

When she looked at Cullen again, he had the phone pasted to one ear.

"Jana?"

Mei shut her notebook and stood, fully prepared to give the family privacy.

"What's so important that you have to speak with me before you talk to the twins? You missed calling from your last stopover." Cullen combed his fingers through Belinda's overlong bangs and gazed at his son, who raptly awaited news.

Teetering on the balls of her feet, Mei wasn't sure if she should leave or stay. Ultimately she decided to return her teapot and cup to the Archer kitchen. She'd almost reached the door when she heard Cullen say explosively, "You want me to wire *how* much? I know what a pearl and jade necklace is likely to cost. Why not pay with one of your credit cards?"

Mei let the door close on his next comment, but she thought it sounded as if he was questioning how she could max out three cards. There was no mistaking his fury when he virtually bellowed, "*All* of them? Dammit, Jana, what kind of junk did you buy?" As quickly as he'd flared up, he appeared to calm down, and he promised to phone his banker on his cell while she spoke with the twins.

Mei actually might have lingered at the door to eaves-drop longer had Freda not bustled out of a room at the end of the hall.

"Ms. Ling. Er…Lieutenant. Have you come looking for more tea?"

"No. I figured while Mr. Archer's on the phone with his wife, I'd return my dishes to the kitchen and perhaps find the bathroom."

"Ex-wife." The housekeeper stared over Mei's shoulder at the door behind which they could hear the children's ex-cited chatter. "It's a crying shame that woman can reach out from across the world and turn this household upside down." Freda relieved Mei of the dishes and pointed her toward a bathroom.

"Will he be long?" Mei asked before the woman rushed off.

Freda shrugged. "Hard to say. Ms. Jana was clearly in a state about something. I'm sorry the kids broke up your meeting. I answered down here, and they happened to pick up on the upstairs extension. They've been waiting for their mother's call for days. They expected to hear this weekend, and they've moped since Friday."

"Um, well, their father may need some extra time with them. I'll just run back to headquarters and check my morning messages. Could you tell Cullen, uh, Mr. Archer that I need to talk to Chief Tanner so I'm clear on how much time she wants me to devote to this case?" Truthfully, Mei needed to ask how Catherine thought she should han-dle the situation with her father. She couldn't barge into his gallery, introduce Cullen Archer as an insurance investi-gator helping Interpol, and watch Cullen start throwing out questions about smuggled Chinese artifacts. Good Chi-nese daughters didn't act that way. Not even if the daughter was a cop. Such discourse moved slowly in her culture and rarely involved women. Westerners didn't understand that there was an order to things, a process to work through to answer even the simplest questions.

Mei felt comfortable explaining that to Catherine. Not to Cullen Archer.

Normally Mei Lu didn't hesitate when it came to dealing with influential men. Actually, she'd dealt well with many of them when she ran the Hong Kong gallery.

So, admit it's this particular man. He only had to look at her with those gray eyes and her stomach turned cartwheels.

Mei knew if she was going to continue to work with Cullen, it was a reaction she needed to quash. Besides, it was a reaction that made no sense. Ask anybody who knew her well. Mei Lu Ling didn't lose her composure over men.

"Suit yourself, dear," Freda was saying. She still held Mei's teapot and cup. "I'll give Mr. Cullen your message. Can't say as I blame you for hitting the road. Ordinarily you can't find a more affable man. But after weeks of phone calls from 'her nibs,' he's a bear. Ah, there I go, running off at the mouth again. Sorry. I should keep my thoughts on that subject to myself. It's not as if Mr. Cullen doesn't frequently remind me—and himself—that Ms. Jana is the mother of his children."

By now Mei was getting used to Freda's slips of the tongue. And to the way she darted in and out like a hummingbird. As she left the house, Mei began to wonder if there was another reason Cullen might want to steer the investigation toward Ling Limited. If he had a high-maintenance ex-wife and a lifestyle to keep up among Memorial's upper crust, might smuggling be a lucrative way to increase his cash flow? After all, he wouldn't be the first of his stature to succumb to the lure of easy money. She'd exposed more preposterous crimes in Houston's white-collar community. And Archer had an ex running around Thailand. How simple would it be for a man with his connections to arrange contacts in the Asian underworld? As simple as it'd be for him to shift the blame—for instance, to an unsuspecting Houston art dealer.

If nothing else, her stomach stopped fluttering over Archer's looks. She had a whole lot more to keep herself occupied on the drive downtown. Such as...which of these musings was she duty bound to share with Catherine?

CHAPTER FOUR

MEI LU FOUND A PARKING PLACE in the precinct's always-busy garage. One thing she loved about the main police station was the amount of activity going on day and night. Men and women rushed in and out of the historic building, some in uniform, others in street clothes, a few in disguise. If their disguises were good, no one except close friends recognized them. The ones easily seen through provided fun for weeks.

Police work, the nitty-gritty part of keeping a city the size of Houston safe from crazies, derelicts and all-around bad folks, took an emotional toll on the psyches of everyone on the force. Laughter was the best cure. Everything, from the smallest oddity to the most bizarre occurrence became fair game to pass around from department to department. After the weeks at the academy, during which Mei Lu took such a drubbing over her deficiency in martial arts, she was careful to avoid being the butt of their jokes.

As a result, no matter how harried or hurried, she sauntered through the building, occasionally stopping to chat, but leaving in her wake an aura of calm efficiency. At least that was her objective.

Cops on all the floors used to stare at her anyway. Partly because at the time she went through the academy, Mei was one of only three Asian Americans with the Houston PD, and the only Asian female. Gradually, no doubt due to the recent influx of Asian immigrants, department numbers had begun to reflect the recent diversity.

Chief Tanner, always big on women walking their own path, used to give Mei Lu pep talks about how she had a golden opportunity to be a model cop. So what if she happened to be Chinese? Except that her minority status had made her the go-to authority anytime there was a disturbance in the Asian quarter. And she didn't always feel like an authority. At times she felt quite removed.

It was Crista who helped her see and come to accept that there would always be cops to whom race mattered a lot. Everyone could name them. Crista confronted them, while Mei did her best to steer clear. It was increasingly evident, however, that as the Asian community expanded, unrest rose among those cops who'd rather everyone of color simply went away.

As she sat outside Catherine's office waiting for the chief to wind up a mid-morning meeting, she considered the various things that could trigger an upsurge of racial violence in the city. Reports of a suspected rapist at large, or a serial killer, or gang activity. She worried that if news of this smuggling operation broke or, worse, became widely known, patrols would triple along Bellaire. Families in Mei's neighborhood, law-abiding for the most part, would be subtly harassed.

Suddenly, Catherine's door burst open and two men in suits and ties stormed past, causing Mei to glance up and forget the concerns running through her head. The shorter of the chief's visitors had a red face and bulbous nose. He was chunky around the middle. The other, taller and leaner, had a pasty complexion. He sported a bushy mustache that made his angry eyes overpower a weak chin.

Mei wondered who they were and what Catherine had said to annoy them. Because they clearly were annoyed, as evidenced by their grim expressions and choppy strides. Their body language said they couldn't wait to put this experience behind them.

"Lieutenant," Catherine's assistant, Annette, said after hanging up her phone. "The chief asks if you can give her five minutes to make a couple of callbacks. Then she has ten minutes to spare. I forgot, she's due to address a Kiwanis luncheon today, and we've already rescheduled it once."

"I don't want to rush her. I can come back this afternoon." In fact, she'd like an excuse to not have to see Archer again today.

"Not good, either." Annette frowned. "She goes from the luncheon straight to a groundbreaking ceremony for the new detention center they're going to build near the intersection of the Brazoria and Galveston County lines. The folks in charge have planned a whole host of events. I doubt she'll make it back here today."

Rising slowly, Mei crossed to stand in front of the administrative assistant's desk, which beat shouting across a noisy room. "I didn't realize the chief had so many duties outside of police stuff."

"No one tells you these things before you take the job, either," Catherine remarked from her doorway. Screwing up her face, she flung the back of her hand to her forehead in a "woe is me" gesture.

Mei and two of the office clerks shared a chuckle.

"Come in." Catherine gestured to Mei Lu. "I assume Annette told you I'm pressed for time. Now that I think of it, what are *you* doing here? As of last night, I thought you were on special assignment with...what's his name?"

"Cullen Archer," Mei said with a sigh as she slipped past Catherine.

"Is the man a problem?" Catherine turned away from her visitor and began sorting papers and loading them into a worn briefcase. "Yes? No?" Pausing, Catherine turned and fixed Mei Lu with searing blue eyes.

"He's a little overbearing—" Mei stopped abruptly, feeling a flush creep along her neck. "That's unfair of me." Mei clasped her hands tight around her ever-present notebook. "He was thoughtful enough to buy me Lapsang tea. Oh, he said I shouldn't go alone to the nightclub where the first courier was killed, but he probably spoke out of concern for my welfare rather than any real chauvinism."

"So then, what's wrong? Why aren't you two nosing around the club?"

Mei shook her head. "I don't know." Swallowing hard, she felt the beginnings of another flush. "No…I do know," she said decisively.

"Then spit it out. This isn't like you, Mei Lu. I've rarely seen you act wishy-washy."

"It has to do with my family. Cullen, uh—he said to call him that—is bent on starting our investigation at Ling Limited."

"Goodness, Mei Lu." Catherine frowned. "Surely Interpol doesn't think…I mean, *you* don't suspect your father in any way…?"

"No," Mei shot back quickly. "But…you know my relationship with my folks. I…can't march into my father's office acting like the cop they never wanted me to be."

"A cop is what you are, Mei Lu," Catherine said with no softness in her tone. "It's the career you chose. You took an oath to uphold the law, which transcends all other loyalties, even filial. You know the rules about recusing yourself if evidence should ever point to anyone in your family."

"It won't. But of course I understand." Mei edged toward the door. "My greater concern revolves around how Archer and I could differ over investigating anyone in the Asian community. Not specifically my family. I'm unsure how to enlighten Cullen, since it's essentially his case. I know if we barge in throwing our weight around, expecting normal interrogative techniques to work, people will close ranks and give us nothing."

Catherine pinched the bridge of her nose. "I'm fully aware yours is a culture that demands treading carefully."

Mei released the breath she'd been holding. "And lightly. And slowly." She'd known all along that Catherine would understand what she was trying to say.

"Tell Archer straight out. If the man is sensitive enough to buy you Chinese tea, Mei Lu, trust him to be open to suggestions that come from your experience."

Mei nodded dutifully. It wasn't what she'd hoped for. She really wanted Catherine to take her off the case. But she couldn't admit part of her reason was that Cullen Archer made her feel more a woman and less a cop.

"Chief, I know you have no one else in the department to translate Chinese, but... Shoot, I've never been so uncertain about how to proceed." Mei hit on something she *could* admit. "On the other hand, I've never worked with anyone from Interpol."

Catherine eyed her young lieutenant long and hard. "I hope that's all it is," she said, collecting her cell phone before walking to the wall to turn off her lights.

As the chief drew nearer, Mei noticed lines around her mouth that she didn't recall seeing there before. And come to think of it, Catherine didn't seem her usual cheerful self. "Is everything all right with you?" Mei asked, taking care to lower her voice. "Did those two men you met with upset you?"

Catherine dropped her ring of keys, knelt and scooped them up just as fast. "What makes you ask?" They walked out of her office, and with a sure hand, the older woman locked her door.

"I thought their movements appeared angry when they passed me."

"Did they say anything?"

"No. Nothing. The way they were dressed—well, I wondered if they were lawyers. Maybe part of the team going after Myron Addison?" The thought had only now occurred to her. Mei knew it was a dicey case. Myron was a sixteen-year police veteran accused of transporting drugs across the border. He'd been off duty at the time, and he was hollering setup. The papers were having a field day. The story seemed to grow more legs every day.

"You know I can't comment on a case IA has under investigation."

"Right. But we all know it's yet another situation bringing adverse attention to the force as a whole. The media keep harping on Addison and on those rumors about missing evidence. It's not fair. You've done so much already to decrease the number of times our citizens have to ask who's policing the city's police."

A meager smile lifted one corner of Catherine's lips. "I'm alternately accused of being a tough old broad, or else too lax. You'd think I'd get used to being in the hot seat." She sighed. "Sometimes I long for the days when all I had to do was be a good cop and teach ethics at the academy."

Annette left her desk to intercept the women. "These are some last-minute calls you may want to return from your car, Chief."

"Thanks, Annette." Taking the message slips, Catherine turned to Mei Lu. "Jordan used to tease me about women's work never being done. Now I suspect he wasn't teasing. Mei, good luck on the case. Keep in touch."

Mei lingered only a moment before turning toward the stairs. She and the other women under Catherine made conscious efforts not to appear too chummy with the chief in public places like the elevator. As Mei Lu clattered down the hollow-sounding stairwell, she thought about Catherine's last statement. She rarely mentioned her dead husband, but when she did it was always with fondness. It sure negated Mei's own cynicism when it came to marriage. Although statistics proved it was common for cops' marriages to fall apart... Having seen a few fellow officers cheating on their spouses, Mei questioned what kept some unions sound and others not.

Her cell phone rang, echoing in the open chamber, and she fumbled it out of its pouch. "Lieutenant Ling here."

"Mei, it's Cullen. Freda said you were called away by your office. Can you give me any idea of when you'll be back? The twins are bugging me to take them ice skating. You and I have barely scratched the surface of what we need to do next. Say, better yet, can you meet me at the rink?"

He rattled off the rink's address, and Mei knew right where it was. She'd gone there as a kid and was now reminded of visions she'd held of becoming the next Olympic champion. "I don't skate," she lied, then qualified her response. "Not in years, anyway. I'd probably break my neck if I tried." She moved to the wall to let two patrol officers entering the stairwell pass.

Cullen's deep chuckle floated over the phone, sending those irritating goose bumps up Mei's arms again. "You think I'd risk life and limb on the ice?" he said. "I just sit where I can keep an eye on the twins, and guzzle a gallon of hot coffee to try and keep warm. How about it? Can I tempt you if I promise to bring a thermos of tea?"

"No need for that. Tea tastes funny out of a thermos. I wonder if the hot chocolate they sell at the concession stand is still as fabulous as I remember."

"So, you'll meet me there? Good. The twins will be forever grateful to you. How long will it take you? Half an hour?"

"Uh, probably longer." Mei couldn't figure out what had possessed her to say she'd go. It seemed too much like playing hooky from work.

Cullen must have sensed her hesitation. "Promise you won't stand me up. If you do, I'll end up being bored to death by a gaggle of mothers who assume I've got nothing better to do than hear every last thing their darling children have done since birth." He lowered his voice. "You have no idea, Mei Lu. Sometimes they even go into those details, too."

She laughed. "Okay, you have my word." He sounded so pathetic. She shut and stowed her phone, but was still grinning when she yanked open the fire door that opened onto her floor and collided with someone rushing out.

"Oops, sorry!" Mei jumped aside. "Lucy?" Gaping at the changes in Lucy Montalvo's appearance since the two women had last seen each other, Mei stood there stunned. "Gosh, you look…different. Gorgeous," she added.

Blushing, Lucy raked her narrow fingers through her shoulder-length brown hair. "New hairstyle. I admit this is a far cry from the way I used to skin my hair back in a ponytail. But there's nothing much different about what I have on. Same old white shirt, navy blazer and blue jeans."

"It's more than your hair, Lucy. I never knew you to fuss with makeup." Of her former friends, Mei had always found Lucy to be the biggest enigma. Quiet, single-mindedly efficient. Risa used to tease Lucy about being too private. But then, she had the tough job of locating abducted or missing children. So, how could her emotions not be involved?

"Well, Jackson likes feminine touches. That's where I was headed. To meet him."

"At the ranch?"

"No, at a florist's." A bright blush added color to Lucy's cheeks. "We're choosing flowers for our wedding, Mei Lu. It's going to be very small. Only family. Still, I have to keep pinching myself. It's really, finally going to happen. Oh, and guess what else? Jackson has a buyer for the ranch."

"That's great! I've been so afraid you'd move out there and leave us like Abby did. Speaking of Abby, did you get the postcard with her new phone number?"

"Yes. I hope all's well with her and Thomas. I know how happy I am, and I wish the same for her."

Mei reached out and clasped Lucy's wrist. "I spoke briefly to Abby. I can't wait to catch up—with her again *and* with you. Anyone can see you're walking on clouds."

"I never told people at work how difficult it was for me to find Tomas Avila dead a few months ago. Jackson's helping me work through that, so I'm not nearly so hard on myself. I saw Jackson make peace with his alcoholic, abusive father, so by comparison, overcoming the high expectations everyone's always placed on me is simple, really. Oh, I've gotta tell you, Grandpa Wiley's having a grand time making new friends at the senior center. I just— well, life couldn't be better."

"I'm so glad everything's working out for you. All falling into place," Mei said. She noticed that Lucy kept glancing at her watch. "I can tell you're in a rush. I have an appointment away from the precinct myself. Let's get together soon—all of us. If not before your wedding, then right after. Please say you will."

Lucy smiled and gave Mei a fierce hug. "I'll do my best. I miss our gabfests even more than I imagined I would. As well, I want everyone to get to know Jackson," she declared, suddenly seeming shy. "He's the best. He's good for me, Mei Lu."

Tears stinging the backs of her eyes, Mei nodded. Blinking fast, she hugged Lucy one last time before her friend dashed away. For a minute, Mei stood in the stairwell, her hand gripping the knob of the door through which Lucy had appeared. She felt strangely bereft and for a moment forgot where she was headed. Just a year ago, the five friends would have thrown Lucy a bang-up wedding shower. Mei echoed Lucy's comment about the group. She missed their camaraderie, too.

She was glad no one stopped her before she reached her desk. Collecting the few messages that had come in, she left again as quickly.

She remained less than enthusiastic about the prospect of meeting Cullen Archer at the ice rink. Several times she considered turning around and just going straight to the nightclub on her own. After all, she'd done hundreds of interviews.

Turning on the radio, she spun the dial to her favorite station, arguing that this investigation was no different from any other. But it was, some part of her brain insisted. Two men were dead. This was not an ordinary white-collar crime.

Traffic was dreadful. Mei pulled into the crowded parking lot a full hour after she'd hung up from making the arrangements with Cullen. He could have come and gone by now. Although, in that case, she would've expected him to phone again.

Remembering how cold ice rinks could be, even in the area where parents huddled waiting for lessons to end, Mei gave thanks for the emergency supplies she kept in the trunk of her car. She pulled out a hooded sweatshirt left over from her street patrol days. She had a lap robe and a windbreaker, too, but didn't bother with them.

Cullen was the first person she saw as she slipped inside the busy arena. She stood in one spot near the concession area, letting the heavy door close on its own.

Spotting her, he shot out of his seat. He seemed relieved, and even a little glad to see her.

"I was afraid you'd gotten hung up at the station." He tossed an empty paper coffee cup in a recycling bin. "That's my third. I'm not sure even a coffee hound like me can drink another. I've managed to save you a seat. If you'll watch my stuff, I'll go get your hot chocolate."

"The rink's packed. So is the parking lot. Funny, I don't recall it ever being this full when I was a kid." She set her notebook on the table and pulled her sweatshirt on over her head. Her last comment came out muffled.

"Quite a few schools are out for Easter break. That's why I have the twins in the middle of a school term. They spend summers, Easter break and alternate holidays like Thanksgiving and Christmas with me. Hey, between the sweatshirt and the cold air you've managed to electrify your hair." He waved his hand an inch or so away from Mei's cheek. They both watched strands of her hair follow his fingers.

"I must look a fright." Still, they both laughed. Mei tried smoothing her hands over her once-sleek hair, only making matters worse. "I don't have a comb on me, either."

"A woman without a comb? No purse? That's gotta be a first. Frankly, I think it's cute. I've tried imagining you a bit ruffled." Cullen's lips curved up in a teasing grin.

Mei felt herself blush. Where she'd been shivering with cold, she suddenly felt warm. "I don't carry a purse but have a car key clip inside my notebook," she blurted, or there was no telling how long the two of them would have stood, gazing into each other's eyes if Cullen's kids hadn't skated up to the Plexiglas barrier and banged on it to get their dad's attention. He wheeled abruptly and acknowledged them. They waved mittened hands, their little faces wreathed in grins. Mei waved back, but they'd already skated off.

"I remember my brother, Stephen, and me being exactly like them. Red faces. Icy feet. And yet we were in seventh heaven. No way would we have come off the ice or admitted to being cold."

Cullen, who had his jacket collar turned up around his neck, tucked his hands in his pockets. "Did your mom sit out here for hours freezing her butt off?"

His query effectively doused Mei's joy. Embarrassment flooded in. "Uh…no. Stephen and I came with friends." She didn't mention how, at that age, she and her brother had been mortified over the funny way Aun dressed and, more so, over her refusal to learn English. So they'd stopped having her come.

Luckily Cullen didn't probe further. He excused himself to go after the hot chocolate.

Mei used the time to refocus on the present. She opened her notebook and read through the few notes she'd made.

But her mind refused to fall into line, instead lingering on how she and Stephen had done their mother a disservice.

Returning shortly, Cullen carried two steaming cups of cocoa. Whipped cream oozed out over the edges and climbed up red-and-white peppermint sticks protruding from the white mound.

Mei immediately cupped her cold hands around the warm cardboard cup. "I'd completely forgotten about the peppermint sticks. My brother and I tried making these drinks at home. Somehow they never quite tasted as good."

"So, are you and Stephen close?" Cullen asked after pausing briefly to lick a blob of whipped cream threatening to spill down the side of his cup.

Mei realized she was staring when Cullen glanced up at her and grew still.

She hurriedly lowered her eyes. "Uh…what did you ask?"

"You and your brother? You're still close?"

Mei angled her head to watch the skaters. She saw the twins, who were laughing and spinning with their arms wrapped around each other. For the first time in a long while, she considered how she and Stephen had become such strangers. "My brother's in charge of Ling Limited's Hong Kong operation. Strong ties are difficult to maintain long distance, especially since neither one of us keeps regular hours. He's engaged, and I've yet to meet my intended sister-in-law. What about you? Are your siblings in Houston?"

"I'm an only child." Hiking a shoulder, Cullen followed her gaze to his children. "That's why I'm thankful Belinda and Bobby have each other."

"Not to get nosy, but you make it sound as if they're the last little Archers. You don't want more children to fill that big house?"

Cullen hid a grimace behind the still-steaming cocoa.

"I wanted a whole passel of kids. It turned out my wife had quite different views."

His scowl convinced Mei to drop the subject. "Shall we discuss our plan?" she said briskly.

"Right." Cullen took a big gulp before setting his drink aside. He dug out a notebook much larger than Mei Lu's. "Have you got anything in your closet that's…less corporate-looking?"

"Pardon?"

"Clothes. Not that you don't look fine for normal police work. But if you've got nothing else on your agenda tonight, I figure there's no time like the present to begin observing who comes and goes at that nightclub."

"Surveillance of the parking lot? All that requires is blue jeans."

"I meant for us to go inside." Cullen slouched against the chair back and laced his hands together behind his head. "I find information flows more freely around people who fit in."

Mei thought about the corporate cocktail parties she'd attended for that very reason—she fit in. "Point taken," she said, sliding a pen from a pouch in her notebook. "What time shall I meet you? Or maybe I should ask, what time did our courier die?"

"Midnight. But I'm not planning on duplicating the situation to that degree," he teased. "Let's say I pick you up at your place around quarter to nine. Write your address in my book. I assume from a previous comment that you live near the club."

"I said the market I frequent is a few blocks from there. I'll have no problem meeting you at the club by nine."

"My picking you up seems to be a problem, Mei Lu. I guess I never asked if you have a…significant other. I remember you said you're not married."

"No. I have a dog."

"Ah. Must be some monster dog if he's the reason you meet your dates instead of letting them collect you at your door."

"This isn't a date." Her pen slipped through her fingers and hit the floor. Mei grabbed up the cup of chocolate to save it from spilling as she leaned over to retrieve the pen.

Cullen shifted in his seat, but he obviously remained amused. "Pretend, Lieutenant. This is my idea. We go inside and have a drink or two. We dance a little, and keep our eyes and ears open."

"Isn't that unprofessional?" Mei said coolly.

"Why are you so prickly all of a sudden?" Cullen removed a pen from his shirt pocket. "That parking lot is one big slab of concrete. Anyone going into or leaving the club would spot us sitting in a car. But we can try it your way."

He sounded offended. The last thing Mei Lu wanted to do was offend him. She bent sheepishly over her book. "No. You're right. We need to blend in. It's just…I'm afraid I don't have your experience club-crawling."

"Wait just a minute," he said huffily, then paused and rubbed the back of his neck. "Guilty as charged. In my younger days, I used to hang out in night spots. After my divorce, too. Until I got my head screwed on straight and told myself I was too old for such crap," he said unapologetically.

"You've been divorced how long?" Mei picked at the edges of her cup.

"Longer than I was married. Six years, to be exact. Jana and I called it quits when the twins were a year old."

"I'm sorry, Cullen."

"Me, too. For my kids' sake. Not so much mine. I look back and tell myself I ought to have been smart enough at twenty-eight to see how different Jana and I were." He stared into space, rapidly clicking his ballpoint pen.

Mei was silent, sucking on her peppermint stick.

Cullen's eyes traced the progress of the mint stick. Quickly glancing away, he shifted in his chair again, making it squeak loudly.

She was about to ask if something was wrong when a blast of cold hit her back. She twisted around.

The Archer twins stumbled in from the rink, bringing a fog of icy air with them.

Cullen leaped up, and Mei followed his lead.

"Daddy, we're pooped," Belinda exclaimed. "But it was the most fun we've had in ages. Mom hates sitting at the rink, so she never lets us go to the one in Austin."

Bobby plopped down and began unlacing his skates. "Mom takes us plenty of places, Belinda."

Mei thought the boy sounded angry.

"Yeah, right, Bobby," his sister went on. "You really like visiting dumb old art museums."

Mei's ears perked up at the girl's remark. Here was yet another reference to Cullen's ex that might fit the profile in this case. A woman who maxed out her credit cards on excesses and spent free time in enough art museums to cause an eight-year-old to complain. A woman like that would surely know which pieces collectors would pay for on the black market.

Or... Mei had another thought and blurted, "Cullen, is your wife by chance an art dealer?"

"She's my *ex*-wife," he muttered. "Jana's not anything, except maybe the world's most accomplished shopper. That's coupled with the fact that she has parents who still indulge her every whim, even though she's a grown woman." Then, as if realizing Mei and his children were shocked by his outburst, Cullen massaged the back of his neck vigorously. Deliberately relaxing his jaw, he aimed a smile at the twins. "Hey, guys. I'll bet you two are ready for a hot chocolate. Mei and I have already sampled some. We can definitely tell you how fantastic they taste. Can't we, Mei Lu?"

Bobby kicked off his skates. "I don't want any old hot chocolate. I want to go home. Why is *she* horning in on *our* vacation? You were s'posed to watch us skate, Dad." The boy's stormy eyes were locked on the interloper in their midst.

"Apologize for that, Bobby." Cullen reached around Mei to clasp his son's shoulder.

"It's okay," she murmured. "I *am* stealing time you should spend with them."

Cullen leaned toward his son. "Bobby, I explained yesterday at lunch that I can't always clear my calendar when you come to Houston. Mei Lu and I are working on a case together. That's the way it is. Now...she's waiting for you to say something."

Bobby shook off his dad's hand. "If you lived with us all the time, you wouldn't have to take crummy old jobs when we don't gotta go to school. Grandpa Vaughn said so. He said you could live in Austin with us if you wanted to and do investigator work for him. You just don't wanna live with us."

"That's not true." Cullen suddenly saw how much interest this conversation was drawing from a room filled mostly with women. He also noticed that Mei had hurriedly removed her car keys and shut her notebook.

"Belinda, do you want hot chocolate or not? Your brother has just forfeited his right to a treat."

The boy's sister seemed to struggle with her conscience. She frowned indecisively, but only for a moment. Then she sank down and untied her skates. "That's okay, Daddy, Freda can fix us something at home."

"No, hon, that's not how punishment works. Your brother's not going to get an afternoon snack at home, either. So if you want cocoa, I'll give you the money and you can buy it while Bobby and I go outside for a chat. Mei Lu will wait for you, Belinda. Won't you?" he asked, turning to the woman now trying to ease around him to head out the door.

Caught, Mei Lu cast about for an escape. Finally, she said, "I think it's better if I leave, Cullen. I have enough data to do some digging into this case on my own. There's no need for you to cut your family time short. If I turn up anything, I can get in touch by phone."

Cullen's eyes glittered. He dumped his notebook into a duffel, hooked it over his arm and lifted his son off the bench by the scruff of his collar, marching him to the door. He seemed impervious to the ruckus Bobby was making.

Mei Lu turned in the children's skates, and walked Belinda out into the afternoon sun.

Already at his vehicle, Cullen unlocked both doors. "I'm done with this nonsense, Robert Madison Archer. You know what I want to hear. Spit it out. Belinda, climb into the back seat and buckle up. Your brother and I will be there after we finish our business with Mei Lu."

"S…s…orry," Bobby choked out in a nearly inaudible tone. "Now can I get in the car?"

For a second, Mei thought Cullen would make him repeat himself. In the end, he didn't. He dipped his fingers into the front pockets of his jeans and sighed, giving the sullen boy permission with a jerk of his chin.

Mei hadn't realized before this moment that Cullen was dressed so casually. Worn blue jeans over scuffed cowboy boots. Not the same pair he'd worn at their first meeting.

Those were dressier. She ought to leave, but something held her in place. Since Bobby had met Cullen's demand, she could just take off.

Cullen, though, held her with his eyes as he stripped off the leather jacket he'd been wearing to ward off the cold inside the rink.

Mei watched in fascination as his biceps flexed and the muscles rippled below the sleeves of a knit shirt that clung to his wide chest. Her stomach tightened when Cullen casually slung the leather jacket over his shoulder. Honestly, did she have to be so in tune with every move the man made?

"Let me apologize for that entire scene."

"No need." She passed her tongue over suddenly dry lips.

"There is a need. Bobby's been testing me a lot this trip. It's not the first mention he's made of Jana's father undermining me. I can see I'll have to have another talk with Hal Vaughn. He's a semi-retired lawyer, a former state senator. Quite used to throwing his weight around. But Hal knows it doesn't work with me. I won't have him putting the twins in the middle of a family feud."

"It's all right, Cullen. You don't owe me any explanations. So, we'll cancel our visit to the club tonight? I'll plan on dropping by after they open tomorrow."

"Absolutely not. What's changed? I love my kids, Mei, but they don't rule my life. I'm still picking you up at eight forty-five. You did put your address on my notepad, didn't you?"

"No." Mei darted a sidelong glance toward the Archer twins. "I don't mind, Cullen. Really."

"I mind. So humor me. Please. Otherwise you'll wreck what's left of my ego."

The chagrin on Cullen's face did more to change Mei's mind than any argument he might have presented. She kicked a loose rock aimlessly and capitulated. "Give me your notebook. I'll write down my address. It's not in the phone book for obvious reasons. So, if you give it to anyone else, I'll have to kill you."

He liked her response; Mei could tell from the way he laughed. She scribbled her address on the page he extended. Then she did a swift about-face and walked over to where she'd parked.

She suspected she'd just made a huge mistake.

CHAPTER FIVE

FOO MANCHU did his usual doggie dance around Mei Lu's feet when she entered her duplex. His tail beat against her legs and he jumped. So high, she felt his warm tongue against the back of her hand. "You are the best greeter a girl could have," Mei crooned. She dumped her mail, notebook, keys and suit jacket on the kitchen table, and gave him her full attention before doing anything else. They played a game that involved her hiding the ball and the dog finding it. Afterward, he romped around the courtyard, tossing his favorite squeaky toy into the ivy.

Mei had discovered that if she lavished love on Foo first thing, he was content to flop down somewhere and let her read mail, fix dinner or do whatever else needed to be done. This afternoon, that entailed figuring out what to wear on her non-date with Cullen Archer.

"Tell me why I stupidly agreed to get all fancied up tonight," she lamented to the dog a couple of hours later.

He sat on the end of her bed, his fuzzy ears flicking forward and back in sync with the rise and fall of her voice. His interest was punctuated by sharp yips. Apparently eager to help her locate something in her closet, whose deep dark corners he loved to sniff, Foo jumped from the bed and nosed his way inside.

Laughing, she rubbed his head. "I've never been to any

of the Asian nightclubs and have no idea what other women wear. When in doubt, black is always good—right, Foo?" Scooping him up, Mei fondled his ears. He shut his eyes and tucked his head under her chin as she contemplated various dresses stored in plastic because they got so little use. After pulling out and returning two possibilities, she settled on a black silk. Her shoes underwent the same scrutiny. She had black, red or white. So she picked black and added a matching wrap in case the brisk wind, which had kicked up on her drive home, turned into a squall. Satisfied with her selection, she closed the closet door.

Mei Lu didn't spend much time in the shower or with makeup. Drying her thick hair took the longest. But when she made a last inspection in her mirror, sticking out her tongue at what she saw, Mei realized she was fifty minutes early. And she had a bad case of nerves; transferring a few items into a small dress handbag, she kept dropping things on the floor.

"Now what, Foo? Men expect women to be late, not early. He'll think I'm eager, won't he? Darn." She sank down on her bed, and her eyes lit on the note reminding her to phone Abby. Snatching up the receiver, she punched in the numbers.

Her friend's phone rang so many times, Mei almost hung up. At the last minute she heard Abby's breathless, "Hello."

"Ab? It's Mei Lu. No, nothing bad's happened here. There's no special reason for my call, other than to catch you up on news, and see how you're doing."

"I'm doing great!"

"You okay? You sound out of breath."

"I just got back from grocery shopping. I've been unloading the car, which is why I'm out of breath. So, hurry up, tell me what's new."

"Maybe the biggest news flash to date—I ran into Lucy at the station today. She and Jackson have set a wedding date. They're planning a very small wedding, she said. Lucy practically glowed, Abby. Anyhow, your name came up. I decided it was high time I quit procrastinating and phoned you."

Laughing, Abby proceeded to rattle off a laundry list of questions concerning the friends she'd left behind in Houston.

"Whoa. Hold everything." Mei propped a pillow behind her head. "You're the one who moved half a continent away. We all want to know about you. I haven't actually spoken with Risa, so I don't have the scoop on her," Mei murmured, unsure about discussing Risa, because Mei felt she'd let her friend down. "Oh, another thing…at the gym this week, Crista flipped Sergeant Denholm on his back. Knocked the wind right out of him. It was fabulous."

"Oh, wow, Mei. I'll bet it shut him up. Sorry I missed that."

"Yeah. I wish you'd been there, too." A dejected note had crept into her voice. "Crista and I went for coffee afterward. It wasn't like it used to be, though. Nothing's the same," Mei said, then curtailed the longing even she heard. "Hey, I made lieutenant."

"Mei, that's fantastic! I can't believe you waited this long to tell me." Abby chided. "So what gossip haven't you spilled?"

"I've hardly been in the station break room at all. Catherine has me out on special assignment."

"That's interesting."

Mei shrugged. "Not so far. Smugglers. Asian art. The guy working the case for Interpol needed an interpreter. That's me."

"But…it's international. Could get exciting. And Interpol! I don't suppose your contact is a James Bond type? I'm envisioning Pierce Brosnan here."

Mei hesitated, giving the image some serious consideration.

"The guy's hot, isn't he. You're holding back, Mei Lu. I can feel it. Come on, give."

"His name is Cullen Archer. I'm afraid I can't compare him to James Bond. No accent. Comes from old money— oil. Lives in the family mansion. He's got eight-year-old twins." Mei knew how all of that would sound to Abby.

"Married, huh? Well, darn. Maybe he has a single buddy. You're too much a loner, my friend."

"From that remark, can I assume all's well in your love life?"

Abby paused only briefly. "Thomas and I are talking marriage, Mei Lu. This time around is all I've ever dreamed of and more."

Mei felt another tiny stab of melancholy as she reflected that Abby had been willing and able to risk her heart not once, but twice. Mei doubted she could ever be that certain of her destiny. She hoped that Abby was right, that Thomas was the one. Mei cleared her throat to make sure her perceptive friend didn't pick up on her doubts. "You sound...I don't know, more relaxed than you used to. *Serene* may be the word I'm looking for."

"I hadn't thought of it in those terms, but I am. Thomas is who I want. It's that simple. And he finally sees we belong together."

"I'm happy for you, Abby." It gave Mei's heart a lift to know that was true. Before she could say more, she heard her doorbell ring. Foo leaped off the bed in a frenzy of barking and raced out of the bedroom. When Mei glanced at her bedside clock, she realized they'd been chatting half an hour.

But if it was Cullen at her door, he was early.

"Something set off your dog? How's the pooch working out for you, Mei Lu?"

"He's the best. We get along fine. Abby, I thought I'd have more time to talk, but someone's at my door."

"Do you want to see who it is? I'll hang on. I still have a million questions to ask you. We haven't even mentioned Catherine or her daughter, Kelsey, yet. How are they?"

"Catherine's fine. Busy, busy. I'm afraid I haven't seen Kelsey in a while. I feel bad about that, too. It's another friendship lost in the fallout from Risa's Internal Affairs investigation. We all pulled back, and if Risa felt abandoned, Kelsey probably did, too—or worse. There goes my doorbell again. Abby...I'll have to call again another night. I'm, uh, going out. To a nightclub."

"You are? See, I *knew* you were holding out. Well, have fun. Oh, I have other news. We'll talk soon. And I want to hear every last detail about tonight. Promise?"

"It's not that kind of going out. Tonight is job-related." Mei grimaced as she deliberately misled her absent friend.

"A job? Jeez, okay. I should've known. I'll let you go, then. Honestly, Mei Lu, you'll wake up one day and find you've worked your life away. Then where will you be? Not rich, my friend. Not even on a lieutenant's salary."

"Yeah, I know what you mean. But I've got to run. I will definitely call again. Or you phone and tell me when you two get married. I want us to keep in touch. Let's make every effort to talk often." Mei listened to Abby's murmured agreement. Then they said goodbye to the accompaniment of the dog's frantic barking.

Hanging up, Mei slid off the bed, tugging down the short skirt fluttering about her thighs. She told Foo to hush and hurried past him to check her peephole. Cullen Archer stood on her porch. All she could see was his chin and his tanned throat. Hauling in a deep breath, Mei opened her door.

"Hi," he said. "I only just noticed I'm fifteen minutes ahead of schedule…." If he'd been going to say more, the words stuck in his throat. Instead, Cullen ended his statement with a fairly recognizable wolf whistle.

Mei, who already hung onto the door for dear life, felt like slamming it and running in the opposite direction. In casually elegant clothes, her "colleague" on this case exuded a sexual chemistry that shot Mei's heart straight into high gear.

He wore charcoal slacks low on his hips. A dove-colored silk shirt was partially hidden by a black linen jacket, which without doubt had been tailored to fit his wide shoulders. And yet…his nervousness showed in the way he buried both hands in his pants pockets, and he rocked to and fro in his shiny black dress shoes.

"All I can say, Lieutenant—well, I can't seem to say anything. You leave me speechless." Cullen wasn't sure what he'd expected her to wear for this outing she'd been so reluctant to attend with him. She had just plain knocked him off balance when he'd first glimpsed all that pale amber skin wrapped in a tiny swath of black fabric.

"Speechless good, or speechless bad?" Mei queried, worriedly yanking on her skirt.

"Good. Definitely good." Cullen ran his gaze down her long legs. But instead of lingering on her high, strappy sandals, his eyes stopped on the bared teeth of a comical-looking dog who gave every indication of protecting Mei Lu's shoes at any cost.

"Ah…I'll step inside to wait while you finish up, if you guarantee I'll be leaving with all my appendages intact."

"Sorry," she said, bending to pick up her pet. "Foo is acting weird. Normally he's glad to see neighbors drop by. I've always said he'd bring a burglar in and show him my silver." She laughed a throaty laugh. "Not that I have any silver. Please, do come in." Moving, she opened the door wider.

Cullen didn't enter immediately, but reached out a hand to let the dog, now safely ensconced in Mei's arms, sniff his fingers. "The twins want a dog. So far I've managed to resist their badgering, even when they double-team me." By not making any sudden moves, he was soon able to scratch Foo behind his ears.

"I'd think a dog would be a better companion for them than a rabbit."

"You saw Mopsy?" He heaved a long-suffering sigh. "She's just one in a series of inappropriate gifts my in-laws lavish on my kids. Believe me, if Jana's mother wasn't allergic to dogs, they'd have a dozen. The fact that Jana's parents buy the twins every single thing they want is a big reason I'm resisting a dog."

"In that case, I understand." Mei closed the door before she set Foo down again. "Kids have to learn they can't have everything they ask for."

Cullen stepped in and swept the living area with a thorough glance. "This isn't the part of town where I pictured you living, Mei Lu. But this house, this room, they're you. Clean lines. Nothing fussy." Shoving both hands in his pockets again, Cullen moved to a wall to examine a painting. A beach scene—the silhouette of a surfer cresting a wave at sunset. Below the picture, the lamp sitting on an end table's base was a ship's wheel. Around the room were other models. "Considering the business your family is in, I'm surprised at your preference for maritime decor."

She laughed. "Building model ships is a hobby that goes back to my junior-high years. Stephen and I got the bug from one of our gardeners. My mother tossed out our collection when we left for college. I've never been so furious. I renewed my interest in it after I finished police training. The tedious work relaxes me. It often helps me recognize the missing pieces when I'm puzzling through a case." She averted her eyes. "I suppose you think that's silly."

Cullen picked up one of the ships. "Not silly at all. But I can't believe you have the patience to build these. It'd take me years."

"The big ones do. That's why I mostly choose little ones." She found her face growing hot at his praise. "Shouldn't we be going to the nightclub now? I just need to grab my purse from the bedroom." Mei made a fluttering hand motion toward one of the two doors opening off the living room.

"All this talent and a woman who can be ready on time? Mei Lu, you're a wonder. I can't understand why some lucky man hasn't married you." Cullen set down the ship and slapped a hand to his heart.

His teasing grin and his remark really threw her. "I don't like to be kept waiting. Why should I keep others?"

"You mean that isn't a secret mothers teach their daughters from birth. Just kidding," he called quickly, as Mei Lu disappeared, presumably to grab her purse.

She came back carrying a lacy shawl and a small evening clutch. "Even if that were true, Cullen, I guarantee it'd be a habit erased at the police academy. They don't take kindly to people not showing up for classes on time. A thousand push-ups have a way of getting the point across."

Cullen took the shawl from her hands and draped it around her shoulders. The lace snagged on the catch to her necklace. "Oops, hold on. I don't think you had the safety on that chain fastened." At the outset, Cullen had noticed the single diamond teardrop resting in the hollow of Mei Lu's throat. His mouth had gone dry at the thought of kissing his way along that chain. Now his fingers seemed all thumbs as he stood behind her. He found the strands escaping her French braid all the more enticing.

Mei Lu's hand flew up to touch the clasp. She went absolutely still when she encountered Cullen's fingers already fiddling with the shawl's entangled threads.

"There," he exclaimed, with a sigh. "Got it. That's a tricky little devil. I can see why you hadn't locked it properly."

"Thanks." Mei Lu nervously ran the pear-shaped diamond back and forth along its thin gold chain. "I rarely wear jewelry. I guess it shows."

"It's a shame you don't wear it all the time," he murmured. "You have the perfect neck and skin to showcase gems of any type or color."

Mei Lu blushed furiously. She bolted out the door, commanding Foo to "Stay!"

Cullen trailed her out, waiting on the middle step while Mei locked up. He'd felt her immediate withdrawal. But he thought it odd that such an attractive woman wasn't used to casual compliments.

As they walked to his car and she avoided letting him place a guiding hand on her waist or elbow, he decided not only wasn't she used to personal compliments, they made her downright uncomfortable. He felt he needed to say something—anything—to break the tension. "If I offended you, Mei Lu, I'm sorry," he said as he opened the passenger car door and she slid inside.

When she glanced up, their eyes met. Mei was able to read the sincerity of Cullen's words, and that caused her greater consternation. In her home, men and women had always been reserved in the company of the opposite sex. At college, when her roommates threw themselves into dating, she'd buried herself in her books, and so had sidestepped the awkward dating stage. She'd been too busy in Hong Kong for personal pursuits. And she hadn't been interested in going out much since joining HPD. While Cullen might be the first man to give her butterflies, the two of them were nothing more than partners. And Mei had witnessed too many messy situations between partners to want to venture into those waters.

"W-we're working a case together. That's all," she finally stammered. "There's no need for you to pretend anything else until we get to the club."

Cullen closed her door. He took his time walking around the back of the BMW. A host of questions darted through his mind. Coming on to her hadn't been something he'd set out to do. Lord knows he was aware of her tony background. He would've thought he'd learned that particular lesson with Jana. Why get involved with another rich, spoiled daddy's girl?

Somehow, though, that profile didn't fit Mei Lu Ling.

Seeing her home, her ordinary middle-class neighborhood, and hearing her say she understood why he didn't want his in-laws to lavish so much on the twins, added to the impression.

Still, she was right about their being work partners only. He'd let her appearance tonight blind him to the truth of that old adage about not mixing business with pleasure. He gave himself a stern shake as he slid into the car. After all, he had his spotless record to think about. Up to now, he'd solved every case he'd taken. It was just that he found it damn difficult to concentrate on anything but her whenever he was in the vicinity of Mei Lu Ling.

Gnashing his teeth, Cullen turned the key in the ignition, vowing not to let this woman knock him off course again.

"I made notes on what we have up to this point, Cullen," she was saying, her tone all business. "Two dead men—we assume they were trying to peddle the goods in the pictures they had on them. And from the letters they carried, we know neither was local. That's not much to go on. Has your contact at Interpol tracked the source of those letters? I'm guessing China."

"They've turned up nothing. The paper is garden-variety stationery that can be bought anywhere. The ink's from a run-of-the-mill pen."

"Hmm. I suppose our dealer could live in Hong Kong or Singapore or Thailand. You're the one in Houston's arty crowd. Do you know who in this city has an extensive collection of period Chinese sculptures? A person or persons able to shell out large sums, probably in cash, for the privilege of owning statues and vases they'd have to hide in a vault?"

"No. Do you?" He lashed back so fast, Mei gaped at him.

"Oh, I see, you think my father—" Breaking off, she frowned at Cullen until he was forced to leave the stoplight where he sat letting his car idle.

"I'm starting to wonder if I shouldn't be suspicious of your dad or someone from his gallery, Mei Lu. Otherwise, why do you seem so unwilling to discuss going over there to talk to him?"

She studied her short, unpolished fingernails. "It's a long story. Or maybe not so long. Catherine, uh, the chief said I should be honest with you. I find it hard because I don't want to cast my family in any sort of bad light." She paused. "Part of the problem is that I'm really the problem. I'm a huge disappointment to my family."

"*What?* I don't believe that."

Mei bit down on her lip, then she gave a thin sigh. "The Lings are a very traditional Chinese family. My mother, especially, subscribes to the belief that through yin and yang all elements are balanced. Night and day, sun and moon, moist and dry, dark and light, fire and water. Sons and daughters fit into a philosophy in keeping with the balance theory. They simply don't rock the boat. Sons and daughters don't chart their own course, but follow a path set by their elders. Sons are yang. Their qualities are brightness, heat, activity, expansion and even aggressiveness. Daughters are yin, and as such tend toward rest, stillness and receptivity."

"I'm afraid you've lost me."

"See, that's what I figured. Most non-Chinese just don't get it. Not only did I upset the balance of our family when I left Ling Limited, I branched out into a field my parents consider solidly yang in nature."

"Oh. I understand. Police work is a man's field, you mean?" Cullen frowned. "But you *are* a cop, Mei Lu. Have been for a number of years. Surely your parents don't suppose they can still change your course?" He slowed the car to take a corner. "But if that's the problem here, I'll go talk to your dad by myself."

"This is a conflict for me because it's my duty to go with you. Catherine already delivered that lecture. I'm not asking that we skip questioning my father, Cullen. I am asking you to let me handle him in my own way. Or rather, in the Chinese way. Business is never conducted in a rush. I can't take you to Ling's and let you shoot questions right and left the way you might do with another person of interest to a case. He'd totally clam up. We face the same situation at the club tonight. To make inroads, to get anyone to speak, we have to be patient. If the bartender, waitresses or clientele are Asian, it's imperative we take a roundabout approach."

"I see. You mean something like sitting down and drinking three cups of tea before we throw out questions about the dead man the cops hauled out of their parking lot?"

"Exactly." Mei's face brightened.

Cullen all but basked in the warmth of her relief. He decided immediately that he was willing to play by her rules. "I see no reason not to let you ask all the questions, Mei Lu. Why don't I sit back and follow your lead?"

"Really? Do you mind giving lessons to my captain?"

"He's all yang, huh?"

Mei Lu laughed, a delightful ripple of sound. "Through and through."

"I suppose it's impossible to tell your superior to buzz off."

"Unwise, anyway. In that respect I'm grounded in reality."

He nodded, and might have continued chatting amiably had Mei Lu not pointed out that he'd driven right past the club.

Cullen snapped a fast glance over his shoulder. "Not exactly the Ritz," he muttered. "I thought you said the grocery you go to is close by. Sheesh."

"You passed it already."

"Tell me this area looks less seedy in broad daylight."

Mei craned her neck and tried to see the street through his eyes. "Would it help if I told you I ran a check, and Wang Xi is the first person ever murdered in this spot or for many blocks in either direction?"

"Marginally." Cullen swung his car in a U-turn at an approved intersection and headed back. Once in the lot outside the nightclub, he sat nervously studying the woman at his side.

"What's wrong?" Mei had knotted her shawl, picked up

her purse and placed her hand on the door release when she felt his eyes travel over her.

"Nothing. Oh, hell. I'm looking at the picture you make in that dress and I'm wondering how many drunk, amorous bums I'm going to have to beat off with a stick."

"If those two women walking into the club are an example of the clientele unattached men have to choose from, I think you can safely leave your stick in the car," she said dryly.

Cullen followed Mei's gesture. Two extraordinarily attractive Asian women with nice figures were outlined in the light spilling from a row of Chinese lanterns swaying from the building's eaves. He uttered a meager grunt and thrust open his door without further comment.

Mei didn't wait for him to assist her out. Nor did she crow about getting the last word the way Jana would have done or manipulate him into swearing she was the prettiest woman here. For all her beauty and the advantages Jana had had heaped on her by doting parents, his ex-wife had been in constant need of validation. Mei Lu, he discovered, seemed oblivious to her appearance. To further punctuate that fact, once they entered the building and Cullen paid the cover charge, she didn't head straight for the ladies' lounge to check her hair or makeup.

"Look," she said quietly. "There are two vacant seats at the far end of the bar. Right next to where the waitresses pick up drinks. Perfect for listening, and maybe striking up conversations." She grabbed Cullen's hand and they swerved in and out between couples dancing to the latest rock tunes.

Cullen found the music at odds with the quasi-oriental interior. It wasn't until they were seated at the bar and he'd been approached by a waitress that he realized how foolish it would've been for him to come here without

Mei Lu. In the ebb and flow of conversation going on around them, he noticed that few spoke English. He was totally dependent on his date. Well, not his date. His work partner.

"What are you having?" she whispered in English, leaning close to his ear.

So close that Cullen recognized the subtle scent she wore, which had intrigued him the first time they'd met. *You,* he nearly said. Instead, he shrugged before asking what they had.

"Three Chinese beers. Shanghai, Tsingtao and Yixing Lager. I see a wine I like. Tsingtao. It's dry and white."

"I'll try the lager."

Mei Lu gave their order, choosing the Tsingtao wine for herself.

Cullen saw the bartender bestow a pitying gaze on her. The guy obviously thought she could do better than Cullen. For that reason, he scooted his stool closer to her, until their arms brushed. Hers bare, his covered by a lightweight jacket. It wasn't really warm, but Cullen claimed it was so he could remove his sports coat and feel the casual touch of her skin against his. Or maybe to give anyone watching the message that they were a couple—if only for tonight.

Not that anyone in the place appeared to care. From the raucous laughter and continuous babble, most people at the club were simply here to have a good time.

Leaning into her, Cullen murmured as much to Mei Lu as he clinked his bottle to her glass. "I don't know if I'd hoped to walk in here and find everyone in the place acting suspicious and sinister, but I doubt anyone here is even aware there was a murder in the parking lot last week."

Mei agreed. "Unless they've relegated it to the background, as something that doesn't concern them."

"But...murder?"

"This isn't River Oaks or Hunters Point," she said, naming two upscale areas in the city. "Some of the people around here could have long histories of being accused of wrongdoing by local cops, for no reason other than that they're ethnic minorities."

Cullen took another swallow of the creamy beer. "Is that your way of saying we're barking up the wrong tree?"

She shook her head and pushed aside hair that had escaped her French braid. It clung for a moment to the curve of her cheek.

"Is this a dead end, though?" he asked, wanting to touch those strands of hair.

"Hard to say. Why are you reading things into every comment I make, Cullen?"

"I'm not. But I am out of my element. I don't want to make a wrong move that might offend you—or anyone—" he hesitated before finishing "—anyone from your culture. Funny, I felt less of an outsider when I tracked that painting into China."

"Because there the people you met were your hosts. Here, families are trying desperately to blend in. Living well is a collective goal, and as such, what is most beneficial to the group is also what's most important to the individual. Even if it means going down a path that individual would rather not take."

"That's rather socialistic."

"Cullen, I'm only trying to explain how things are in my part of town."

Nodding, he took another swallow of beer, and concentrated on setting it back into the same damp ring so as not to mar the dark wood of the beautiful teak bar.

"If you're going to brood, I'll pop into the ladies' room

to see if I can learn anything useful." She patted his arm as she slid off her stool.

He reached for his coat. "Will you be okay going alone? What if you rattle too many skeletons?"

Her eyes twinkled, or maybe it was the flashing Shanghai beer sign that made it seem that way. "I spent two years on Houston's mean streets, doing everything from busting crack houses to posing as a hooker. This is tame by comparison. Drink up, Cullen. And order another round. I may be gone a while."

Cullen watched her melt into the highly charged throng of dancers. It wasn't until he could no longer see her slender form that he consciously willed the tension out of his body. That was also when it dawned that he should've had her do the ordering before taking off.

When the bartender got around to his end of the bar, Cullen decided to try giving the usual sweep of a hand over their empties. As luck had it, in bar talk, he'd found the universal language. Like magic, a fresh beer and a sparkling glass of wine appeared, and the twenty he'd set out vanished. Money was another universal way to break the code of silence. He'd wait to see what, if anything, Mei found out in the ladies' room before he flashed any cash.

And then he wondered how the good lieutenant might feel about bribing information out of potential witnesses. She'd probably pitch a fit.

He'd been sitting alone for quite some time when suddenly he noticed that the couple to his left was gone, their seats claimed by two pretty women. Because he couldn't help being a red-blooded male, he eyed them with a smile. And saw that the one seated closest to him looked much less Asian than did her friend. So he wasn't really surprised when she struck up a conversation in English, as the other woman drifted off to join a group seated near the back.

"Did you stumble in here by accident?" she asked, one eyebrow rising.

Debating whether or not to respond, Cullen picked up his beer and lingered over a long pull.

She studied him through lashes thick with mascara. "You're awfully well dressed to be a new cop on this beat. Unless you transferred in from a tonier unit than those last guys who swaggered in here."

"I'm not. A cop," Cullen added with emphasis. Although technically he was on a cop's mission tonight. "What brings the cops here? Is the club generally staked out?"

Lighting a thin cigarette, the woman shook out the match and blew smoke toward the ceiling. "I hope not. If so, it could eat into a working girl's profits. Nope, far as I know, the cops were on a case. Something happened outside." She faced Cullen. Her intent was obvious when she let her free hand caress his thigh.

He hadn't been so obviously propositioned in a long time—not since tracking a painting into the red-light district of Amsterdam. He'd planned to ask more about the incident the woman mentioned, but noticed she'd backed off, probably the instant his shock showed.

Her low, sultry laugh raked Cullen's spine like fingernails on a chalkboard.

"It's clear you aren't here to score—more's the pity. That leaves pushing drugs. Unless…" She stubbed out her partially smoked cigarette and blew the final wisp of smoke into the air. "Unless your sexual appetites don't run toward women, honey. That'd be a crying shame," she whispered huskily, tracing a finger over one of Cullen's shirt buttons.

He'd gone stone-cold at her last insinuation, and nearly

toppled from his perch when Mei Lu slid her tense body between him and the stranger.

Cullen was aware of the glitter in Mei Lu's eyes just moments before she flipped open her dainty beaded handbag and flashed her badge. "If I were you, honey," Mei said with exaggerated sweetness, "I'd avail myself of this one and only opportunity to take a hike. A quick phone call to Vice, and I can shut you down."

"You left him, sweet cheeks. Don't blame me for poaching." The woman trying to poach didn't appear intimidated by Mei Lu's threat. But in their clash of wills, she gave in first, and slipped off her stool. "Guess I was wrong on both counts," she said to Cullen, around Mei Lu.

Bold as you please, the hooker extracted a card from a black satin purse. Reaching around her nemesis a second time, she tucked the card in Cullen's shirt pocket. "Call me if your woman's ever out flexing her muscle with the boys in blue and you're in need of a diversion. I'll make it worth your time…and money." She sauntered in the direction of the front door, with a lot of hip-swaying.

"What nerve," Mei Lu exclaimed. "For two cents, I'd sic Vice on your friend."

He smiled. "We both know the punishment would be to Vice. They'd be doing the paperwork long after her lawyer bailed her out."

"You liked her," Mei Lu exclaimed, faintly accusing.

"Nope. But don't you admire her grit?"

"Oh, is that what we're calling it?" she murmured, diving her fingers into Cullen's shirt pocket. "Her working name is Fidelity. At least it's not Chastity." Mei wafted the pink, perfumed card under Cullen's nose, then made a big point of pressing it back into his hand.

Holding Mei Lu's slightly hostile glance as he got off

his stool, Cullen ripped the card into tiny shreds which he deposited in the ashtray Fidelity had used to extinguish her cigarette.

Mei Lu's heat fizzled. "Sure you won't regret that before you get home?"

"Positive. Ready to leave? I know you blew our cover to save my honor, but I can't say I like the way that bouncer's eyeing us. Either the bartender or those two women have probably tagged us as trouble."

"While you were making nice with a streetwalker, I got a lead. A waitress who happened to be going off duty at the time our courier was shot."

"Wait. Don't say any more until we're in the car with the motor running."

Mei Lu let Cullen drop her shawl around her shoulders. And she didn't object when he pulled her tight against his side as they exited the bar. Then they practically ran to Cullen's BMW.

Both expelled pent-up breaths as he peeled out onto the main drag.

"What did you find out?" he demanded.

"Wang Xi's part of a triad. The waitress was scared spitless. I gave her fifty bucks before she'd tell me he had the mark of a tiger on the web between his thumb and forefinger. A white tiger. Trust me, that's significant," Mei insisted when Cullen looked clueless.

Cullen was busy reflecting that Mei Lu Ling never ceased to surprise him. Again she showed him how little he'd learned while he was in China. If he wanted to make headway in this case, he'd do well to start relying on her cultural expertise—and her experience as a cop.

CHAPTER SIX

MEI LU FACED CULLEN, who appeared to mull over the information she'd gleaned from the waitress. "The ME's report on the second courier should tell us whether he had a tiger tattoo as well," she said.

"Why a tiger?"

"For centuries in China, red dragons have depicted good and white tigers have stood for evil. I kid you not—that waitress was shaking in her shoes when she brought up the tattoo. She desperately wanted the money I was offering, but I could see how nervous she felt about giving me information."

"While I was chasing after that painting I told you about, I ran into roadblocks thrown up by people whose every move was determined by what a fortune-teller had outlined for their day. You don't believe in all that, do you?"

"No. But we're dealing with people who do."

"After we check the medical examiner's report, this is the neighborhood where we'll have to dig for further leads. Did you get the name of the waitress, Mei Lu?"

"Are you kidding? Not for ten times the money! Tomorrow, you call for a copy of the report, Cullen. I'll visit local merchants on either side of the nightclub."

"Will you be safe?"

Mei Lu nudged his ribs. "I keep reminding you, I'm a

cop. Trained to investigate criminal elements. I carry a weapon." She opened her purse, which contained only her badge, Taser and a small tube of lipstick.

"That's supposed to make me feel better? Guns beget violence. Violence begets more violence. Not to mention a criminal's gonna take one look at you and think…" Cullen stared straight at her, then turned aside without finishing his sentence.

"Go on. What is a criminal going to think?"

"Never mind," he muttered. "If we're referring to men, their minds are going to be on that dress, or how hot you look in it. My mind certainly is."

She ignored him. "It's a mistake to think pretty does as pretty is," she said, twisting the old cliché. "Come with me to the kung fu studio one night. I'll show you a two-hundred-pound cop my friend Crista put out of commission in one flip. And she's smaller than me."

"Kung fu, huh? I imagine you're really proficient."

"I could lie and claim that I am. However, I'm finally making progress. I don't tell many people, Mr. Archer, but in martial arts I was a joke at the Police Academy. Everyone started out way better at hand-to-hand combat and self-defense than me. It's also a mistake to think all Chinese are like Jackie Chan."

"I prefer it when you call me Cullen. And another thing it'd make me happier if you were a grand master kung fu fighter. You're planning to head off tomorrow to poke into a mess that's already gotten two people killed."

"Two that we know of," Mei Lu murmured, all teasing gone from her demeanor.

Cullen pulled to the curb in front of her duplex. "The sooner we sort this out and come up with a suspect who might be transporting the statues, the better I'll feel."

Mei Lu started to agree, then held back—because it dawned on her that when the case was solved, there wouldn't be any reason to see Cullen again. She'd never experienced anything like this over a man. The swiftness and depth of her reaction bewildered her. Her earlier concerns flooded in, the reservations she'd come away with from their first meeting. Nothing had changed, really. And Cullen's ex was still in Asia.

Except that the more time she spent in his company, the less Mei Lu could picture him involved in anything underhanded. She hated all this emotional confusion. Mei told herself she needed to focus on the facts of the case.

"Noon tomorrow, then, at your house?" she said, clutching her purse and shawl tight as she prepared for her getaway.

Cullen watched her grope for the door handle before he swore and thrust his open. Joining her just as she scrambled out unaided, he grasped her elbow, escorting her along the walkway despite her protest. He skimmed his hand along her arm and nonchalantly linked their fingers. Never glancing at her profile, he said, "That dress deserves a whole evening in a classier place than the dive we ended up in tonight."

Mei didn't know what to say. She tried to separate their hands, but he didn't release hers.

"Why do you shy away from compliments, Mei Lu?"

"Because we're trying to work together on a case."

"Are compliments against police regulations? I hope you don't consider a simple compliment harassment."

"No, of course not. I'm sure flattery is a common practice in your crowd."

"I beg your pardon? First, I don't have a crowd. Second, that term, 'flattery,' suggests I'm insincere. Let me assure you, I'm very sincere."

Mei reached her bottom step and stopped. "I didn't mean to insult you. The chief said you're an art patron. That's what I meant by 'crowd.' As for the other…" She stammered a bit. "M-my friends all say I need to loosen up."

He'd finally let go of her hand, and she shot up two steps.

Cullen considered what she'd said, and what she'd implied, as well. He'd sworn off women after his divorce, but something about Mei Lu Ling stoked long-forgotten longings that reminded him all women weren't like Jana.

Although he knew the smart thing to do would be to say goodbye and walk away, a desire to kiss her—just to see what response that might bring—overrode his good sense. Acting on instinct, he bounded up beside her and, for a moment, merely ran his hands up and down her arms, keeping her off balance. The minute he felt her begin to tense, Cullen pulled her against him and covered her lips in a kiss. Had she tensed more, or struggled in the slightest, he'd have released her at once. She did neither.

Cullen noticed her initial shock and softened his kiss. That was when her lips parted and she began kissing him back.

His smile came involuntarily, as did a feeling of satisfaction. The instincts that guided him told Cullen light and short was best, even though hunger for a whole lot more spread through every part of his body. He recognized when the time had come to end the kiss—when he felt her purse slip out of her grasp and strike his shoe, followed almost immediately by the gentle swish of her shawl pooling around his ankles.

Easing away, he bent at the waist and retrieved both things, which he then tucked firmly into her limp hands. Turning, he leaped off her porch with a casual "See you tomorrow." Cullen whistled jauntily, although he wasted no time getting back to the BMW.

As Mei Lu stood on her porch, it seemed to spin out from under her. Through a fog—although it was a glass-clear night—she watched Cullen's car lights switch on. His engine's throaty roar echoed inside her skull. Why had he kissed her? How could he act so casual before, during and afterward? Mei Lu felt anything but.

Clasping her purse and shawl, she felt too rattled to hunt for her house key—until she saw that Cullen wasn't driving off and she realized he wasn't leaving until he saw her enter the house. She had to pull herself together. Foo was barking his head off and pawing at the door.

Ah! The key. At last she inserted it in the lock and made it all the way inside without looking totally foolish. She hoped so, anyway.

After all, it wasn't as though that was her first kiss. "Just the first one that caught me completely off guard, Foo," she said as she closed the door behind her. She dropped her belongings on the couch and switched on a second lamp before hugging the dog. It was then that Mei heard Cullen drive off.

She thought about his delay as she walked dreamily into the kitchen to check on Foo's food and water. Granted, she hadn't dated much. A couple of the nicer cops she'd met. Working screwball shifts the way she did made it difficult to meet men not on the force. And the guys she'd gone out with had treated her more like a buddy than a date. At the time, she'd seen nothing wrong with being dropped off at the curb. One had even experimented with kissing her. Nothing romantic.

Cullen was certainly aware that they weren't calling tonight a date. He just operated differently. Good manners, for instance, were automatic with him. He opened doors, guided her in and out of buildings with a hand at her waist. Which was nice. Very nice.

But that kiss!

Mei Lu paused in the middle of spooning out a quarter can of the dog food her vet said Foo could have once a day. In the morning he got kibble. He loved the canned treat, and now lapped it up before she'd recapped the can and set it in the fridge.

The little dog padded to the back door and stood there patiently while Mei rinsed the spoon. "I know you want to sniff the backyard for night creatures. But you'll have to wait for me to ditch these shoes."

Given the hour and the fact none of her neighbors could see into her patio courtyard, even if they were up, she donned a nightgown, robe and slippers.

As she sat in a deck chair sheltered by her mimosa tree, waiting for Foo to do his business, she tried to plan a schedule for morning. But Mei's thoughts kept drifting off in another direction.

Cullen had said several times tonight how much he liked her dress—the one she'd chosen from a closet containing ninety percent career clothing. Mei had grown up around silk, satin and brocade, but she'd rebelled at an early age against wearing the things her mother selected. As a result, Mei had probably gone overboard with severe styles. She'd worn no-nonsense suits in Hong Kong. At the academy, jeans. After graduation, a uniform. Then back to jeans, and now suits again. Mei watched the moon flicker in and out among the tree leaves. What did that say about her femininity?

It wasn't something she'd worried about before. Why now?

Well, wasn't that obvious? Being with Cullen Archer made her want to look and act like a woman, not a cop. A woman able to bring that certain expression to a man's eyes.

Hadn't Lucy said something similar the other afternoon? Lucy, who before she met Jackson Davis had never fussed with her clothes or hair. Yet now she did. In fact, Lucy had admitted making changes for the man in her life.

Good grief! Mei didn't *have* a man in her life. And for the first time in maybe forever, she was bothered by the reality of that.

Vaulting out of her chair, she sashed her robe with a yank. Placing two fingers against her lips, Mei Lu whistled Foo back to the patio. "Come on, mutt. It's bedtime for us. What I need to do is crack this case. Spending all this time with Cullen Archer isn't good for me."

The dog sat back on his haunches, flicked his ears and uttered a few muted whines to commiserate before trotting into the kitchen behind Mei.

CULLEN took a circuitous route home. He drove down Bellaire Boulevard toward the 610 freeway and couldn't recall ever being in this part of town. Surely he'd been here when he was younger. Yes, he knew he had. Although then there hadn't been the profusion of Asian signs touting new businesses and restaurants. What had happened to the Hispanic population that used to call this area home?

The farther he drove, the more Cullen realized his city had changed around him while he—what? Tried to make a life with Jana that ultimately fell apart? After he'd failed to keep his marriage together, he'd pulled back from all but a few social obligations. Now he lived complacently on Max Archer's estate and ran as many of his business ventures as possible from his home office. Phone, fax and Internet made it easy to be a recluse. A woman on the juried art committee had accused him of that recently.

Darting fast glances from side to side, he felt as if he were back on the narrow streets of Hong Kong. This smuggling case, which his old friend Brett Davis at Interpol had dumped in Cullen's lap, might well be harder to solve than he'd supposed. When Brett had first called and then faxed him the file, Cullen had assumed it wouldn't be terribly difficult to spot a few slippery Asian privateers in Houston. Now he felt like an idiot. This was a veritable city within the city.

According to his car clock, by the time he got home it should be almost 6:00 a.m. at Interpol headquarters in St. Cloud, France. Cullen figured he'd better call Davis before he left his apartment in Paris and tell him this wasn't going to be the walk in the park they'd initially thought.

Despite that, his curiosity got the best of him and he didn't take the freeway, but instead followed the surface streets, wanting to see how far the Asian community extended. It wasn't long before the area really started to deteriorate. After several more blocks, Cullen decided it wasn't wise to continue. Not with the way those young hoods hanging around an alley entrance were eyeing his BMW. They wore black headbands and red kerchiefs around their upper arms. They could be harmless, but it was past midnight, and Cullen's gut said they weren't choirboys.

Deciding this area would be better explored in daylight, he made an abrupt U-turn and sped straight to the freeway. Damn, he hoped Mei Lu wasn't planning to follow her lead into this section. Cullen had no trouble imagining smugglers with tiger tattoos finding a welcome haven here.

A LOUD, PULSING RING ejected Mei Lu from a deep sleep. Groaning and yawning, she waved a hand around in the dim light, trying to find her alarm clock. It'd taken her hours to get to sleep last night, and she knew she was going to pay for it today. She hit the snooze button, but it didn't silence the sound. Not until Foo dropped her cell phone near her head and whined did she understand the ringing wasn't her alarm, but her phone.

Sitting up fast, she flipped the phone open. Assuming it was someone at the station, she shooed away the mental cobwebs and answered in a sure voice. "Lieutenant Ling."

"I knew you had a flaw somewhere. I hate people who sound so chipper this early in the morning."

The minute she heard his voice, one hand flew to her mouth and visions of his parting kiss last night jolted her fully awake. Mei didn't respond because "chipper" didn't begin to describe her current state. Sinking back against her pillow, she scraped her tangled hair out of her face. Her illuminated bedside clock showed it wasn't quite six o'clock. She read all kinds of implications into his phoning at this hour. None should have left her mush-brained and tongue-tied, but apparently they did.

"It's Cullen. Mei·Lu, are you there?"

"Uh, w-we're not meeting until noon, right?" she stammered.

"That's why I'm calling. Belinda woke up during the night with a terrible earache. I had to take her to Emergency. The on-call doctor gave her an antibiotic, but because the eardrum is so inflamed, he felt she should see her own pediatrician today."

So much for her rampant and outrageous thoughts. "Oh, Cullen, I'm sorry. Do you want to call me after you get an appointment? My schedule can be flexible."

"The twins' doctor is in Austin. I'm packing to leave now. I'll phone him from the road. I'm sure his staff will work us in."

"You mean you don't have a doctor in Houston? If the

kids are with you all summer long, I should think you'd want someone closer than Austin."

"I've never needed a doctor before today." He sighed. "I phoned their mother to update her and said I'd take Belinda to my own doctor, but Jana carried on so much... well, it doesn't matter. It's easier just to drive to Austin. I've made the trip so often I could probably drive it in my sleep. But here's the problem—depending on what the doctor says, I may stay overnight at Jana's. She's still in Thailand, but I have a key."

"I see. So you need to postpone our meeting...until when?" Mei Lu was surprised by the disappointment that washed over her.

"Just until tomorrow. Say, three o'clock?"

"Fine. That gives me more time to make inquiries among merchants near the club." Mei heard someone speak to Cullen in the background, and he covered the receiver and said something back.

"Sorry, Mei Lu." He said into the phone. "Freda's asking about packing for the twins, but they have plenty of clothes in Austin. I do have another question for you. After I got home last night, I phoned my Interpol contact. Brett said he's aware that tongs are mixed up in organized crime. I was sure you said 'triad.' Are they connected?"

"No. Tongs are the equivalent of our street gangs, Cullen. Triads are old, venerable secret societies that evolve out of a common practice in China called *guanxi.*

He repeated *gwan-chee,* and murmured, "Yes, I've heard of it, although I don't know a lot. Tell me about it."

"I don't know if I can explain it briefly, but I'll try. *Guanxi* is a centuries-old remittance system that guarantees the reciprocal exchange of favors and an automatic acceptance of one's family. Over the years, triads have evolved beyond blood ties. That's what makes them so difficult to investigate or track. For instance, take you and me. If you did me a favor today, here we'd say 'I owe you one.' Half the time it's a meaningless phrase. In a Chinese triad, that favor would be remembered, maybe even written down. You might never need me to return the favor directly, but say your children or a cousin or a good friend needed help. They could show up on my doorstep with a letter such as the ones carried by our couriers, and I'd be expected to make good on the favor I owe you."

"Good God, that sounds complicated. How can anyone keep track?"

"Years of practice. Can you see how beneficial such a method of support would be among non-English-speaking immigrants? What *guanxi* does is ensure familiarity and a stable source of income in a foreign culture. Now maybe you can understand why I said getting any information in these tight-knit circles may prove next to impossible."

"Are we talking Asian Cosa Nostra?"

"No, although some triad networks operate with a hierarchy and probably have a secret oath. Triads more often come from specific regions."

"So," Cullen mused, "if you go back to the waitress and find out from her what region of China our courier with the tiger tattoo is from, we can work backward and locate his triad? Then we find his family. Very likely, they're our smugglers."

Mei Lu laughed. "If only it were that simple, Cullen. Remember, I said *guanxi* doesn't necessarily run a straight course. It's what makes the triads almost impenetrable. You break off one piece and the trail ends." She paused for a moment. "Reactions like fear, anger, sadness are schooled out of triad members. Displaying negative emotions causes one to lose face. The need to maintain personal pride and dignity comes from centuries of hardships endured by the Chinese. Face has an importance equal to life itself, Cullen. Loss of face is considered the most terrible weakness, and may disturb others in the triad, causing them to lose face, too. The waitress took my money, but she let me see her fear. I can almost bet she went inside and quit her job. Today, her sister, her cousin or a friend will replace her. Someone stronger who won't crack under my questioning."

"That's hard to believe."

Mei Lu could hear Cullen's frustration. "It wouldn't be if you grew up in a traditional Chinese home and were surrounded by people who were entrenched from birth in those beliefs."

"You're not like that at all. You wear your emotions on your sleeve. Yet you claim your family is traditional."

"My mother, mostly. As I mentioned—"

"Sorry." He broke in. "I hear Belinda crying again. I really have to go. But the more I learn, the less I like about this case. Do you have something else you could work on today? Then tomorrow I'll pound the pavement with you."

"This is my only case at the moment, Cullen. And for the reasons I've just explained, I may have better luck conducting this part of the investigation alone. Also, I doubt Belinda's ear is going to be better by tomorrow. And I'm sure she'll want you to stay close by."

"You're probably right. Listen, why not pay a visit to your father today, as well? You said you'd rather do that alone. Before you get huffy and think I'm insulting your dad, all I mean is that with his contacts in the import-export business, maybe he's heard something through the grapevine. It'd be a big help if we had even the slightest idea of when the next museum piece might hit Houston."

Mei Lu sighed. "Okay. I'll add it to my schedule. Although I'm sure that if my father heard about any movement of ancient artifacts, he'd notify someone."

"The police? As you remind me often enough, Mei Lu, *you* are the police, and he dislikes the fact that you are. In any event, you have my cell number if you need to discuss the case. Even if you don't, I'd like to hear from you this evening." He hesitated, then said gruffly, "Humor me, huh? I want to know you're all right. Last night after I left your house, I drove out along Bellaire. I don't mind admitting that I was uncomfortable at the thought of you digging around there."

Mei twisted the phone cord. The excitement she'd felt on hearing his voice returned. Did his remark mean he was worried about her?

"Drive carefully," she murmured. "Oh, tell Belinda I hope she feels better soon. I never had earaches as a child. But a cop I worked with on patrol, his son was plagued by them. They finally had to put tubes in the boy's ears."

"I frankly don't know if Belinda's had problems before. If she has, Jana wouldn't bother to tell me, and Belinda's never said anything herself."

Once again Mei Lu detected frustration in his tone. "It must be difficult to share custody," she said softly.

"You don't know the half of it. And if it weren't for Jana's parents wielding such clout, I probably could've gotten full custody. But that's another story. I wish you success today. Just…take care."

Mei Lu's tongue seemed stuck to the roof of her mouth. She hadn't imagined his meaning that time. Cullen cared about her personal safety. But perhaps that was as far as it went. She shouldn't make more of it just because the man happened to send shock waves through her. She, who had next to zero experience with these kinds of feelings.

Determined not to dwell on something she couldn't control, Mei hung up, climbed out of bed and dived into a cool shower. She came out shivering and still pondering her reaction to Cullen Archer.

Her next attempt to cleanse him from her mind was more drastic. She phoned her parents and arranged to visit them before she tackled finding others who might have been in the nightclub parking lot on the night the courier died. Mei usually made excuses not to go home. Whenever she entered the residence where she grew up, she instantly became the daughter of the house again, and consequently her ideas and suggestions counted for little. Even her absent brother's opinions carried more weight.

Today's visit began the same way. Her father smiled in welcome. Her mother entered the room behind him. Aun clapped her paper-white hands and a housemaid Mei had never met instantly appeared with a tea cart.

Mei sat, but only after Michael Ling had pulled out a carved teakwood chair. Even then she sat rigidly, her spine never touching the pale-blue satin brocade chair back.

After her mother had filled three antique cups from the matching pot, Michael cast another smile toward Mei Lu. "From the suddenness of your visit after weeks of absence, Daughter, is it fair to assume you've decided to return to Ling Limited where you belong?"

Mei nearly dropped her cup. She recovered and managed not to spill tea on the wooden table. It was impossible to miss the deep frown creasing Aun Ling's face. Plainly she was unhappy with her daughter's clumsiness.

"After six years, Father, I hoped you might see that I'm

happy in my work. As you would've seen had you come to my promotion ceremony last week."

"Bah," Aun said unexpectedly. "You should be in China, following your brother's lead. He's found a proper bride in Beijing. I have someone in mind for you, Mei Lu."

Mei Lu couldn't resist countering sweetly, "What would I do with a proper bride, Mother?"

"No need to ridicule your mother," Michael said tartly. "You know we wish both of our children eventually to make happy unions."

It was on the tip of Mei's tongue to ask if her father was happy himself. But it would provoke him, and she'd come for another reason. Why cause more hard feelings?

"Tell me about Stephen's fiancée. I tried calling him several times after he left a message on my recorder saying he was getting married. He's never in his office, and he hasn't returned my calls. He didn't even tell me her name. Does she work for the company? I don't know why I expected that she'd live in Hong Kong. Beijing, you said?" Mei's ever-analytical mind processed that new fact, but she wasn't altogether pleased with what the facts suggested.

Aun clapped her hands again. She carried on a brief conversation with the housemaid. The woman left and returned almost at once, to set a thick envelope on the tea tray. Mei's mother opened the envelope and removed a photo, which she handed to Mei Lu, picture side down. According to the daintily brushed Chinese characters on the white surface, the enclosed was a likeness of Li-li Yu, and she was twenty years old.

"She's so young," Mei gasped. "Stephen is thirty-two." Glancing up, she noticed her mother and father both pursing their lips. "I can't help it. I find it very surprising. When we worked together, Stephen dated modern, savvy women his own age." She'd turned the picture over by the time she'd finished her diatribe. It didn't surprise Mei to see how beautiful Li-li Yu was. Her brother had an eye for beauty, whether it came to silk, jade, pearls or people. She'd always known Stephen had good taste. *Had he also developed a taste for museum treasures?*

Where had that traitorous thought come from? Looking down at the photo, she saw a gorgeous, serene face staring back at her. A woman in traditional coolie pants, unlike any worn here. Li-li's hair was twined in a long, single braid. "She's exquisite," Mei murmured, fighting the nagging suspicions that crowded in. "I'll send Stephen a note of congratulations," she added, checking to see if the Chinese script bore any resemblance to the letters found on the dead couriers, then returning the photo to her mother.

A sense of profound relief washed away the tightness that had come into Mei Lu's chest. It was plain that the delicate strokes on the back of the photograph were far more feminine than the squared-off characters in the two letters she'd seen.

Nevertheless, she needed to broach the subject and be done with it. From the way her father repeatedly looked at his watch, her visit must be keeping him from a prior commitment. But he would never rush her. That simply wasn't his way.

Mei took a last sip of tea. "I'm working on a new case. One that might interest you, Father. Rare artifacts have been taken from China. They're turning up in Houston. Well, I don't actually know that the pieces are. But a former art dealer in the city was approached, a man who had heart surgery a little while ago and gave up his business. That smuggler—the one who approached him—and a second were murdered."

Aun gasped. Her lips moved, and for a moment she said nothing. The teacup she held clattered against the thin porcelain saucer, or against the five rings she wore on her fingers.

As her husband and daughter sat staring, Aun recovered. She bowed her head. "My husband, you must make your daughter leave this police work. She is not safe. What kind of world approves of letting young women deal with death?"

Mei shook her head. "Mother, it's all right. I spent a lot of time training for this career. I'm also working on this case with a man attached to Interpol. He's experienced at tracking stolen art. He…we…neither of us will take chances."

Her father rose suddenly and lifted the cup from Mei Lu's hand. "Come, Daughter, we will go down to the gallery where we'll speak further. It's impossible to think any reputable dealer would find a buyer. But there's no need to upset your mother."

Mei recognized her father's tone. The subject was closed. In that respect, Mei didn't admire him. Before she'd broken with the firm, she'd learned that business woes were never discussed at home. Michael protected his wife from all concerns about money, as well. Aun was only ever touched by the pleasant side of doing business. She hosted dealers and prominent customers. Mei never understood why her father kept her mother in the dark; it wasn't how Mei wanted to live. Which was another reason she'd left the business.

"I have my car, Father. I'll follow you," Mei Lu said. "Mother, I didn't mean to upset you. Please don't worry about me. I'm quite capable of taking care of myself." She left quickly, dropping a kiss on her mother's cheek.

At the gallery, her father escorted Mei directly into his office. He gave her no time to chat with his personal assistant, or the sales staff with whom she'd once worked. Michael shut the door.

"Tell me, who dares to do such a thing? We at Ling's have spent our lives elevating our gallery to a prominent level in this community. Who is compromising our reputation?"

"I don't know who, Father. So, you haven't heard of anyone seeking buyers for museum pieces? You haven't been approached?"

"My daughter, you should not have to ask the ridiculous. I would shake such a person by his slimy ears."

Her smile was grim. "In my heart I knew that. But you must be careful if anyone should contact you. Two men tied to this smuggling died violently. If you hear *anything,* call me at once. It's my job to handle these kinds of criminals."

"And have your mother filling my home with smoke from a hundred bronze Hsuan Te incense burners? She would lay offerings for your safety—and my demise. You cannot ask that of me, Daughter."

"Then will you contact Chief Tanner if you hear anything? I know you've met her at various city functions."

"I have. If the need arises I will take proper steps. Will I know these items on sight?"

"Most definitely." Mei Lu quickly ran down the list of the pieces she knew had been stolen.

Her father turned ashen. "Impossible! Those are priceless icons. It would take someone very brave or very stupid to move such objects through Customs."

"But there are collectors who would pay any price to own even one, right?"

He nodded. "I know of some, although we've long since parted ways. No...don't ask me their names. I've drunk tea from their pots, and they from mine. I will make discreet inquiries to see if the men I know have recently acquired anything of great value."

"How——?" Mei started to press for his method, but his face turned stony, and she knew that would be overstepping a daughter's bounds. Lowering her eyes at once, she murmured, "Thank you." Soon after that, Mei voiced her goodbye.

She left feeling better. She had trusted him implicitly, but it strengthened her faith to hear his shock and to see the genuineness of it in his eyes.

Now, if only she'd be able to repeat the experience with her brother. Mei couldn't shake the image of Stephen's serene, too-young fiancée, a girl who wore the plain cotton garb of the poor working-class Chinese.

Mei recalled an argument with her brother, which had been the catalyst for her leaving Ling's. On a buying trip into China, Stephen had ended up with three very old ivory combs. Mei had run across them accidentally when she'd been hunting in the warehouse for a particular lavender jade vase. Her brother claimed he'd purchased the combs with other items from a farmer, who swore they were made of bone. Mei hadn't believed Stephen. She'd demanded an appraisal. Such overt distrust had resulted in a major disagreement. She'd threatened to quit before, but this time Stephen merely said he wouldn't have any trouble running the operation alone. Mei had left Hong Kong in a flurry of hurt feelings. But she'd never told their father any of this— partly because she knew her parents would side with her brother.

As she dialed his number and again only reached his answering machine, she wondered if those three combs had been the start of something bigger.

Several weeks after she'd entered the Police Academy, Stephen phoned unexpectedly to make amends. He admitted he'd failed to inspect everything he'd bought from the farmer. At the time, his explanation had sounded plausible to Mei. Especially when Stephen said he'd been embarrassed by the error. He thanked her for not telling their father. She knew how hard her brother worked to please Michael. Now, though, Mei Lu wondered if she hadn't been too gullible.

Cullen had said to phone if she stumbled across any new development in the case. Was this one bona fide? She agonized all the way across town. What if she was wrong? What if her brother was innocent? Leaking any suspicion to Cullen meant he'd have his Interpol contact investigate the Hong Kong gallery immediately.

Even if the investigation turned up nothing, the stigma would ruin Ling's reputation. How would that make her feel—to have wrongly blown the whistle on her brother? Plus, was it truly a coincidence that Cullen's ex just happened to be vacationing in the right part of the world? Or was that a clever ruse set up by the Archers? If so, she'd be handing Cullen the perfect scapegoat.

By the time Mei Lu reached her next destination, which was the nightclub, she'd effectively talked herself out of sharing her misgivings too hastily. At the academy, Catherine had stressed the importance of thorough investigation before jumping to conclusions about a suspect's guilt or innocence. In her six-year career Mei had never felt a greater need for taking that advice to heart than she did now. On this, she needed to be absolutely sure.

CHAPTER SEVEN

MEI LU MEANDERED in and out of establishments near the club. She got the sense that people were afraid to talk to her, and even speaking Chinese didn't loosen tongues. The one time she showed her badge, hoping to convince a woman she was on the right side of the law, the people in that shop not only wouldn't say a word, they vanished.

As she'd said to Cullen, her assumption about the waitress was on the money. The young woman did quit her job. An older relative, who'd shown up to replace her, stared straight through Mei Lu as if she didn't exist.

It was well after dark before she emerged from an equally fruitless interview with the bartender. Her cell phone rang as she unlocked her car. Feeling hostile eyes watching from the gathering dusk, she slid inside and locked her doors before she answered.

"Hey, good. You do have your phone turned on. Two more rings and I'd have given up. It's Cullen," he added unnecessarily.

"Hi. You caught me crawling into my car to go home. How are Belinda's ears? Are you still in Austin?"

"We're almost home. The pediatrician changed her medicine and after one dose she's better. The doctor said she can't go swimming the rest of this week, though. Now she's sure Bobby's going to have more fun. How did your day go?"

"Disappointing," Mei said without hesitation. She'd definitely decided that until she had real facts she'd leave her brother out of any conversation with Cullen.

"Did you see your father?"

"Yes. You'll be happy to hear no one's approached him with photos or requests to find buyers. I wish you could've seen his shock when I named the items floating around on the black market. He also brought up a good question." She started the Toyota and backed out of her parking space, catching the eye of a couple climbing into the adjacent car. As people had been doing all day, they avoided direct eye contact. But maybe she was reading more into it than was warranted. New immigrants often tried to appear invisible.

"Are you going to tell me your dad's good question?" Cullen prodded.

"Oh, yeah. Sorry. I'm navigating out of the nightclub parking lot. Dad wondered how anyone could get those artifacts through Customs."

"We've got no proof they've actually come through yet. It's not against the law to bring letters of introduction or photographs of art treasures into the country."

"Wouldn't you bet money that those two statues are here? Or at least that they were? Why else are two men dead?"

"I've had time on this trip to try to put the puzzle pieces together, Mei Lu. They just don't seem to fit. Which makes me wonder if maybe the couriers were accidental victims."

"I don't buy that theory, Cullen. It's too big a coincidence."

"Maybe, but why wouldn't someone savvy enough to know the net worth of those pieces not be savvy enough to destroy the photographs? They're the damning evidence. Without them, Houston PD would have nothing to link the two deaths."

"You're right. According to my friend Crista, knife

fights are a common weekend occurrence, especially here on the east side. But the killing on the dock—the new security measures taken since 9/11 make it harder to believe it's a random act, don't you think?"

"Given our lack of leads and the dead ends we've hit, I really don't know what to think. I almost hoped someone trying to sell Chinese antiquities in Houston *would* make overtures to Ling Limited. But since you're positive Michael heard nothing—"

"I am positive." Mei cut Cullen off. Even as the declaration left her lips, she felt heat creep up her neck. She was sure her father was innocent. The same might not be true of her brother or his fiancée. Maybe Li-li Yu had found a way to use Stephen. Mei was thankful she and Cullen were talking on the telephone and not face-to-face. Otherwise, he would've seen that she was holding back. Lies and half-truths didn't come easily to her. But, until she had a chance to question Stephen, she owed her brother the benefit of the doubt.

"I'm just pulling into my driveway, Mei Lu. How about if I help Freda get the twins fed and into bed, and you and I meet somewhere for dinner?"

"Why?" The word exploded from her before Mei Lu realized how it sounded.

Cullen didn't take offense. He laughed. "You haven't eaten, have you?"

"No, but I'm nearly home. I've been gone all day, and I haven't even stopped by the station to collect my messages. Plus there's Foo. But…I suppose if you have ideas we need to pursue, then…sure, I guess I can rearrange my evening."

There was a long silence on Cullen's end of the line. Mei thought maybe the connection had broken off, until she heard him say haltingly, "I have no…uh…new ideas.

I looked forward to our morning and hated like hell to cancel out the way I did. I guess I just…uh…hankered after adult conversation over a real meal, not the fast-food variety the twins talked me into all day."

As she considered his explanation, Mei felt her heart beat faster. Was Cullen trying to say he missed her? Oddly, even though she'd made an effort to overlook the truth all day, she'd looked forward to seeing him, too—with an equal mix of excitement and apprehension. Tension crept in whenever she remembered how they had parted the previous night. If Mei was honest, she'd admit how much she'd enjoyed kissing him.

There, she'd admitted it. Remembering Crista and Abby's admonitions about the bleak future she'd have to look forward to if she didn't let go of some of her reserved attitude when it came to men, Mei allowed another half second of silence to go by, then said, "Where shall we meet? I'm in front of my house now. I can run in and let Foo out for ten minutes or so, and then feed him. If you know of a restaurant halfway between your place and mine, I can probably be there by seven-thirty." She held her breath. If he had any clue what a step forward this was for her, he'd probably laugh. Most women her age were experienced in ways she wasn't.

"How does Joe's Crab Shack sound? Of the dozen or so around Houston, there must be one midway between us. Ah, good, according to my GPS, there is." He gave the cross streets and the freeway exit number.

"I love seafood. That sounds perfect. I'll see you as near to seven-thirty as possible."

After they'd said their goodbyes and she'd sprinted into her house, Mei had second thoughts. Meeting a man for anything other than business was so unlike her. She wished now that she'd listened to the byplay when their group used to meet for happy hour or dinner. The six friends frequently discussed dating. During trainee days, Mei and Lucy had never had much to contribute. Neither of them had ever had a serious relationship. Risa warned them all off cops. Before Grady, Risa's dates had been pretty disastrous. Boy, she hoped Risa was happy now. She deserved it if anyone did.

Unlocking the door, Mei tossed her keys and purse aside and dropped to her knees for her usual welcoming tussle with Foo.

Mei's mind returned to this impromptu meal with Cullen, then back again to whatever words of wisdom the others, namely Crista and Abby, had shared about their dating experiences. Catherine didn't count. She'd been happily married, she always said. Only her in-laws had caused trouble. Mei's own folks had never dated. Hadn't even met before their arranged union. Mei knew that Aun had felt torn away from a family she loved. She talked about her brothers as if they were saints. But Michael Ling would never discuss such things as love and marriage, period.

Setting aside thoughts of her family, Mei let Foo out to run. She thought again of what her friends had said. Abby usually complained because Thomas was gone a lot. Mei couldn't recall her ever saying anything negative about her first husband.

Mei had probably had more heart-to-heart talks with Crista, though. Bad experiences like those Crista had suffered at the hands of an abusive stepfather and ex-husband only fueled Mei's belief that love was elusive, if not nonexistent.

At least, that was her belief before this past year, when one by one she had watched each of those friends do a one-eighty over a man. Except for Risa, since Mei had had virtually no contact with her after the IA investigation started... With the others she'd witnessed the overt changes caused by love. They swore their lives were complete, and better, because of that certain, special man.

But doubts flitted through Mei's head as she changed clothes. Perhaps it was more of a question: how did her friends *know* Grady, Jackson, Alex and Thomas were the men they wanted as husbands, lovers, fathers to their children?

Mei pulled on a short black skirt and a red silk blouse that was comfortable and that friends said looked good. Black, high-heeled boots and a shoulder-strap purse big enough to hold essentials like car and house keys, and her Taser, completed her metamorphosis from cop to woman headed for pleasure.

She bent to pet Foo, who'd come to find her. The dog obviously thought Mei was getting ready for bed, and had staked out his usual spot. He raised his head and barked at the ceiling.

"Sorry, boy." She rubbed his ears. "I'm leaving you again. This is one time I'm really glad you can't ask me why. Because I just plain don't know."

Mei did know, though. The prospect of seeing Cullen again filled her with an inexplicable joy. Did she only imagine that the night air smelled fresher and the moon looked brighter?

Her cell phone rang, and for a heartbeat, Mei's stomach dived. She was certain it was Cullen phoning to cancel dinner.

But the airwaves crackled with a hollow static of the type she associated with international communication. Stephen's voice, sounding distant, surprised her.

"Mei Lu? I've been away and only returned today from

a five-week buying trip to Qiqihar in the plain of Manchuria." He pronounced it *Manzhou* as the Chinese did. All Mei Lu remembered about that region was that it was historically known for shamanism, opium…and tigers. The first courier had had a tiger tattoo on his hand. But was she looking for significance where none existed?

"Five weeks," she muttered. "Who ran the office in your absence?"

"Why do you care?" Stephen snapped. "You left Ling Limited without a concern about me. Father refuses to replace you, yet I can't very well be in two places at once."

"That's not fair. You *said* you could handle the office alone. And it's not my fault Father chooses not to replace me. After six years, he ought to realize I'm not changing my mind about returning to Hong Kong."

"Forgive me for biting your head off, Mei Lu. I'm really tired. And…I could use your help now."

She felt an immediate surge of her old love for him. "You should've waited until after you had a good night's sleep to phone me."

"I thought maybe your attempt to reach me was urgent. Sang Chi gave me the messages she took at the gallery. You'd called there twice. Then I came home to find three calls from you on my recorder."

Her brother seemed in such a cross mood, Mei Lu lightened her approach. "I phoned when I learned congratulations are in order. Sang Chi should have said you'd be away for five weeks. I called again today because I visited Mother and Father. Mother showed me a picture of your bride-to-be."

"Oh. What do you think?"

She thought he sounded strained. "Of you getting married, or of Li-li's picture?"

"Either, or both."

"Honestly? I've always assumed you and I would remain single forever. She's beautiful, but...not exactly your type."

"You can tell that from a picture?"

"Come on, Stephen. The women I saw you date were sophisticated products of the twenty-first century. Li-li is...very young."

He spoke tightly. "Father disapproved of every other girl I had any interest in. Li-li comes from the same province as Mother. I figure that should please them both. When's Father coming over to meet her? I've asked him to. As well, I want his approval to train her for the position you left."

"Stephen Ling, you're marrying that poor girl to get an office manager?"

"How totally westernized you've become, Mei Lu. Father married because he needed a wife to entertain clients, and to produce sons who'd eventually help run the business."

"Oh, I think there was more—" Mei Lu stopped, asking herself whether she really thought there was more to her parent's almost sterile, brokered marriage.

Her brother didn't appear to have heard her swift intake of breath. He continued talking. "I'll do what I have to, Mei Lu, to keep this end of the business afloat. And I don't need lectures from you. You let me down, not the other way around."

"I didn't," she said in defense. "Surely you haven't forgotten why we quarreled?" Mei decided their conversation was breaking down. If she expected to seriously question Stephen, she had to jump in and do it fast.

"Three silly combs."

"Three *illegal* combs carved from ivory and inlaid with non-exportable black pearl," she shot back.

"I didn't export them, did I?"

"No, but I found them in our warehouse. They weren't on the manifest of items you brought in from Hangchow."

"I see you're still sanctimonious. In spite of what Father says, it's clear to me that leaving Ling's and becoming a crime-fighter is your calling. We should've said goodbye following your congratulations. Like I told you, I'm tired. I have my job. You have yours. Leave me alone, okay?"

Mei Lu felt the vibrations of Stephen hanging up in her ear. She gripped her phone so hard her fingers ached, but let it fall to her lap when the car behind her honked, startling her. It was then that Mei saw she'd passed the exit Cullen had told her to take. As a result she had to drive on to the next one and backtrack along unfamiliar streets.

Her phone rang again. This time, since she was late, she was sure it'd be Cullen. Again she was surprised.

"Lieutenant Ling? This is Sergeant Marshall. Chuck," he added, his words rushing together. "I'm phoning for Captain Murdock. He needs you on an undercover assignment. He said to tell you straight away that he cleared this with Chief Tanner. She gave permission to have you attend a big shindig tomorrow night."

"What's the case, and where will I be going?"

"The captain asked me to leave all the particulars in an envelope on your desk. I stuck it in your center drawer. Can you pick it up tonight?"

Mei saw that it was seven-forty. She was already ten minutes late to meet Cullen. "I'm on my way to a prior appointment," she said. "I'll swing past the station before I head home. I hope everything's in the envelope. Who do I talk with if I have questions?"

"Ma'am, I'm just the messenger. I suppose you'd need to track down the cap'n."

That was the last thing Mei wanted to do, but she wouldn't tell the sergeant that. "Okay. If you speak with him, Chuck, tell him I'm on for whatever the mission is." She signed off, thinking the assignment was probably a cocktail party. Mei had never kidded herself into believing Shel Murdock had requested her for his unit to diversify his all-male bastion. It was well-known that he needed someone better able to infiltrate gatherings of corporate bigwigs. Mei had hated leaving her old unit—Fred Benson was the best captain, but she'd been up for lieutenant and deserved the promotion, and Benson had no opening.

A night spent working another case might be just what Mei needed to help her refocus and decide how to proceed with Stephen.

As soon as she rolled into the parking lot, she saw Cullen's car. Someone was just pulling out of the space next to him, and Mei swung into it. She couldn't help noticing how out of place her Toyota looked as she locked it. She laughed, wondering why she bothered. Surrounded by sports cars, his BMW, and a Mercedes or two, Mei was again reminded of how badly she needed to make time to find a new car. At least she didn't have to worry about a car-jacking tonight.

Cullen stood in the restaurant foyer jiggling the change in his pants pockets as he examined a line of Houston wharf photographs on the wall. Spotting him, Mei walked straight up and said, "I hope you haven't waited long. I missed the exit and had quite a time working my way back here."

Spinning, he let his eyes cruise over her from head to toe before murmuring, "It was worth the wait." Taking her arm, he turned them toward the hostess. "They announced my name a minute ago," he said. "If we're lucky, she hasn't given our table away."

"Oh, there you are." The hostess smiled and handed two menus to a hovering waiter.

The interior of the restaurant pulsed with raucous music and laughter. As they wound between tables, Mei noted that a majority of the patrons were young, maybe college age. That surprised her because of the cars in the parking lot. Which brought to mind Abby's recent admonition that she wasn't likely to get rich on a cop's salary.

"Is this table all right?" the waiter asked Cullen, who deferred to Mei Lu with a little quirk of his eyebrow.

"It's fine. Anything's fine. Passing those steaming platters of shrimp made me realize I'm starved."

"Me, too." Cullen let the waiter place the menus on the table, then pulled out Mei Lu's chair. After she sat, he wedged himself into the chair tucked in the corner. Their knees collided, and she moved hers aside.

"Do you have enough room? Would you rather trade seats, Cullen?"

"This is fine." He grimaced slightly. "Either I'm feeling the effects of my round-trip drive to Austin, or I'm getting older. I'd forgotten how loud they play their music. But I remember they have good food. I haven't been to a Joe's in years. And don't ask how many," he cautioned with a playful grin.

"It's a great choice, Cullen. I don't mind the noise. I like seeing everyone having a good time," she said, looking around with a wistful expression.

Cullen caught her expression. "I know you said you don't date much. I dismissed the remark, because I find it hard to believe." He studied her instead of his menu.

Mei, who'd begun to peruse hers, glanced up. "Oh? Why? Goodness, do I strike you as the party-girl type? Is that how I come across?" she asked anxiously.

"You're not serious?" He paused as the waiter set down glasses of water and took their drink orders. "Let me say there's definitely something wrong with the men you know if they allow you to spend your evenings alone at home. Now, there you go, blushing again. Stop. It's true, I swear."

"I don't sit home waiting for my phone to ring. More often than not, I'm busy."

"Is that so? All right, let's take tomorrow night. What if I asked you to accompany me to a business engagement?"

Mei Lu's jaw sagged a little. "I, uh, would have to decline. I have something going on tomorrow night," she said, purposely not saying it was another case.

Cullen seemed a little skeptical. He also looked disappointed—enough for Mei Lu to wish the sergeant hadn't phoned her.

The waiter brought their drinks and took their food order, and Cullen dropped the subject of their going out again. Mei filled the silence. "Belinda must be much better or I doubt you'd leave her tonight *and* tomorrow night."

"I won't claim a miraculous recovery. She's improved enough that I'm comfortable going off." He grinned. "She begged to come tonight. Both kids did. Belinda is such a little faker. Once she saw I wasn't giving in, she tried telling me her ear hurt again."

Mei sipped her iced tea. "How do you know she was faking?"

"Outside of the fact that she learned the art of manipulation early on from the world's best—her mom? I called her bluff is how. I grabbed her jacket and said that meant she needed a second trip to the ER."

"I wouldn't have known to do that," Mei Lu lamented, rubbing at the condensation coating her glass.

"Sure you would. You develop a sixth sense as a parent.

Similar, I imagine, to the techniques required to be a good cop. You learn to cut through the bull."

This time it was Mei who laughed. But inside, a niggling voice made her wonder if she *was* a good cop. Instead of sitting here taking pleasure in Cullen's company, she ought to be probing him regarding his absent wife. Specifically, why Jana had chosen now to travel in Asia. As well, Mei should contact someone in Hong Kong to check Stephen's recent buying trip to Manchuria. She would, she told herself. First thing in the morning.

Two heaping, sizzling platters of seafood were delivered to the table, causing Mei to put her concerns aside once again.

Cullen had ordered crab. He cracked it out like a pro and ate with gusto. Mei nibbled on her grilled shrimp, unsure when she'd ever taken such pleasure in watching another person eat. Mealtimes at her parents' home were silent affairs. It had taken a long time out of that environment for Mei to accept that it was okay to talk during a meal. She still tended to eat quietly and listen.

Catching Mei staring, Cullen set down his crab leg and pick. "Is something wrong with your shrimp?" He wiped his hands on a wet towelette sitting in a bowl.

She lowered her eyes quickly. "Uh, no. Everything's fine. I'm letting mine cool, that's all."

"Good." Satisfied, Cullen swiped a napkin across his lips, then dove into his pile of crab again. Juice flew as he broke off a claw.

Giggling at his look of surprise, Mei wiped her cheek and reached across the table to do the same to his chin. "You're a wild man."

He waggled both eyebrows. "And do you like your men wild?"

She recognized his sexual innuendo and froze. Was she

reading too much into mere playful flirting? While happy to be here with him, Mei wasn't ready for more. She had tons of reasons. After gulping a bracing swallow of watered-down tea, she broached one of them.

"Cullen, what kind of relationship do you maintain with your ex-wife?"

His eyes narrowed appreciably. There were several tense moments as Mei Lu kept her gaze trained on him, and she thought he wouldn't answer her. But he did.

"It crossed my mind to ask why you think that's any of your concern. But, given the impression I left you with last night, I suppose you have every right to bring it up."

"I don't mind stating my reasons. You're divorced, yet you admit to having a key to her house. Plus, I was there, remember, when she phoned you from halfway around the world to say she'd run short of cash." Mei toyed with a shrimp. "From what I've observed of other people who are divorced, they can't stand the thought of being on the same planet together. Do you and your ex share business dealings?"

Sitting back, Cullen picked up his glass. Time stretched as he carefully weighed his answer. "I don't hate Jana. I try to have a cordial relationship with her for the sake of Belinda and Bobby. I don't always have an easy time of it, but…I married her, after all. Living together is an adjustment, and I don't claim to be without faults. I'd never have stayed at her home in Austin overnight if she'd been there. You have my word on that, Mei Lu."

She nodded solemnly, noting, however, that he'd skirted the issue of his covering Jana's maxed-out credit cards. "You were right in your first assessment, Cullen. Your private life is none of my concern. Only if it affects our case. If it weren't for that, I wouldn't be so nosy. I believe, though, that you have a few suspicions regarding my father. As I have mine about your wife. *Ex*-wife."

"I beg your pardon?" Cullen had dipped into the vegetables on his side plate. He stiffened and a spear of broccoli tumbled off his fork.

"Jana," Mei said, "is in Thailand. Last time I checked an atlas, Thailand was a stone's throw from China. Someone in that part of the world is directing artifact-smuggling operations into Houston. You, Cullen, live very well, and you own high-end art. I heard you authorize your bank to cover a substantial overdraft for a woman you claim you don't care for. That doesn't add up." Mei Lu picked up a fat shrimp and popped it in her mouth.

Cullen's chin nearly hit the table at the same time his fork fell with a clatter. "You believe I—that I—that Jana…"

His well-tanned, sculpted cheekbones turned so florid, Mei Lu thought he might self-destruct. He teetered in that state only seconds, though, before throwing back his head and roaring with full-throated laughter. It went on long enough for Mei to grow nervous. People around them had stopped eating to stare their direction.

"Cullen, shh," she hissed. "Don't."

He did, mopping tears from his eyes with his napkin. "Mei, why didn't you mention this earlier? I am well-off. I explained that my estate's maintained through a trust fueled by oil leases set up by my great-grandparents. I also figured I'd bitched quite enough about my ex the day you and I met at the skating rink. I try not to say things that might influence the twins against her. I tell myself that if I teach them properly and keep their feet on the ground, one day they'll look at their mom and understand being selfish and spoiled is no way to live." He shook his head. "Family court judges don't see spoiled moms as an issue, especially when the children's maternal grandparents wield the power Jana's folks do. To be blunt, Mei Lu, Jana's too narcissistic to organize or operate a smuggling ring. It'd be more her style to pout and cry until Daddy shelled out the bucks for a black market artifact she coveted. But as disgusted as I get with Hal and Sue, I don't question their honesty. They'd draw the line if Jana asked them to fork over for anything illegal."

Mei Lu pushed back her plate. "I'm sure it wasn't easy for you to sit here and say those things about someone you once loved. Really, I'll understand if you call Chief Tanner and ask to have me taken off the case. But I feel I'd overheard enough at your home to warrant some suspicion."

"I agree. Why would you think I'd want you removed from the case?" When she shrugged, he said, "As you pointed out, I considered Ling Limited a possible gallery of interest, even though Michael didn't appear on the list Brett at Interpol sent me. I, uh, find it difficult to talk about my failed marriage. On the other hand, it resulted in one of the best things I can point to in my life. The twins. I love them, and for that I owe Jana."

Mei reached across the table and covered Cullen's drumming fingers. "Say no more. I'll take your word that it's pure coincidence Jana chose Thailand for a vacation. I hope my cynicism didn't ruin your dinner."

"Mine? What about yours? I polished off three-fourths of my meal. You ate practically nothing."

She'd been honest with him about her father. She hadn't been so forthcoming about her brother. Cullen had never mentioned Stephen by name, though. Mei supposed she should voice her nagging worries—and she would…the minute she could rule Stephen out. Or if she uncovered greater reason to suspect him.

The waiter appeared at her elbow. "May I take your plate? Would either of you like a take-out box? Did anyone save room for dessert?"

"No box for me. I'd like coffee. Mei Lu?"

"Nothing for me, thank you."

"You don't want him to box your shrimp for Foo?" At the shake of her head, Cullen turned to the waiter. "Bring her the dessert menu. I'm going to tempt her so that I don't have to sit here drinking coffee alone."

"Absolutely." The young man with the crooked bow tie and spiky blond hair zipped off.

Mei sat back, frowning faintly at Cullen. "I'll stay if we're going to discuss the case. But I'm not ordering a dessert I don't want, just to make you happy. And…Foo only gets dog food." She adjusted her watch, which had turned around on her narrow wrist. "I should probably go, Cullen. I have work waiting at the station. Will you let me pay my portion of the bill?"

"In a word, no. Out of curiosity, why do you have work waiting at the station? I thought Chief Tanner assigned you exclusively to this case."

"Apparently not. My captain cleared this new assignment with her. Maybe she knows we're not making much headway. I feel a little like I'm goofing off. I mean, I met you at your home, at the ice rink, a nightclub and here. What have we got to show for our time?"

"We've gotten to know each other better. I've enjoyed that. Haven't you? Particularly at the nightclub and tonight. Wait, don't bruise my ego. At least not before I point out that those trips weren't on company time. Unless you aren't allowed any nights off for pleasure."

His somewhat self-conscious smile pierced Mei's armor as perhaps nothing else could have. The tension that had plagued her all through the meal seemed to ooze out through her toes—toes that suddenly tingled in anticipation of imagined pleasure. "The city doesn't own me twenty-four-seven except in extreme emergencies." Mei pushed a lock of hair out of her eyes and looped it over one ear. "I've always had difficulty mixing business with pleasure, Cullen. I tend to be single-minded when I'm working."

The waiter brought Cullen's coffee and dropped off a dessert menu for Mei Lu, saying he'd be right back to take her order. Smiling lazily, Cullen held the single page in front of Mei Lu's eyes. "Pick the richest, most sinful item on the list. Guaranteed to help what ails you."

She hesitated, but all at once felt like throwing caution to the wind. Why not? It wasn't every night she sat in a dimly lit restaurant across a table from a man who could make her toes curl with his lopsided smile. "If you promise to help me eat it, I'll try this one called Death by Chocolate. We could say it's appropriate to our case."

He screwed up his face. "Mei Lu, that's sick humor." Even as he said it, Cullen hailed the waiter and placed the order.

When it came, they both sat and stared at the huge brownie, bulging with chocolate chips, topped with a mountain of chocolate ice cream and drowning in dark chocolate syrup.

Between them, and amid a lot of laughter, they polished it off.

Smacking her lips after swiping them with her napkin, Mei Lu fell back in her chair with a groan. "I can't believe we ate that. Ate the whole thing. I'll probably be up all night with a stomachache. If you are, darn it, I want to know."

"I happen to have a cast-iron stomach, but even if I got sick, the joy of seeing you dig into that gastronomic phenomenon would more than make up for any discomfort.

See, it's okay to relax, Mei Lu. You should do it more often." Cullen dug out his wallet and signaled for the bill.

"You're right," she said. Mei was never coy. Scooping up her purse, she murmured, "I wish you'd let me split the check."

"Don't spoil the fun we just shared." He carelessly thumbed out a sheaf of twenties, tucked them under the bill, then rounded the table and slid his hand under Mei Lu's arm. "What about tomorrow?"

"What about it?" She blinked up into his warm eyes, feeling her point of gravity shift dangerously.

"Our agenda. What's next?"

"Oh. I don't know. We didn't discuss that tonight," she said, knowing she sounded piqued.

"We're discussing it now. I propose we meet at eight. My office."

"Did you forget I'm headed for work? They may have plans for me." She knew Sergeant Marshall had said they needed her to cover an evening function. But she felt dizzy whenever Cullen touched her. She needed to establish some control.

"I had forgotten. After that big meal, I'll be up reading or going over old ground on this case. Call me tonight after you get your assignment. If you're tied up tomorrow, and if Belinda feels better, I might take the kids to the zoo."

"That sounds like fun."

"Hey, if your time allows, come with us. I've been there so many times, just me and the kids, I've got to admit I'd welcome the company of someone over three-and-a-half feet tall."

Mei smiled at that image as they walked out to the parking lot. She knew if she worked tomorrow night, it meant her afternoon would be free. "I'll phone you, and we'll see. You have to promise me one thing, though. If I go with you, I need your word that we'll work on our case."

"I promise." When she stopped beside her car, he said, "How about if we shake hands on it?"

She eased out of his grip, stepped back and extended her hand.

Clasping it in both of his, Cullen gave a sharp tug, drawing her toward him just enough so that he checked her forward motion with his lips, locking them tight against hers.

Mei didn't fight it. She gave him an *A* for ingenuity. Besides, ever since last night, her thoughts had lingered on what it would be like to kiss him again. Now she knew. Terrific was the word that thundered through her brain. *Terrific!*

CHAPTER EIGHT

MEI LU LET CULLEN LEAD her to her car and unlock it and open the door. She said something about calling him as soon as she found out if she'd be available to go with him to the zoo tomorrow, but her brain wasn't exactly focused. She was all thumbs when she went to start the Toyota. It took three tries.

She had kissed both of the other men she'd dated. One didn't move her. The other was more like a friendly, "we're friends" kiss. Both times Cullen kissed her, she'd felt her feet leave the ground. Her heart beat so fast she thought it might fly out of her chest. And her mind—well, it spun faster than a top and didn't work right for an hour afterward.

Dragging her cell phone from her purse, Mei drove out of the lot at Joe's, aimed in the general direction of her office. She punched speed dial for Homicide, Chicano Unit. "This is Lieutenant Ling. Is Detective Santiago—Crista Santiago—on duty tonight?" Pulling up at a stoplight, Mei tapped her fingers to the low throb of a tune playing on her car radio as she waited for the dispatcher to check. "She is? Oh, she's out on a call?" Mei said, making a left turn behind the car directly in front of her. "No, don't patch me through to her car. I'm on my way to headquarters. I'll pop in when I get there to see if she's reported back. It's not urgent. Thanks." Mei pressed the End button. She needed to talk to someone about these riotous feelings Cullen evoked in her. Crista was the friend Mei trusted most, even though they'd had a difference of opinion as to how they should proceed at the time Risa was accused of shooting her partner. Up to then, the friendships among the six women had been solid. Mei fully understood that Catherine had to be excluded from any discussions about Risa. The chief had to remain absolutely impartial. But it was as if they all got touchy when Risa's name surfaced. Worse, they went from being touchy to outright disagreeable. Rather than fight openly, some of them stopped speaking. That was slow to change, even after Risa had been cleared.

Although they all spoke in passing, the friendships weren't like they'd been before. Mei realized she'd just phoned Crista as she might have in the old days—to discuss the reactions she was having to Cullen. But...what if Crista laughed, or told her to take off her rose-colored glasses and step into the real world, as she'd done at dinner the evening that four of the friends met for what had turned out to be their final girls' night out.

Mei backed off on her plan to confide in Crista. She dropped the whole idea several blocks ahead of pulling into the HPD parking garage.

Minutes later her footsteps echoed in the corridor leading to her unit. Most areas of the midtown station teemed with activity around the clock, although the white-collar crimes unit tended to be dark at night. Those cops worked bankers' hours; their jobs entailed mostly computer investigations or forensic audits. Occasionally some of the officers followed leads at night, because certain executives were wising up about not leaving paper trails. Mei assumed that was why she was needed tomorrow night. Murdock or someone else probably got word that questionable business might be discussed at a cocktail party or banquet.

She turned on the lamp on her desk and pulled the manila envelope out of her middle drawer. Two items fell out when she emptied the envelope on her blotter: a scribbled note from Captain Murdock and a ticket to a benefit gala at the Contemporary Arts Museum. She caught her breath. What if this benefit was where Cullen planned to go? No, he'd said a business dinner. Of course, he might have those in conjunction with those family oil dealings he'd mentioned.

Mei also saw that the sponsors listed were some of the area's largest, most influential manufacturers. Cullen probably had no reason to be involved with those companies.

The ticket said that proceeds from the by-invitation-only event were to provide art scholarships to local, talented but underprivileged artists, some of whose work would be on display. Mei tapped the ticket against her chin, thinking that it appeared to be a worthy reason to hold a benefit. Such galas were commonplace among the city's wealthiest. They didn't mind shelling out big bucks in charitable contributions, especially when it provided an opportunity to wear designer gowns, mill around drinking champagne and looking important. Plus, it got their names and/or pictures in the newspaper—a given with this list of bigwigs.

She dragged Captain Murdock's note closer to the light to decipher his scrawl. Over the last few years, federal immigration services had been cracking down on companies that knowingly hired illegal immigrants to work at low-paying jobs that many company officials went on record to say they couldn't otherwise fill. The INS said tough. The feds might turn a blind eye if a few undocumented aliens showed up on a firm's payroll. Not, however, if the firm's officials facilitated transporting non-citizens for that purpose. The INS had conducted several successful raids in Texas. From Shel's note, Mei couldn't decide if her unit had been tapped to aid the INS, or if Murdock had picked up a clue and wanted to cast his own net and advance his role in the Houston PD. Anyway, it wasn't Mei's job to question his reasons. Her instructions were to lurk near five specific men named in the note and to listen for any incriminating chatter among them. She was to tape their discussion.

Mei put the ticket in her purse and shredded Shel's instructions. She knew from past experience that high-powered male execs could usually be counted on to ignore a woman standing alone sipping champagne. Lucky for her. As Mei stood, reaching to turn off the lamp, the telephone on her desk rang. She picked it up, expecting to hear her boss. Instead it was Crista Santiago.

"Dispatch said you phoned earlier, Mei Lu. I decided to clock out and go straight home from my crime scene. What are you doing at your desk this late? I ran into Charlie from your unit at our local Fiesta store last night. He said you were still on special assignment."

"Charlie who? From my unit?"

"Marshall. He shoots pool with a bunch of guys from Homicide."

"Oh, Sergeant Marshall. He was introduced to me as Chuck. He's right. I am on special assignment. I'm also helping with another investigation."

"Is that why you phoned? About a case?"

"No." Mei Lu let a sigh escape. "It was personal, but I decided not to bother you."

"Now I'm curious. Does it have to do with your family?"

"More personal than that." Mei cleared her throat and

glanced around to make sure she was indeed alone in the office.

"What's more personal than family? I'm intrigued."

Mei fidgeted a bit, then finally blurted, "I need advice, Crista. You know me. Know how I am. How can I tell if the feelings that…come over me anytime I'm around a particular man might be more than, uh, respect or friendship?"

"Is it by chance that guy you were telling me about at the gym?"

"Cullen Archer? Yes. He confuses me, Crista."

"Don't they all? Men, I mean." Crista laughed. "I'm probably the last person who should give advice, Mei Lu. I said a lot of things before I met Alex that I have to take back now. I just know I've never been happier. A year ago I'd never have believed it. You and I had similar views on love and marriage. Now, I…well, maybe you ought to take a chance on this guy, Mei. See what happens. Hey, I'm pulling into my driveway. Alex is waiting."

"Then don't let me keep you. Thanks for taking time to call me back. I don't know when I'll get to the studio to work out again."

"Yeah, we're both really busy."

"Right. Bye, Crista. And thanks again." Mei Lu hung up before things could get awkward. She'd come to accept that was how it was now between the once best friends. Mei realized she was afraid to find out how deep all the hurt feelings went. What if their friendships were irreparable? She'd hate that.

In spite of Crista's ambiguity, Mei Lu trusted her instincts. Which meant that if she took Crista's advice, she'd pick up the phone and call Cullen. Tell him she'd have the morning free and she'd love to visit the zoo with him and the twins.

Before her fears could weigh her down, Mei Lu did just that.

"Hey, that's the best news I've had all day," he exclaimed. "Don't get me wrong, I love doing stuff with my kids. It's just more fun if there's another adult along to...to... Hell, I'm making a bad job of explaining, aren't I."

"Not at all. I may not have children, Cullen, but I learned a thing or two over the two years I spent patrolling neighborhoods. Being a single parent isn't easy, no matter what circumstance brought it about. Mostly I saw women who couldn't keep a lid on the family. Ones who couldn't control angry teenagers. Of course, cops only see the families with problems."

"Compared to what you're describing, my life's a breeze. I promise I won't bend your ear tomorrow about my insignificant trials and woes."

"Cullen, I didn't say what I did to make any point. I thought I was commiserating with you. Raising kids is a scary proposition. Marriage is scary." Mei laughed uncomfortably. "Why do you think I'm still single? My friends would say it's because I want the guarantee of a storybook ending, and there aren't any such guarantees in real life."

"Truer words were never spoken. Of course, nobody thinks about that when he or she falls in love. So, you never have, huh?"

"What? Fallen in love? No," she admitted, dragging in a sharp breath.

"Why? Never mind, I can answer that. You don't let a man get close enough to risk that loss of control."

Mei, still seated at her desk, stiffened. Again she darted a furtive glance around, making sure she was by herself. "I don't think you know me well enough to make that judgment, Cullen. Furthermore, I'm not sure how our conversation worked itself around to my love life or lack thereof. It's late," she added, "and I'm still at the station."

"Mei Lu, hold everything. I can hear you getting defensive."

"I'm not. It's just not something I want to discuss—" She gripped the phone between her ear and her shoulder, willing the rest of her body to relax. "Okay, I am getting defensive. I'm sorry. What time are you planning to leave for the zoo?"

"Ten, I thought. The kids like to eat lunch there. Mei Lu, I know you think you've managed to distract me from the subject. But I learned something in the trenches, brief though my marriage was. The only hope of forming a lasting relationship is if the couple involved starts out talking honestly about anything and everything."

Mei didn't know what to say to Cullen. Yet she felt him waiting for a response. "I wasn't aware we had a relationship," she finally blurted.

She heard him sigh, then give a low laugh. "It obviously needs more work," he said. "I hear Belinda calling out. I'll have to let you go. We'll look forward to seeing you in the morning."

Her fingers tightened around the receiver. She might have murmured goodbye, but wasn't sure. It wasn't until the overhead lights came on, flooding the room, that Mei Lu realized she was still sitting there listening to a disconnected buzz.

"Oh, hi. Didn't mean to interrupt. My partner said he heard someone talking over here. I told him he was nuts, that you folks keep bankers' hours."

Mei recognized a detective from Narcotics. They had quarters next door—larger than the cubbyhole allotted to the two white-collar crime units. Mei grinned and set down her phone. "I'm not a ghost, Detective Winters. I just dropped in to pick up some messages."

"I saw your name on the most recent posting of new promotions. Congratulations, Ling. You shouldn't waste your time and talents on the likes of Shel Murdock, though. Narcotics always has room for a sharp investigator."

Dale Winters was short and round, with a ready smile and a quick wit that Mei Lu appreciated. "I'd consider switching, I really would, if only you guys in Narcotics didn't deal with such unsavory characters. The dogs you get to work with are the best thing you have going for you." She stood and tucked the ticket for tomorrow night's gala in her purse, which she slung over her shoulder. As the detective laughed, she scooped everything out of her in-basket. It was impossible to read all the junk mail and memos filtering down to individual officers every day. "You're right about our hours, Dale. But out of curiosity, why did your partner care if someone was moving around over here?"

Winters popped two antacid mints in his mouth, returning the roll to his jacket pocket. "Hal's edgy. We all are because of the memos coming out from Stan Richards and his crew."

"Stan Richards?" Mei thought the name sounded familiar, but in a police department the size of Houston's, she didn't know everyone by sight or by name.

"Richards is captain over at Internal Affairs." Detective Winters muted his voice even though Mei Lu had reached around him to switch off the main bank of lights and was already several steps ahead of him down the hall.

She stopped walking and let the lumbering detective catch up. Recalling Risa's problems, Mei said, "I've been out on special assignment, so I'm out of the loop. Is IA investigating a new in-house situation?"

"Oh, you know how it is with those snoops."

"No, I don't." Mei Lu shivered, remembering how miserable IA had made Risa's life.

"Be thankful. If they get on your back for any reason, they stick like a monkey. My motto is, do your job and keep your nose clean."

Mei noticed Winters had stopped at the door leading into his department. "Good advice, Dale. Well, I'll see you around. Take care," Mei said.

At home a short while later, she took Foo out for his nightly constitutional. Knowing he'd sniff forever if she let him, she whistled him back inside after ten or fifteen minutes.

Aware that tomorrow would be a long day, especially with the evening gala, she was tempted to put off reading the stack of handbills and department circulars she'd brought home. But she wanted to be aware of what was going on, so she brewed a pot of soothing oolong tea. And while it steeped, she sorted out the junk mail from pieces deserving a more thorough inspection.

A memo from U.S. Customs caught Mei's eye. They'd recently arrested a shop owner on Bellaire Boulevard, having found fourteen-hundred-year-old clay artifacts smuggled from Honduras hanging in the man's store among cheap wind chimes and bird feeders. Customs was urging Houston PD to be on the lookout for other such infractions. But who on the force would know that Honduras had outlawed exporting artifacts in 1984? And who would know real clay treasures from fakes?

The memo started Mei wondering if the Chinese statues she and Cullen were looking for might be hiding somewhere in plain sight. She set it aside to show him tomorrow, and made a mental note to spend her early morning poking through some of the shops that sold Chinese knickknacks.

The only other memos she spent much time perusing were the ones from Internal Affairs. As Detective Winters had said, the in-house sleuths seemed to be on some kind of witch hunt. Although, to be fair, IA had posted a list of the infractions under investigation. They included disorderly conduct while in uniform. But being drunk at a crime scene. Sex on the job with a married partner. Boy, had Catherine warned the five female recruits in her training class about *that* pitfall. Cathy wasn't one to mince words. She'd been blunt in saying that sex relieved stress, and a cop's job meant daily brushes with danger. She warned her friends to find other outlets for relief.

Mei had never been remotely tempted to have sex with a co-worker. But she knew it was an issue that had surfaced in Risa's investigation. A messy triangle involving Risa's partner, Luke.

Finishing her tea and walking to the sink to rinse her cup, Mei recalled the two times Cullen had kissed her good-night. He had accused her of not wanting to lose control, but she hadn't felt in control then. She'd all but come unglued. The last couple of nights he'd even appeared in her dreams.

Mei placed her cup on the drainboard, snapped off the light over the sink and called to a sleepy-eyed Foo. "I'm beginning to understand the type of feelings Catherine lectured us about," she told the dog. "I honestly never thought I'd have to worry. And look at me. If anything comes of… of…Cullen and me, I guess you know my friends will have a field day."

For probably the first time in Mei Lu's life, she discovered she didn't care what anyone else thought. That shocked her. She raced through her nightly ritual, slid into bed and pulled the sheet up to her chin, wishing the sleep hours away so she could get to her outing with Cullen faster. And his kids, she reminded herself. The twins would be there to chaperone, and that was good.

THE NEXT MORNING, Mei wanted to hit as many Chinese-owned shops along the boulevard as she could work into a short morning that would still get her to Cullen's no later than ten o'clock.

Since she didn't want to constantly refer to a list of items stolen from Beijing museums, she did her best to memorize the copy Cullen had faxed her. She had a good memory for art pieces she liked. It so happened that she'd seen many of these in a traveling exhibit that had passed through Hong Kong. The few she didn't recognize on sight, she looked up in a book she owned of treasures from the Forbidden City.

Armed with her plan, she dressed comfortably for trekking around the Houston zoo afterward. Mei bid Foo goodbye and set off.

A display in the first shop window supplied her with the perfect reason to poke through the store's nooks and crannies. Toys. A full array of Chinese toys, any one of which might delight Cullen's twins.

The proprietress—a small, birdlike woman with a high-pitched voice that got on Mei's nerves—tried too hard to sell Mei Lu something. Anything. The pushy woman spoke impeccable English, yet she employed a range of tactics Mei recognized from having dealt with merchants on the backstreets of Hong Kong. The woman, Mrs. Wen, believed her sales for the day would improve if she could sell Mei Lu, her first customer, some trinket. It was an old superstition prevalent among Asian traders and shopkeepers.

Near the back of the shop, Mei Lu found some authentic hand puppets. In spite of taking an instant dislike to Mrs. Wen, Mei relented and bought Belinda Archer a Fan Princess puppet. And for Bobby, she settled on the Monkey King. These were as sought after by Chinese children as were Barbie dolls and Matchbox cars in the U.S.

The second store Mei Lu visited specialized in Chinese kites. She was able to tell at a glance that this shop wasn't hiding stolen artifacts. However tempted she was to purchase kites for the Archer twins, Mei Lu resisted. She decided to see how they received the puppets first. Not only didn't she want to waste money, Mei didn't want Cullen to think she was trying to buy his kids' affections.

She spent too long chatting with the delightful old couple who made the kites in a back room they gladly let her tour. At about nine-thirty, Mei had to go or risk being late. Bowing respectfully, she said in Cantonese, "I've never seen more beautiful kites. But I want to be sure my friend's children will truly appreciate the butterfly and good-luck flyers before I buy them."

Mr. and Mrs. Wu trailed her to the door, bowing and beaming their pleasure for the praise she had heaped on their work. Mei thought from their immaculate but worn clothing that they probably had far more talent than money. She vowed to return and buy kites, even if she tucked them in a closet to fly in the park herself some windy day.

To describe the Archer twins as excited over the prospect of their zoo outing would be to minimize their reaction. They hopped up and down, talking nonstop as they threw open the front door and raced out, converging on Mei before she could step from her car. Even Bobby greeted her enthusiastically.

Wearing a bemused smile, Cullen came out onto the porch and closed the door the kids had left wide open. "Listen up," he called, and then followed that with a shrill whistle to get their attention. "There's no leaving until after you hit the bathroom and collect your jackets. Let Freda know we're taking off. Belinda, tell her I have your noon pill with me."

The two responded by shrieking and tearing back into the house, and Mei Lu decided to wait until things were calmer to present the puppets. She walked slowly toward Cullen, not willing to admit how fantastic he looked. He shook his head and rolled his eyes heavenward once his twins had thundered past and left the front door standing wide open again.

"You'd think those deprived children had never been taken on an outing in their lives." Reaching out, he took Mei Lu's hand and drew her up the last two steps. "Hi," he said softly, running an unabashedly approving gaze over her.

"Hi, yourself." Mei Lu was aware that she sounded short of breath.

"What's in the sack? Did you bring me a present?" Cullen nudged the bag in her hand, wearing a grin of boyish expectation.

"These are Chinese hand puppets for the twins. I bought them this morning. I do have something for you, though." She fumbled open her purse and pulled out the folded memo from Customs.

Cullen read it, nodding. "Interesting tidbit. So that's why you weren't home when I phoned earlier."

"You phoned? Why? You didn't try my cell." Even as she made the declaration, Mei Lu took out her phone and checked it for missed calls.

Slipping his hands around her narrow waist, Cullen swayed her back and forth, apparently satisfied to simply smile down into her eyes. "I didn't want to bother you in case you'd gone to the station for an early meeting. I don't really know why I called. I just had an urge to tell you good-morning."

Mei smiled as a heady feeling stole over her. "That's a nice gesture, Cullen. I wish I'd been home to receive your call."

"Well, if you'd stumbled over our stolen figurines I expect I'd be far less disappointed. I take it you didn't find anything suspicious."

"No, but I only scratched the surface. There are scores of shops to investigate."

"You'll go broke if you buy something from every one."

She poked him hard in the ribs. "I'll have you know, Mr. Archer, that I'm a damn fine bargainer. I offer that bit of information on the authority of a wizened little man I used to do business with in the Hong Kong jade market. He said that to me every Saturday."

"Tough lady, huh?" Cullen made a show of testing Mei Lu's arm muscle.

She batted his hand away, then moved quickly down one step the instant she heard the kids rattling the door in an attempt to jerk it open. Belinda probably wouldn't mind seeing her father's hands on another woman, she thought. But Bobby might not be so forgiving. And she didn't care to spoil the day for either of them.

"Mei brought you guys something," Cullen announced when he had finished inspecting their hands and faces to be certain they'd washed.

"What? What? What?" Belinda danced around on her toes.

"You act remarkably recovered for a girl who was sick enough yesterday to see a doctor."

"Is that why you brought me something?" Belinda asked. "Can't I have it if I'm feeling better?"

"Don't be dumb," Bobby exclaimed. "Dad said Mei Lu brought us *both* a present. I wasn't sick."

The fact that Bobby crowded forward, staring at the bright red sack covered in gold lettering, surprised Mei Lu. "Okay, here's the deal. Close your eyes, and no peeking."

They immediately complied and Mei Lu passed Cullen her purse, then carefully opened the sack and slipped one puppet on each hand. Calling on days gone by when she and her brother used to entertain themselves for hours playing with hand puppets, Mei Lu tapped each twin on the head. She then carried on a conversation between the puppets using different tones of voice.

Cullen liked this unexpected, more playful side of a woman he was already attracted to in other ways. As well, he delighted in observing the rapt expressions of his kids.

"We're going to have a heck of a time finding a parking place in the zoo lot if we don't get under way soon," he finally said. Otherwise Mei Lu and the twins would likely have spent the whole morning making up stories for the puppets.

She glanced up, a guilty look crossing her face. "Sorry, Cullen. I guess I got carried away. May they take the puppets in the car? Unless they get too rambunctious, the puppets will keep them occupied for the ride to Hermann Park."

"Noise in the car is something I've never minded," Cullen said, pointing his little entourage toward the garage.

Unexpectedly Bobby Archer chimed in. "Mom sure hates it. She's always yelling at us to be quiet. And she doesn't like it if Belinda or me say that she's making just as much noise hollering at us."

"Belinda or I," Cullen corrected as a matter of course. He did it so swiftly, Mei Lu figured it was a common occurrence. Again she weighed Cullen's easy style of parenting against that of her own folks. Although, come to think of it, her father was far more lenient whenever her mom wasn't around.

"Bobby, driving's always made your mother a nervous wreck. It'd be better, certainly safer, if you'd cut her some slack."

"I'll try, Dad. But, like, when she picks us up from school and Belinda and me...have a lot to tell her, I forget."

"Yeah," Belinda reiterated as she and her brother climbed into the back seat and laid aside the puppets while they buckled in. "If we've got important stuff to say, we need to tell Mom between school and our driveway. Otherwise, there's no chance, 'cause she goes to the club to play tennis or meet her friends. By morning Bobby and me always forget what the teacher said."

Mei Lu noted that Cullen didn't correct Belinda's grammatical error. She also saw him glance in the rearview mirror and frown. Mei wondered if Cullen didn't know about his ex-wife's habit of dropping the kids and taking off for the day. If so, he didn't make an issue of it.

Cullen drove the way he did everything else. Calmly and with confidence. Mei wasn't sure why the fact hadn't registered when she'd ridden with him to the nightclub. But she supposed that after last night's brief chat with Crista, she was letting herself relax about spending leisure time with him.

"No one would ever accuse you of being a chatterbox," Cullen said suddenly, casting a sidelong glance in her direction.

"It's the result of years of conditioning and constant reminders that good Chinese girls are seen little and heard less."

Cullen glanced at the mirror again, which allowed him

to check on the children. In the back seat the noise level of their puppeteering had greatly escalated. "Either I started off wrong, or I need lessons in how to accomplish that feat."

"No. Take it from me, Cullen. Your method makes for a happier childhood."

"You just referred to Chinese *girls*. Did your brother have more privileges than you did?"

"My first instinct is to say yes. But on second thought, I'd have to say no. My parents definitely held Stephen to higher standards." Mei considered how she'd defied her father's wishes by leaving Ling Limited, whereas her brother had such a need to please Michael that he'd marry someone he didn't seem to love in hopes of a favorable nod. Mei Lu knew she'd never do that.

"Maybe it's different with twins," Cullen mused in an undertone. "I find myself bending over backward to ensure that neither Jana nor her folks can ever accuse me of unfairness—of treating the kids differently."

"Would they do that?"

"That's a good question. It could just be in my head— but I think they would."

Neither he nor Mei Lu said more, because just then Cullen turned the corner and they were facing the park's entrance.

"Kids, put your puppets away and try to spot an open parking space."

"There's one," Bobby cried, stabbing a finger toward the right side of the car. "In the next aisle, Dad. Someone just tried to pull in with a van, but I think he didn't fit."

"It might just be that the cars on either side are parked too close to the lines. We might not fit, either."

But they did, with room to spare.

"It's really changed around here from what I remember," Mei Lu said. "I won't even say how many years it's been since I visited with my fourth-grade class."

"You taught fourth grade?" Belinda asked.

"No." Mei Lu laughed. "I mean I was *in* the fourth grade."

Bobby squinted up at her. "That must've been about a hundred years ago, huh? We come every summer. If you wanna know anything, ask Belinda or me."

"Son, you just insulted Mei Lu," scolded Cullen. "First, never insinuate that anybody's a hundred years old. And you need to be doubly careful saying anything like that to a woman. They're touchy on the subject of age."

"I don't mind telling my age," she said to the boy, who'd begun to scowl. "I'm thirty-one, Bobby. To someone who's eight, I imagine that seems old. Not that there's anything wrong with being old. I'm Chinese. We believe the old are wise. And we appreciate and respect wisdom."

"You're cool," the boy said, moving alongside Mei to take the hand his sister wasn't clinging to. "Mom won't tell anyone how old she is. I can't figure out why it's such a big secret," he said, not quite loudly enough for his father, who was in line buying their tickets, to hear.

"At the zoo, everyone's allowed to be a kid again," Mei Lu said indulgently. Then, for what remained of the morning and the early afternoon, they all did laugh, act zany and in general have a good time.

"I should've asked how long you planned to stay," Mei Lu remarked, surprised to check her watch and see that it was nearly four o'clock. "I hate to spoil anyone's day, but I need time to drive home from your house, Cullen, and then get all the way back downtown for a work-related assignment."

Cullen studied his watch, even lifted his wrist to his ear to test it. "Where has the day gone? Kids, we have time to stop at one last habitat, as long as it's on the path leading back to the parking lot. Check your zoo maps. Decide in two seconds, or Mei Lu and I will."

The kids pored over the map. "The gorillas," Bobby shouted. "Yeah, or the baboons," Belinda tossed out. "Can we see both, Daddy? They're on the same path."

"Mei Lu?" Cullen turned to her with a furrowed brow.

"Why not, if we pass both of them anyway?" She was stunned when the children ran up and hugged her before darting on ahead.

Cullen looped an arm around her neck, easing her into the curve of his body. It left Mei with a cozy feeling of belonging—a contentedness that intensified after Cullen rubbed his cheek along her hair and brushed a kiss across her temple.

"Thanks. You gave each of them their wish. The minute I said they had to agree, I bit my tongue and pictured ending our day with an argument. Their mother would've made a big stink about me saying they had to pick one exhibit, but then letting them visit two."

Mei Lu reached up and held his hand, which he'd draped over her shoulder. "They've been really good today. There were so many kids in the park, and most of them ran wild. Did you *hear* some of them? You're lucky, Cullen." She squeezed his fingers.

Mei couldn't identify the change that crept into his eyes. But he urged her to the side of the path and this time kissed her full on the lips. The kiss was gentle and sweet and unrushed. A sluggish warmth filled her and Mei experienced a languid tugging low in her abdomen. She had no difficulty recognizing the need. At the zoo, for pity's sake. With Cullen's children and a thousand others around.

"To be continued," Cullen murmured, releasing her slowly and with noticeable reluctance.

Mei found it beyond her capability to do more than smile stupidly and nod. The kids ran back then, assailing them with tales of gorillas and baboons. They bubbled all the way home, giving Mei an opportunity to collect her scattered senses. She was coolly in control again by the time they parted. Still, her heart tripped over itself when Cullen stole a final kiss, and said, "Promise you won't spend all day tomorrow poking through shops. Come to my house for lunch, okay? I won't take no for an answer."

She accepted his invitation. Driving off, Mei Lu was secretly glad Cullen had insisted on the next day's meeting.

CHAPTER NINE

THE TOYOTA'S ENGINE started choking and running rough four blocks from Mei Lu's home. She muttered kind, encouraging words and patted the dash, but still barely coasted to a dead stop three houses away from her duplex. It was as if the motor had died and no amount of coaxing could breathe life into it again.

Climbing out, Mei slammed and locked the doors. She stomped home, aware that the clock hands ticked ever closer to the time she should be dressing for the gala.

She dished up Foo's food while juggling a phone at her ear. The auto club said they'd send a tow truck to transport her car to her service garage, but it'd be an hour. "Okay," she said, heaving a sigh. "I have an appointment downtown, and I'll be leaving the house about then. May I leave a note on the car for your driver." She was relieved when the dispatcher said she could. She'd leave another note inside the car for the mechanic.

While she paced the length of the phone cord, she discovered that Abby had called and left a message. Mei wished she had time to return her friend's call. Not tonight, however.

Resigned to traveling to the gala by cab, Mei Lu stood under a steamy shower—where it dawned on her that between paying cash for the puppets and insisting on paying for her own lunch at the zoo, she probably couldn't scrape together enough for cab fare. Not that she could get a cab clear out here during rush hour, anyway. But if she could make her way to the Contemporary Art Museum, she knew her bank had a branch with an ATM at the end of that block.

Wrapped in a towel, she began a frantic search for any spare change in pockets or otherwise lying about. When all was said and done, she'd amassed a mere five dollars.

Well, that left her with no choice but public transportation. Darn, she hated the thought of riding a city bus all dressed to impress. But it was clearly her only other option.

She called for an updated schedule and learned that if she could be ready in half an hour, she'd make a bus that stopped just two blocks from her place. It connected to another one that passed the museum.

Mei Lu got busy pulling out and examining possible dresses. There was the black one she'd worn to the nightclub. A firehouse-red floor-length gown, which she put back immediately. She did the same with a green sequined chiffon that was way too showy. Reaching into the storage bag again, Mei discovered she'd pared her choices down to one dress, made of eggshell-colored satiny charmeuse. The inset V-neckline formed three-inch straps that doubled as cap sleeves. The dress itself skimmed her curves as the material fell from a built-in bra. If she'd ever bought a dress that felt as if she were wearing nothing, this was it. She slipped it on, relieved to find it still fit.

Next, she ran a brush through damp hair, and threw a small tape recorder, her money, ATM card and badge into a skimpy satin purse. She had no room for the Taser. But her assignment was just to listen in, not to take anyone down tonight. Snapping the purse closed, Mei straightened, wondering if she could get away with wearing a trench coat. In this dress, almost any evening wrap risked getting her run in for standing on a street corner. She could hear the guys from the vice squad now, joking about her working decoy.

Of all nights for her car to conk out.

"Foo, sorry I keep running out on you every night. This is why so many cop marriages fail. You, at least, don't complain about late meals."

Mei had debated whether to wear jewelry. She didn't want any punks jumping her at the bus stop over a little bit of gold. At the last minute, she tucked a small pair of pearl studs in her purse, hoping she'd remember to put them on once she got into the museum.

She had a hand on the outer door when she remembered she hadn't written the notes to leave with her car. Back to the desk she flew and scribbled instructions to the tow truck driver and another note for her mechanic.

As soon as she stepped onto the porch, she knew the night was too warm for the trench coat. Yanking it off, she dashed back into her bedroom and chose, instead, a short ecru cape.

As she got outside again, the tow truck arrived. The driver caught her in the act of leaning into the Toyota to place the mechanic's note on the dash.

A young, muscle-bound, gum-chewing guy in his mid-twenties climbed from his truck and whistled. "Hey, babe! Seems you got yourself some trouble. Don't know where you're headed, but how about I give you a lift?"

Mei eased out of the car, taking care to pull down her skirt, even though it ended several inches above her knees. She actually considered his offer for all of two seconds. Had she been dressed for a normal workday, and had he not leered as he wiped his hands on a greasy rag, Mei might have accepted.

"Thanks, but I have time to catch a bus that will deposit me downtown where I need to be." That was stretching the truth, but why be rude?

"Okay, doll. Suit yourself. This the car that let you down?" He finally quit eyeing Mei's dress and turned his attention to the Toyota. "Phew, I wouldn't let *my* girlfriend drive this piece of junk." He blew a bubble with the gum he'd been chewing. When it popped, he muttered, "Unless you've gotta have those pricey duds for, uh, work, you'd be better off spending your dough on new wheels."

Mei knew by his suggestive tone where he thought she worked. Her first inclination was to let it go. But what right had he to judge anyone? Drawing even with him, she flashed her badge. "I'm a cop. All cops own cars like mine. Makes it easier to do surveillance. By the way, you're double-parked." Returning her badge to her purse, Mei Lu strode off. She knew exactly how long it took Mr. Smart Mouth to hop back into his truck and pull it to the curb so he could hook onto her car. She grinned all the way to the bus stop.

She reached her destination having to fend off only two additional propositions. One from a man too drunk to stand without reeling. The last as she left her bank. A bald hulk on a low-slung Harley, stopped at a red light. She delivered a dirty look and again hauled out her badge. Lover-boy did a U-turn and tore out so fast, she decided to phone his plate in to the station. Dispatch said he had warrants, and promised to send a cruiser to the area to locate him.

At the museum, she handed over her ticket to a perky brunette.

"Welcome. Turn right and take the first set of stairs for

the exhibit. Hors d'oeuvres, cash bar and entertainment are at ground level to your left."

"Thanks," Mei Lu murmured, accepting a program. "Where's the ladies' room?"

The ticket-taker uttered a small, sympathetic laugh. "Lounges are at the back of the room on every floor. I only laugh because they're always my first priority, too. My husband says he can't understand it. By the way, I love that knockout dress. If I could wear that and look like you, I doubt my husband would complain about *anything.*"

Mei, who'd never learned to accept compliments gracefully, breathed out an inadequate thanks and rushed off. Crista was always nagging her about her responses. But no matter how many times her friend bugged Mei to hold her head up and speak out with a straightforward *thank you,* Mei never felt right doing so. Cullen had mentioned her inability to accept compliments, too.

She passed a cloakroom and left her cape, receiving a ticket, which she stored in her purse. That reminded her to put on her earrings.

Making her way across a crowded, noisy room where guests balanced food plates and drinks, Mei Lu wondered where Cullen was right now. He hadn't said, and she assumed he'd asked someone else to his business dinner.

That was a disturbing thought. Trying not to dwell on it, Mei found the lounge and went straight to the mirror, where she slipped on the pearl studs and fluffed her bangs. She used this opportunity to situate her small tape recorder in such a way as to make it easy to turn on when the need arose.

Back in the crowded room, she moved into the drink line and purchased a glass of merlot. Then she searched out a corner with a window. The sill provided a place to set her glass and allowed her privacy while she scanned the crowd for her mark. In this case, marks—plural. Suddenly hungry, she was relieved when a waiter offered hors d'oeuvres.

There were mostly couples at this benefit. Normally it didn't bother her to attend events alone. Tonight, though, she felt out of place and longingly wished for Cullen to appear out of thin air. Deliberately, she pushed him out of her mind and surveyed her food.

She'd barely tasted a cheese-topped bite-size rye cracker when luck smiled on her. Three of the five men she'd been told to seek out formed a huddle less than a foot away. She hastily chewed and swallowed the cracker, and slipped deeper into the shadow cast by the drapes, discreetly switching on her tape recorder.

The men were engrossed in a heated argument. Mei doubted any of them noticed her. At least she hoped they didn't. She listened even more closely when the most recognizable of the executives swore while remarking on one of the trio's two missing friends.

"Dammit, I want out of this contract, Rollie. If Truesdale and Jessup want to load their conveyor lines with undocumented workers, let them. I answer to a nosy board of directors and they're already making me nervous with all their poking and probing through my contract-labor records. They'd gladly feed me to the wolves if they got a hint of what I've pulled with the personnel files."

"Yeah, I agree," his portlier companion said. "After those raids and crackdowns, I'm leery, too. I don't feel right about leaving Jessup holding the bag if we opt out, though. He's got a boat due in next…"

Because the man shifted, Mei Lu didn't catch all of his sentence. She stepped away from the drapes, and suddenly felt two hands clamp over her shoulders. A booming voice rang out. "Lieutenant Ling, what a nice surprise! You should've told me your evening assignment happened to be at this benefit," Cullen said in a more level tone.

Mei Lu whirled, nearly dumping the contents of her purse. Struck dumb, she blinked in confusion. Cullen, meanwhile, calmly snapped the catch on her bag—effectively silencing her tape recorder. At the same time, the three CEOs bore down on them with fire in their eyes and purpose in their steps.

"Cullen," she muttered, hoping she'd recovered quickly enough. Moving her wine to her right hand, she held up her plate and offered him an hors d'oeuvre. Growing desperate when he didn't take one but rather waited for her answer instead, Mei rose on tiptoes and planted a kiss square on Cullen's mouth.

He was obviously stunned, but his hands automatically spanned her waist. When she tried to end his enthusiastic acceptance of her greeting, he wasn't willing to turn her loose.

Not until a gruff voice growled, "Archer? What the hell?"

He rearranged his features and faced the speaker. "Fred Burgess. I actually hoped I'd run into you." Cullen thrust out a hand. "Cloris told the art committee about your generous support of our benefit. Cloris Gaston," Cullen stated the chairwoman's full name when it appeared that Fred had blanked him out and was staring at Mei Lu.

Not that Cullen blamed the poor devil. She was a sight for weary eyes tonight. And Fred, as well as his two companions, looked more than weary; they looked highly stressed.

"Archer, I don't think we've had the pleasure of meeting your friend," Fred said in a steely voice. "If I heard you right, you weren't aware she planned to attend." His smile slid away. "How, if I may ask, did she get a ticket to an invitation-only affair?"

Mei, who could put on an act when the job demanded it, laughed gaily and snuggled up to Cullen. "Darling, your teasing has these gentlemen ready to toss me out on my ear." She offered Fred Burgess her most engaging grin. "Cullen is *such* a joker. He knows I've been standing here for ten minutes with my nose glued to the window, waiting for his *very* late arrival. You naughty man," she chided huskily, laying it on so thick that even she couldn't believe it. Cullen, too, seemed dumbfounded. So, before he got them both thrown out, she tilted her wineglass ever so slightly, spilling merlot down the front of his expertly tailored tuxedo.

"Oh, heavens, how clumsy. Give me your jacket, Cullen. Hold my wine, please. I'll run to the ladies' room to sponge those spots. If we act fast, maybe it won't stain. Nothing's worse than red wine." Mei Lu shoved her glass into Cullen's hand and darted behind him to begin pulling off his jacket.

Slow to react and slower to catch on to Mei's strange behavior, Cullen belatedly began to take note of the three scowling men. Things started clicking into place. He had no idea why three such prominent Houstonites had attracted the interest of the law. He'd bet his great-grandfather's Double Eagle gold piece, however, that they were the reason Mei Lu was here.

Actively assisting her now, Cullen passed her glass to Fred. "Here, Fred. Hold this, would you? Damn, I just got this jacket from the cleaners. I'll go and wait outside for her to bring it back."

She tugged off Cullen's second sleeve, aware he'd added things up. Now, of course, he'd want answers—answers she wasn't at liberty to give. Mei was glad he was familiar enough with the investigative process not to say anything more damaging within earshot of the trio.

The minute they rounded the corner, headed toward the lounge, Cullen lengthened his stride and overtook her. "Okay, what gives?"

Ducking around him, she hurried into the lounge. Thank goodness the sink area was vacant. She dampened one of the thick Turkish towels thoughtfully provided for this up-scale event, and carefully sponged the dark stain from the worsted wool. His coat didn't smell of cleaning fluid, but of the subtle aftershave that Cullen always wore. Her pulse skipped a beat. She'd like to know all those intimate details about Cullen—and more. What did he wear to sleep in, and how did he sleep? On his side? His back? Sprawled across a huge bed? Too many questions swirled through Mei Lu's mind when she ought to be figuring out how to counter *his* questions about her presence. The wayward thoughts that crept in sent hot, then cold, prickles racing down her spine.

Or maybe the cold came as the door behind her opened.

"Mei Lu?" Cullen whispered. "What's taking you so long? People are starting to give me funny looks for lurking outside the ladies' room."

Mei glanced down guiltily at the jacket she'd long since finished sponging and now clutched under her chin. "Coming," she sang out, trying to muster together enough dignity to face him.

She slipped out the door, which Cullen still held ajar, prepared to discuss the condition of his jacket. All Cullen did was rip the coat out of her hands and quickly shrug into it, never so much as glancing at the lapel that had suffered the wine spill. Mei couldn't help comparing with the way her fastidious father or brother would have acted if anyone had dumped wine on them.

"Before we discuss exactly why you're here, Mei Lu,

satisfy my curiosity—how did you get a ticket? Fred's right about this being invitation-only with a price tag of a thousand bucks a ticket. The hell of it is, you had an invitation—from me—and turned it down."

Mei pressed two fingers to Cullen's lips. "You asked me to go to a business dinner. Shh! Everything to do with my being at this gala concerns an ongoing criminal investigation. I'll pick up my cape and leave quietly, but please don't ask for particulars. I can't tell you anymore."

"I have no intention of letting you leave." As if to punctuate his statement, Cullen slid a hand around her waist, forcing her to walk hip to hip with him into the main room. "I'm here out of duty," he said. "Because I'm on the committee. Seeing you across the room made the whole evening worthwhile."

"I'd feel the same way if you'd waited five minutes before blowing my cover," Mei Lu said, gazing up at him with wry humor.

"Ouch. I know an apology won't help, but I'm really sorry, Mei Lu."

Her gaze flickered to the group she'd been eavesdropping on. She realized they'd been joined by two other men, probably those whose names she'd been given. The five were talking and gesturing. She knew they'd been warned off. She might as well go; she wouldn't get any more information tonight."

Cullen had been stopped by a stylish older couple. He introduced Mei Lu as a friend and murmured her name.

"Ling?" the woman said, bestowing a bright smile on Mei. "Are you a representative from Ling Limited?"

Mei started to correct the woman, but Cullen tightened his grip on her waist. "Michael Ling is Mei's father. You must know him, since you two collect Chinese art, don't you?"

"My, yes," the woman gushed. "I probably have the most extensive collection of white jade in the city."

"And lacquerware," her husband put in, smiling indulgently. "Although our real passion is silk hanging scrolls."

"Yes, your father has a standing order to acquire them for us. Of course, really genuine old scrolls are getting harder and harder to come by."

"The most exquisite are part of a collection found in the Baoning temple," Mei said, understanding why Cullen had wanted to detain this couple. "The scrolls were authenticated as fifteenth-century Ming. They disappeared during World War II, and were assumed lost. But luckily they were found again in 1955 in an underground vault."

The woman beamed. "We were privileged to see one of the Baoning scrolls in an exhibit that toured the U.S. with the Imperial Arts of China. In fact, Cullen, you and Owen were instrumental in making sure Houston was one of the cities on the tour."

"By the way, Owen," Cullen said, breaking in. "You haven't heard of Chinese art flowing into the city through less than legal channels, have you?"

The wizened little man looked appalled. "How would I? Louise and I only use reputable dealers."

"A former dealer was contacted by an envoy who, interestingly enough, turned up dead." Cullen pulled out a business card, one that listed his insurance investigator's license number. "They're dangerous folks to get mixed up with, no matter how attractive they may make a deal sound. Feel free to call me if you get any offers that seem too good to be true." Smiling pleasantly, Cullen bid the couple good-evening.

"You scared them, Cullen. Did you see how pale they both went?"

"Good. I hope they're scared enough to think twice

about buying black market art. They're prime candidates. Owen's as rich as Warren Buffett. He's ripe to acquire a piece for no other reason than that Louise covets it."

"Well, you know them better than I do. I know there are plenty of collectors who don't care where a piece comes from if they want it. Otherwise, there'd be no profit in stealing art."

"Can I interest you in taking a turn around the art display? Cloris, the woman heading the committee, arm-wrestled a promise out of each member to be seen viewing local artists' work."

"Sure, I'll go. Or I could call a cab and say goodbye here. I'm certain my targets won't let me get near enough to learn anything else."

"Why would you call a cab? Didn't you drive yourself?"

"It's a long story. The short version is, my car didn't quite make it home from your house."

"You should've called me to come get you. How much did it cost to take a cab from your place all the way down here?"

"I took the bus."

"In that dress?" Cullen seemed genuinely alarmed.

"What's wrong with my dress?" she returned hotly.

A grin started slowly. "Not one damn thing if I'm the one escorting you. Otherwise…plenty."

"Quit that, Cullen!" Mei Lu shook her head. "You're drawing attention."

"*You're* drawing the attention. I'm basking in the fall-out. You think there's a man at this affair between nineteen and ninety who isn't tripping over his teeth, envying me? Oh—just so you know, I'm driving you home."

"But it's out of your way," she protested.

"I'm making it *on* my way."

"Okay. Thanks for being so thoughtful."

"You never said why you didn't ask me for a lift in the first place."

"I knew you had an engagement this evening. I naturally assumed you'd found another date."

Cullen guided her up the final step to a cozy loft above the main floor. A few people wandered about examining artwork displayed on pedestals or hanging on the walls. Cullen brushed Mei Lu's ear with his lips to say what he had to say privately. "I only wanted *you* to come with me tonight. I didn't want anyone else. Since my marriage fell apart, Mei Lu, I usually attend these art functions alone."

"Is it a case of once burned, twice shy?"

"No. It's a case of not finding a woman I wanted to spend my free time with—until now."

"I'm flattered."

She didn't look it, Cullen thought when they stopped in front of a canvas splashed with dark colors that resembled the outline of a man's chest. Through a gaping slash in the center dribbled globs of red paint that looked altogether too much like blood. Each knew from the other's horrified expression that they shared the opinion this painting was ghastly.

"I'm for making a quick circuit," Cullen whispered. "How about you?"

"Okay. Can you believe this thing sold?" she said, shuddering.

"Artistic taste is in the eye of the beholder."

"I know, but what fool paid hard-earned money for something so awful?"

Fred Burgess entered the room and made a beeline for them. "Great, huh? It's the best painting here. I bought it. What do you think?"

"Fred," Cullen said, "I'm speechless. I hope you have the perfect spot."

Mei decided it was a good thing Cullen answered for them, because she was at a loss for words.

"Yep, over my office desk. I figure it'll keep my employees in line." Burgess laughed, but he laughed alone. "Lieutenant, are you an art connoisseur?" Burgess singled Mei Lu out.

"I am, but I prefer Chinese tapestries. Perhaps you're not aware that my family operates Ling Limited Imports. I used to acquire for our Hong Kong branch."

"You gave it up to become a cop? Wasn't that a big drop in pay?"

"Money isn't everything, Mr. Burgess."

"Oh, but it is, little lady. Which do you figure brings down more cops—greed or bullets?"

Mei said nothing, again having nothing to say.

The paunchy Fred smirked. "I can see you've gotta think about that real hard. Well, I'll go pay for my painting and collect the missus." He turned and clattered down the stairs.

Cullen gave Mei Lu a puzzled look. "That sounded like a warning. I admit it went over my head. Of course, I'm not surprised, given Fred's taste in art."

"It was a threat of sorts, but it didn't go over my head. He's warned me off."

"Off?" Cullen wrapped his arm around her tighter as if to keep Mei Lu safe.

"Off an investigation," she murmured. "Don't ask, Cullen."

"Not our investigation?"

"No, another. I really need to get home so I can listen to a tape I made earlier. I appreciate your offer to drive me, but I think I'll catch a cab, after all."

"No. I've seen enough of our local talent. I believe you said you had a wrap? Retrieve it. I'll tell Cloris Gaston I'm taking off."

Mei might have objected more vociferously had Burgess's veiled threat not shaken her. Shel Murdock wouldn't be happy to hear she'd botched her assignment. On the other hand, if her tape player had continued to record after Cullen interrupted her, maybe she'd picked up some reference to when the next human shipment was due. Although, since she'd made Fred Burgess and his pals nervous, they might well scrap their plan.

She noticed Jessup watching her as she produced her ticket and collected her cape. He headed toward her. Mei Lu was glad Cullen appeared right then, saying he was ready to leave, and Jessup veered off.

Mei casually slid her arm through Cullen's. That left her feeling more secure, especially when he closed his free hand around hers and smiled into her eyes in a way that lit a match under her already smoking passion.

She managed to forget about the case soon after Cullen helped her into his car. "Ah, no doubt about it, this is far superior to slogging here on the bus. Have you ever taken one, Cullen?"

"In England I took public transportation to and from college. And when I was a kid here, it was safer. With everything going on in Houston today, I'd never let the twins leave home armed with nothing but quarters and a bus schedule."

"Is it because there's more crime or more people?"

"More gangs. Did you get hit on in that dress?"

Mei Lu's laugh was low and throaty. "*That* question came out of left field."

"Did you?" he asked again, his right hand running back and forth over the top edge of the steering wheel.

"I'm against blaming the dress. People deserve to travel a city in safety, regardless of what they wear."

"Touché. But I read the paper and watch the news and

I know it's a far from perfect world. So give me hell for not wanting you needlessly in harm's way. Promise that you'll phone me if your car's not fixed by tomorrow. The kids and I will come and get you."

"All right...you softie." Before Cullen could object to her purred accusation, she said, "If you do, let's detour and take the twins kite-flying. It's turning blustery. Perfect kite weather. I know just the park."

Cullen reared back. "Where did that notion spring from? And where will I get kites?"

"I'll provide them. You show up at ten. I'm sure my car won't be fixed that soon."

"I don't think the kids have ever flown kites. They'll like that, Mei Lu. Me, too," he said, his voice dropping, sounding velvety in the darkness.

"Are you hungry?" Mei threw out suddenly. "I'm starved. I didn't eat before going to the benefit, and you interrupted me before I'd sampled more than one cracker with a bit of cheese."

"I could eat. I didn't have anything, either. Is there someplace around here where we can go dressed like this?"

"I don't go out enough to know. I guess it's not such a good idea, after all. Unless...there's a market two blocks ahead, on your right. I could run in and buy eggs. I think I have everything else at home to make a couple of omelettes."

"Deal. That sounds like it'd hit the spot. I'll get the eggs. That way you can stay in the car, out of the wind. Sure that's all you need? No wine? You didn't get to finish the glass you bought."

Cullen followed her directions and spotted the market. He pulled up right at the door.

"I may have a bottle at home. Not chilled, though," said

Mei. "Maybe you should buy something you like. This market stocks cold wines at the back."

He climbed out whistling, looking forward to drawing out the evening with Mei Lu. Suddenly, he turned back and tapped on the window, motioning for her to lock the doors.

She did, more to humor him than because she feared for her safety. Not for the first time, she decided the twins' mother had to be seriously nuts to have let a man like this go.

Cullen sauntered into the store and saw he was one of two customers. An East Indian couple stood behind the counter, checking out the other customer's groceries. Assuming that if the fridge with the wine was in the back of the store, the cabinet where he'd find eggs would probably be there, as well, Cullen ambled down the center aisle, barely glancing at the shelves. He didn't know why a display on the top shelf caught his eye.

Condoms of varying brands and descriptions. Not something he was in the habit of buying or carrying around.

Passing the shelf, he found the eggs and selected a carton, then looked inside for cracked ones. That nearby display made him wonder whether Mei Lu, being a modern woman and a cop, kept condoms stored in her bedside cabinet. Somehow, she didn't seem the type.

In the months right after his divorce, Cullen had jumped straight into the dating scene. Quite a few of the women he'd asked out had let him know that they took responsibility for their birth control. Their saying so should have been comforting. But he remembered it had been awkward for him. Yet he had to give the women credit for looking out for their own safety.

Cullen knew what was on his mind back then when he'd asked a woman out a second or third time. He'd hoped they'd end up in bed. What man didn't?

"Hell," he grumbled half under his breath as he chose a European wine he was surprised to find in a convenience store. The same thing was on his mind right this minute. And had been there for days. Every time he thought of Mei Lu…

On his trek to the checkout counter at the front of the store, he ignored the display that had sent his thoughts down this rocky path. Cullen started to pass the shelf, then stopped and grabbed the smallest pack of a brand he'd once used. Immediately, he sped up, so the guilt nipping at his heels wouldn't send him racing back to return the package.

The store proprietor greeted Cullen in broken English. "You, sir…find all you need?"

Then as the woman, maybe his wife, slid Cullen's purchases across the bar code scanner, the man made an innocuous comment about the weather. "Outside, the wind is picking up. Good night to be inside savoring spirits, I think."

The woman got to the last item Cullen had dumped on the counter, and a grin lit her dark face. She said something not in English, but because her husband, if he was indeed that, chortled and wished Cullen a very lucky evening, there was little doubt as to what the woman had murmured.

Cullen took the condom box from the proprietor, right before the man would've tossed it into the grocery sack—and spilled coins all over the counter and the floor. Muttering something indistinguishable, he slipped the box into his tux pocket. As he did so, he shot a furtive glance through the front window to the BMW sitting there in plain sight.

He hoped Mei Lu hadn't witnessed any of this.

Kneeling down, Cullen scooped five dimes and two

pennies off the floor. Once he'd straightened, he finished counting out the exact amount. "Thanks," he said, hoping he hadn't turned forty shades of red as the smiling proprietor observed aloud, "Pretty lady in your car. Nice, too. She come here often."

Cullen knew exactly what the two of them were thinking. He felt as though—to protect Mei Lu's honor—he ought to say something. Assure them it was purely an impulse purchase on his part. But that would be downright stupid. Wasn't it better *not* to call any more attention to the condoms?

He thought it was, but that didn't make him feel a whole lot better.

When he returned, he found Mei Lu had turned on the car radio. Cullen could feel the solid beat of drums as he shifted from foot to foot waiting for her to pop the locks. Sliding behind the wheel, he handed her the sack with the eggs and wine, aware that his blood pounded louder than the drums—or so it seemed.

Peering into the sack, Mei asked, "What took you so long? Oh, I imagine you had a hard time finding a decent wine."

"Actually they have a fair selection," Cullen mumbled, his left hand patting his bulging pocket, where the reason for his overlong stay burned a hole the size of Texas.

Damn, but he felt like a jumpy, awkward teenager again, he thought as he bungled trying to restart a motor he'd left running to begin with.

Mei Lu gave him a curious stare.

Cullen cursed under his breath. Right then and there, he figured it'd be a miracle if he lived through the next few hours.

CHAPTER TEN

FOO GREETED the couple's arrival at Mei's with enthusiasm. He appeared to remember Cullen and treated him to the same happy tail-thumping and knee-pouncing generally reserved for his mistress.

Laughing at the dog's antics of rolling on his back and pawing the air to get Mei to rub his stomach, Cullen nudged her. "I see he has you trained. Why don't I just go put the eggs and wine in your kitchen?"

Mei rose from the floor, where she was tussling with Foo. "Oh, Cullen, let me do that. Where are my manners? First, though, let me hang up your jacket. It's warm in here, don't you think?"

"N-no, the temperature's fine. I'm fine." Cullen stepped back.

Mei, who now clutched the sack with both hands, shrugged, although she thought Cullen was acting strange. "Give me a minute to freshen Foo's water and let him out. Once I do that, I'll assemble everything for our omelettes."

It was almost automatic with Cullen to remove his tie and open the top button of his dress shirt on coming home from any formal event. He did that now, even though this wasn't his home.

Edging backward toward the kitchen, Mei watched him tug off his tie. "I like the fact that you seem to feel comfortable here," she said, sending Cullen a smile. "But are you sure you wouldn't rather lose the jacket, too?"

Considering all the trouble Cullen had gone through to buy what was stowed in that jacket, he wasn't about to let Mei Lu put it somewhere out of reach. He shoved his tie in the other pocket. "I'll probably get rid of the coat when it's time to eat. I'll just toss it on the back of the couch."

"Big mistake. Foo sheds. No matter how much I vacuum, my furniture's covered in dog hair. I think he sleeps there during the day. Better let me hang it up." She shifted course, starting toward him again.

"I'm not fussy, Mei Lu. Stop worrying. And I'm not in a huge rush to eat. So unless you are, feel free to go change clothes. I doubt that dress is what you'd normally wear to cook in."

"You're so right." She smiled. "Even though I like to cook, I'm messy. Maybe I will change. And since you aren't starved, I ought to take a minute and report in to my captain."

"Sure, sure." Cullen gestured with one hand. "Why don't I pull the cork and pour us some wine? Give us both a few minutes to unwind. You've had a hectic day."

"I have. Thanks, Cullen. There's a CD player next to the bookcase on the far wall. After you pour the wine, feel free to see if there's anything you'd like to hear."

"Sounds good. There's no rush. I figure I owe you a chance to call your boss, since I apparently blew your cover." He trailed her into the kitchen, where she stored the eggs in the fridge and got out wineglasses from a small breakfront.

"Not totally wrecked," she said, bestowing another faint smile on him when she'd straightened from refilling Foo's water dish. "In fact, calling out my title and name the way you did probably forced those men to show their hand more quickly than they otherwise might have done. Besides," she added, propping open her back door so Foo could come and go at will, "you improved my evening immensely by simply being there, Cullen. I usually get tapped for these kinds of assignments, but they're always so boring. I have to look like a woman enjoying herself. Tonight, I actually did."

"Glad to be of service," he said, setting down the cork and suddenly blocking her exit as she headed out of the kitchen.

Startled, Mei raised her eyes. The unexpected passion she saw in his sent shivers of excitement to the pit of her stomach. "Cullen?" His name was a breathless question.

"Mei Lu," he whispered.

As he lowered his head and brought his mouth to hers, his hands were busy elsewhere—everywhere, it seemed to Mei Lu. Creating delicious friction between her skin and the soft fabric of her dress.

His kiss drove a corkscrew of longing so tight and deep within her, Mei thought she heard herself cry out. In pain or need. She wasn't so repressed that she didn't know that one sometimes accompanied the other. It wasn't something she'd ever experienced. Not until now. Until Cullen. Mei felt herself slipping. Slipping toward a place she didn't recognize. For balance, she grabbed hold of Cullen's open shirt collar and hung on.

He rucked up her dress, then let it fall as he moved his hands around to her back instead, pulling her even closer. Tight against him…

She wrenched away from the demolishing kiss and said his name again. Just that. "Cullen."

"Am I scaring you?" he murmured, nipping his way

down her neck to a point where her pulse beat fast and he tasted her and inhaled the scent she wore, which he always found fascinating. Sandalwood and something...elusive.

"I'm not...frightened," she tried to assure him as she made a vain attempt to chase his lips.

Her seeking didn't go unnoticed. Cullen lifted her easily off her feet and wedged her against the refrigerator so their bodies touched everywhere and he could free one hand to anchor her head. He tasted sweetness on her tongue, and a long-banked need erupted and threatened to send him to his quaking knees.

Forced to break for air, Mei Lu gazed blankly into gray eyes as glazed as hers must be. "Is this...are we...?" she asked, although her throat was so dry it barely came out a croak.

"I think we are." He nodded. His restless hands followed the curve of her breast and waist and thigh before retreating to gently touch her trembling chin. "I should have more finesse," he said, chest heaving. "I wanted to. Intended to." Excuses that all sounded horribly lame to Cullen.

Mei could see he'd told the truth, and that made all the difference. "I wish I'd known you wanted...uh, intended to..." Giving up, she buried her open mouth in the flesh peeking out from Cullen's open collar. Mei gripped his jacket front, wrinkling the wool in her fists. "What we're doing, where we're headed has been on my mind lately. A lot."

"No kidding? So...why are we stopping then?"

"Because. We can't." Mei enjoyed the feel of his pulse banging against her lips. Even as she denied they could go forward, she opened two more buttons on his shirt.

"Can't *why?*" he choked out, the soft trail of her damp tongue instantly making him rock-hard.

"I'm, uh, totally unprepared, Cullen." She wrapped her arms around his neck, clasping him to her in apology, but knew at once it was a mistake as an expletive escaped his lips. "Sorry. I'm really, really sorry," she panted.

"I know why so many say confession is good for the soul," Cullen whispered. "Here's where I've gotta confess, Mei Lu. I am prepared." He awkwardly patted one pocket. "Jeez, this is more embarrassing than I expected." He heaved a sigh and rolled his eyes. The instant he sensed her shifting and easing away, Cullen rushed on with his admission. "It's not what you think. I didn't leave the house ready to…well, *ready.* At the convenience store—hell, Mei Lu. Wine and eggs weren't all I bought. You asked what took so long?" He fumbled a second or two, then dragged the small box out of his pocket. "*This* took me so long."

She let a few seconds pass, then tried to smother a laugh. Mirth sparkled in her eyes as she snatched the box from his loose grasp. Ducking sideways, Mei Lu took advantage of Cullen's surprise to dart down the hall. She called mischievously over a shoulder, "Last one to the bedroom has to make the omelette."

If he'd been as familiar with the house as she, Cullen thought he could've won the race. As it was, they were both winded and laughing, which somehow made it far easier to tumble into the middle of her big soft bed in a tangle of arms and legs.

Although a small amount of light leaked into the room from a gap in her curtains, Cullen reached for her bedside lamp.

She stilled his fingers, even while she tried to divest him of his tux jacket. "This isn't something I do often," she said apologetically.

"Lord, me neither. It's been a long time for me, too."

Cullen let his jacket land wherever it fell on her carpet. "I want to see you, Mei Lu. All of you. And it's important to me that you're comfortable…with us," he told her. "Otherwise, difficult as it'd be to stop now, I will. I want us to feel that this means something."

"It does," she said huskily. "I'm here. You're here. Sorry about the light," she murmured, finally releasing his hand. "Maybe later."

At that moment, Cullen couldn't have refused her soft pleading. But he thought he owed her an explanation. He hadn't been joking about the length of time since he'd gone to bed with a woman. And even then he hadn't come close to feeling what he felt for Mei Lu.

"I want you to know I went sort of wild with women right after my divorce, Mei Lu. Then…I grew to hate the dating scene, so I gave it up—"

Cullen stopped talking then, because Mei Lu stripped off that alluring dress. He couldn't have said what word exploded from his lips, not if his life depended on it. His eyes had adjusted to the lack of light. In bra and panties and with her lustrous hair a wild dark cloud, Lieutenant Ling was very possibly the most tantalizing, seductive female he'd ever seen.

While Cullen might be rusty, he'd retained the knack for kicking out of his shoes and pants at lightning speed. Which he did.

And from then on, talk ceased. Except for a murmured word of appreciation here and there as they experienced new pleasures.

The only tense moment came when it appeared they'd lost the box of condoms. A frantic and thankfully brief search uncovered it in the hidden fold of a blanket. There ensued giggles and a brief skirmish.

Mei used her teeth to tear open the packet. And that wasn't the only clever thing she did with her teeth. Cullen thought he'd lose his mind and everything else as she nipped her way down across his ticklish belly—and lower, pausing only to put him out of his misery as she delicately rolled on the condom.

That was it. Cullen's last straw. He yanked her up and buried himself deep within her. He felt her sharp little teeth leave their imprint on his shoulder. But Cullen had lost the ability to do anything except pray he'd last long enough to make this first time good for both of them.

It obviously was, if their slick, boneless bodies were any indication when, sometime later, they both fell back spent against Mei Lu's plump pillows.

"Wow," she exclaimed, and Cullen felt the bed rock as she shot upright, even though he lay there immovable. "I'm energized," she exclaimed. "Ready to take on the world. Oh, and I'm famished. Really ravenous. Hey!" She ran a fingernail over Cullen's ribs. "We made a bet, and as I recall, you lost."

Cullen didn't have the strength to roll toward her. He barely managed to move aside an arm that he'd flopped across his eyes. "I really hope you're kidding, because if you told me the house was on fire I don't think I could save either one of us."

"Hmm." Mei Lu leaned forward, grasped her toes and rocked back and forth. "What does this say about me? That I've suddenly become a sex fiend? Not only am I starved, I think I could even go for another round of—"

She broke off right there, because Cullen discovered a surge of energy. He grabbed her narrow rib cage, lifted her high and hauled her down on top of him.

"Talk like that, woman, is bound to have an effect. I'm

sure willing to give it my all. Then, we'll see who's anxious to pay up on that food debt."

"Good." She growled like a tigress and ran her tongue around the inside of his ear. That definitely sparked a response.

"Uh-oh, Cullen. We may have to cut this short. I hear Foo Manchu snuffling outside my bedroom window. That means he's ten minutes from working his way back to the door. Which means eleven minutes max to a cold, wet nose poked…well, who knows where?"

"I've got the picture. Say no more," Cullen admitted with a husky laugh as he rose on his elbows to help shorten the process.

They made enjoyable work of the time they had. Strangely, Cullen came away from that session as invigorated as Mei Lu had been previously. And now she flopped sideways like a rag doll, barely able to snuggle under the arm he stretched out to gather her tight against his damp chest.

"Ohhh," she moaned. "Foo's back in the house. I've gotta find clothes. You should, too."

"Nobody ever told me dogs are as much trouble as babies," he grumbled. Sliding up against the headboard, Cullen snapped on the bedside lamp without warning. He laughed wickedly as Mei Lu leaped off the bed and raced across the room to fling open her closet doors.

His laughter died soon enough. Cullen couldn't swallow. He'd never have believed the mere sight of Mei's love-mussed hair and curvy backside could make him hard again so soon after two tumbles across the bed.

"To hell with dogs and getting dressed." Bounding off the bed, Cullen followed Mei Lu right into the closet and burrowed beneath the clothes. His thumbs stroked the peaks of her breasts as he nosed aside her hair so that he could do some nibbling of his own on her inviting neck.

Mei started to push him away, but then a liquid heat consumed her, turning her insides to slush.

They both had a clear idea where they would've ended up again had Foo not charged into the bedroom, barking his fool head off when he found them.

"He won't give up until one of us tosses his toy," Mei said, her head lolling back against Cullen's shoulder. "And if he keeps on barking that loudly, my neighbors will be over shortly to investigate."

"Damn."

"Cullen—I honestly don't know what—" she paused, then began again. "I'm not…this isn't like me."

Cullen stopped swaying with her and spun her around. "Regrets? So soon?"

She shook her head. Eyes big, she brushed a finger along a deep hollow that suddenly twitched below Cullen's cheekbone. "Not the slightest. And that's what surprises me most. I've taken so much teasing from my friends in the past six years over—well, let's say my virtually nonexistent love life, that I really expected regret, if not plain old guilt. I feel neither," she said slowly, turning to yank a pair of sweats off a hanger.

Scampering off, Mei Lu slipped into the bathroom, leaving Cullen to ponder her admission as he dressed, all the while trying to quiet the still-vocal dog.

He was just zipping his pants when Mei strolled out of her bathroom looking refreshed and renewed. Beautiful from any angle and in sweats, no less.

"Your turn," she told him, jerking a thumb over her shoulder. "I'm going to go get started on the omelette, so don't take all night."

"Hey, I don't welch on a bet. Anyway, I thought you had to phone your captain."

"Darn, I should. I guess you could say I got distracted."

Cullen grinned. "*We* got distracted. But I'd hate being held responsible if you don't check in. Go make your call. I'll be out in a flash. I'll pour our wine and cut cheese and mushrooms and whatever else we can throw in."

"Crumbled bacon and slices of avocado," she called as he was shutting the door.

Taking him at his word, Mei located her dress purse and extracted the tape from her recorder. Walking over to shove it in her tape player, it dawned on her how quickly they'd become occupied with each other. A huge smile blossomed and Mei just couldn't seem to hold it in. Crista and the others would never believe it if she told them all the things that had happened tonight. Not that she could ever tell them *all* of it.

How to explain such a complete metamorphosis, anyway?

After Mei Lu ran the tape, she backed it up again and again. She muted the background to pick up what Fred Burgess's pal had said. *Thursday.* Mei could only assume he'd meant Thursday of the following week. Of course she couldn't be sure of that, as Cullen had shown up and his voice drowned out the men's conversation.

She heard him come out of the bedroom and pass through the living room on his way to the kitchen as she dialed Captain Murdock. "I'm sorry," she told Murdock. "The men weren't forthcoming about the exact location of the shipment, and I'm only guessing they meant next Thursday. I was lucky to get as much as I did. I didn't expect to see a friend at the benefit. He addressed me as Lieutenant, and after that, the men were careful not to say anything I could overhear. Oh, except that Fred Burgess made a subtle threat right before I left the gala." Mei Lu gave Murdock the gist of it. "I wasn't careless!" she said in response to the captain's reprimand. "I realize since all of them will recognize me on sight, you'll have to assign another officer to tail Truesdale and Jessup. No, sir, I am not presuming to tell you how to do your job." Rubbing at a sharp pain between her eyes, Mei glanced up as a shadow fell across the stereo. She showed no reaction as she accepted the glass of wine Cullen placed in her hand. He moved away, returning to the kitchen before she could break off her call and thank him.

Her good mood had well and truly vanished by the time Murdock finished berating her. But Mei Lu was determined not to let his surliness ruin what remained of her evening with Cullen. She slid in a jazz CD and turned the lights down low.

"Ah, you're just in time to eat this while it's piping hot." Cullen deftly cut the omelette in two, depositing half on each of the plates he'd prepared with canned peaches he'd unearthed from Mei Lu's fridge.

He set the plates on her small table and pulled out her chair. She sat, and their knees bumped familiarly as he took the chair opposite her.

"I hope it's okay that Foo went outside again." Smiling softly, Cullen remarked that the CD she'd put on was one of his favorites.

Nodding absently, Mei let him talk. She poked the tines of her fork listlessly into her omelette a few times and remained silent.

Frowning, Cullen set his fork down. "What's on your mind, Mei Lu?"

Her head flew up and her eyes narrowed slightly. "You," she said simply.

"Me? Ah…well." Wadding up his napkin, Cullen wiped his mouth as he waited for her to elaborate. When she didn't, he prompted her. "If I'm the subject of your thoughts, I'd prefer you didn't look so serious."

"According to Captain Murdock…" Mei glared down at her plate. "Never mind. It's my problem."

"Mei Lu, don't do that. Don't insinuate that I've caused you a problem and then not fill me in. I can't fix something if I don't know what it is."

She attacked her food with vigor. "You make a mean omelette for a man who has a full-time cook."

"Mei Lu!"

She swallowed. "I'm not trying to be secretive or coy, Cullen. My supervisor was annoyed because I didn't get all the details I should've gotten tonight."

"That's bullshit. I blew your cover. I didn't do it on purpose, but it happened."

Mei Lu took another bite. After savoring it, she said, "I could've handled everything differently from the get-go, Cullen. The minute I saw the ticket to a benefit showcasing local artists, I should've realized you'd be there. The truth is, even before you barged in, I wasn't focused on work. I've let you—thoughts of you—confuse me."

The food turned to ash in Cullen's dry mouth. He didn't want to ask, but he had to. "That sounds a whole lot like you're about to give me the old heave-ho."

Lifting her head sharply, Mei Lu reached across the table and covered his hand with hers. "No. At least not if you still want me in your life," she said, eyes large and luminous. "I just need to find a better way to organize myself. When I'm assigned a case, I have to devote all my time to it until it's solved. Since we share this other case, I'm sure you'll understand and agree."

"And if I don't? Hell, Mei Lu. Everyone deserves a life outside of work."

She shrugged. "Are we fighting?"

"No. I thought I was stating a fact."

"A fact from *your* perspective. When a person's a cop, Cullen, life and work are entwined."

Cullen picked up his glass and drank some wine to give himself time to sort through the questions in his head. He'd worked side by side with cops. He knew the stats on their failed relationships. And he knew, too well, that he had one collapsed marriage behind him. Setting down his glass, Cullen twirled it idly by its stem. "Is this something you need to decide tonight?"

Foo raced back into the kitchen, tracking muddy paw-prints across the tile. He landed first on Mei Lu's lap and then on Cullen's knees.

"Oh, blast," she exclaimed, jumping up to shut the door. "I forgot how late it is. I try never to let Foo out after the automatic sprinklers around the perimeter of my court-yard come on. Jeez, Cullen, first I dump wine down the front of your tuxedo and now my dog deposits mud on your slacks. I'll pay for dry cleaning. Really," she insisted, when he eyed her as if she had to be kidding.

"What? I shouldn't pay because I'm a woman you slept with?"

"Mei Lu, that's crazy talk. I gave you that look because you have no idea what this tux has been through. Are you forgetting I have eight-year-old twins? Last year, Bobby's nose bled on the collar and one shoulder. Before that, Be-linda ate too much pie at Thanksgiving and barfed all over me. She made a much worse mess of both the jacket and pants. In fact, if I didn't have a dry cleaner who likes the amount of business I bring him, I expect he would've told me to burn the damn thing and be done with it."

Mei Lu laughed at the expression on Cullen's face as

she gingerly carried her dog to the sink, where she began washing his feet. "Okay, Cullen, I'm sure you're exaggerating, but you've made your point."

"I'm not exaggerating. Tomorrow, feel free to ask the kids if those things didn't happen."

"About tomorrow—" Mei hedged, drying off Foo's feet before she put him down near his bowl and fed him the remains of her omelette. "I spoke too hastily, offering to set aside our case to go kite-flying in the park."

"No, you didn't." He stood and stabbed a finger toward the door. "You don't have a car at the moment, so you can't go investigating on your own."

Mei Lu picked up Cullen's abandoned plate. "Has anyone ever told you that you'd make a good lawyer, Cullen Archer? You do an excellent job of twisting a truth into something that fits your purpose."

A rakish grin grew slowly, and he was equally slow to lean over and kiss her thoroughly. "I dare you to find fault with my logic in this case, Lieutenant," he said in a sexy drawl.

"I can't," she admitted, closing her eyes in an attempt to prolong the kiss.

He obliged, but stopped when he sensed they were both getting carried away. "A good lawyer knows to quit when he's ahead and I'm going to do exactly that. Anyway, I left my cell phone in the car. Freda won't know where to locate me if anything goes wrong at the house or with one of the kids."

"Cullen! Why didn't you say so earlier? Why didn't you go out and get it?"

"My mind was on other things," he returned, trailing a hand down her hair and even more lightly over her breast.

Mei Lu blushed, fumbled and nearly dropped a plate.

He removed it from her hands and carried it to the sink.

"You know what makes you an incredible woman? Well, one thing, anyway?"

She tilted her head and studied him through her lashes. "Now you've intrigued me. I shouldn't bite, but name one thing that's…incredible about me."

He let her wait until he'd gone into the living room and plucked his tux jacket off the chair where he'd thrown it after he'd dressed and come out of her bedroom.

At the door, he turned and took a last look at the woman framed in the kitchen archway. Even in baggy sweats that sported muddy paw-prints up one leg, she left him aching and wishing he didn't have to go. Wishing he could disrobe where he stood and simply take her to bed again.

"You really are going to leave without satisfying my curiosity?"

"Yes, because I'm reasonably sure that if I stopped to explain, I'd end up trying to satisfy more than your curiosity. So, this conversation's to be continued."

"Tomorrow?" she prodded. "On the way to the park."

"Uh-uh! Too X-rated for the park." Cullen pulled open the door and stepped into the cool night air. "Ask me the next time we figure out how to schedule an evening alone."

She came to the door, using a bare foot to keep Foo from escaping into an unfenced front yard. "I don't know when that might be, Cullen. Have you already forgotten what I said? I need to concentrate more on my assignments."

Striding back, Cullen slid his hands into her hair. He gave her a kiss that left both of them out of breath and wanting more. His stormy eyes glittered in the porch light. "Then consider me an assignment, Mei Lu. I know what you said, but I'm not going away. And I'm not ready to be a notch on your belt, Lieutenant. So pencil me into your damn schedule."

"A notch on my belt—" The kiss had obviously addled her. So much so that she dropped her guard and recovered barely fast enough to grab Foo by the collar, preventing his getaway. She wasn't fast enough to prevent Cullen's. Moments later, his car lights cut through the night and his engine broke the stillness along her otherwise placid street.

She slammed the front door. Did the man really think she—believe she—? Mei Lu was too furious to even finish her thought.

Then she stomped into her bedroom, saw the disheveled bed and sank like a sack of lead down on sheets still rumpled and musky. She remembered every last detail. Critically reviewing her part in their bedroom scenes, she understood where Cullen might have gotten the mistaken impression that she was far more practiced than simple instinct let her be.

A notch on her belt!

Should she try to combat that? Her first thought was to run it by Crista, who'd said Mei Lu should "go with the flow." She'd done that, but seemed to have given someone she liked a lot the wrong impression.

Dragging over the bedside phone, she started to punch in Crista's number and noticed the message light flashing. She recognized Abby's number on her call display. Mei remembered seeing this same call earlier.

It was too late to phone Abby. Come to think of it, it was too late to call Crista, too, especially now that Alex had entered her life.

Considering the list of friends she would've been comfortable calling at this hour, Mei Lu realized they'd all moved on. All except Catherine. Replacing the phone on her nightstand, Mei thought ruefully that it'd be more than a little unwise to call the chief and babble about indiscretions she'd committed with a man Catherine had sent her to work with on an important case.

Hadn't she always known in her gut that getting tangled up romantically led to nothing but trouble?

Trouble in capital letters.

Mei grabbed a pillow and curled around it, uncaring that the lights were still on in her kitchen and that she wore a muddied pair of sweats and that she hadn't performed her nightly ritual. Her path was clear. She ought to fade out of Cullen Archer's life. She could accomplish that by asking Catherine to take her off the case. There were any number of reasons Mei Lu could cite—all far from the real truth. If only giving him up and stepping out of his sphere were a simple thing. The longer she lay hugging a cold pillow, the more she realized she had to discard that option.

"See, Foo," she said to the dog who'd finally tracked her down and now sat studying her with his head cocked to one side. "I thought I could stay in control. I've found out I can't." Mei sat up, then stood and began pulling the sheets off her bed. Arms full, she marched into her minuscule laundry room and stuffed the sheets in the washer.

It was in the process of remaking her bed with sheets that didn't smell of Cullen's scent that her mind wandered from him to their case. A case with no leads. Well, they had photographs and two dead bodies. And a stumbling block. Her brother.

Stephen, who so wanted acceptance from his father that he was willing to do…what? Besides marry a woman he probably didn't love…?

Mei knew without doubt that her folks, especially her mother, would hate Cullen. The difference between her and Stephen was that she didn't care what Aun thought of her choices.

Is that a fact?

"Yes," she said aloud, causing Foo to paw at her leg and whine. She was tied to her family by her culture's beliefs. But unlike her mother, Mei didn't accept that parents are owed blind respect or that family should be honored, no matter how worthless or foolish the belief, because it's set down in the Tao. *Destiny rules,* Aun said often enough. Eventually, she insisted, one's true path would be revealed.

Mei had always thought that was nonsense. Still thought so. She and Stephen used to be in total agreement on this. Now, it seemed, they'd gone in different directions. Mei wished she knew how many other values they'd ceased to share. That was the big question looming in her head— alongside her feelings for Cullen.

In her heart of hearts, she didn't believe Stephen capable of killing or having anyone killed.

Although maybe he believed the same of her? In that case, she thought sadly, he'd be wrong. It was one aspect of Tao she had abandoned the day she'd raised her right hand and taken an oath to enforce the law and preserve the peace—even if that required the use of force. Even if it meant turning against someone she loved.

Mei switched off her light. Renewing that oath privately tonight brought with it a resolve to seek out the truth about Stephen. Mei knew she couldn't allow her feelings for either Stephen or Cullen to sway her. She wasn't sure why this case had been dropped in her lap by Chief Tanner. But whatever the reasons, her oath hadn't changed.

Just as she closed her eyes, her bedside phone rang. Mei reached for it apprehensively, but found herself smiling when Cullen's low, sexy voice rumbled in her ear.

"I called to say that *everything* about you is incredible. So get used to hearing me say it." He hung up with a soft click.

Mei smiled again as she replaced the receiver. It was a lovely ending to her day.

CHAPTER ELEVEN

MEI LU ROSE EARLY, dressed in jeans and a scuffed pair of cross-trainers for a brisk hike to the kite store. Mr. and Mrs. Wu, remembering her, greeted her effusively.

"Today is excellent day to fly kites," the kite maker said with a toothless grin.

Mei Lu felt her excitement swell. "I need four. The other day I fell in love with a butterfly and one of the good-luck kites. But I want to check your inventory again and be sure I choose right for each person. No multilines, reels or ground stakes. We want to run down hills in the park and let the wind take our kites up."

"You want happy kites," the owner's wife said, fluttering her fragile, paper-white hands. "This is good. I have favorites. Come see them."

"You have so many—how does anyone decide?" Mei marveled at a ceiling covered with colorful hanging kites.

"The right kite speaks to you." Mr. Wu trekked behind the women, giving his advice. "My grandfather and his father made kites from muyuan wood. Hard to find now. Very expensive. I use bamboo, as do most makers of kites."

"And silk," Mei Lu said, lightly touching the exquisite butterfly. "Yes, this one for Belinda. Oh, I see a different one I like for Bobby. The owl." She then debated between an eagle and a brightly colored phoenix that had a long, trailing tail. "The phoenix," she finally said. "For the children's father."

"And what will you fly?" Mrs. Wu asked, holding up first a swallow, then a bluebird, and last a goldfish, slender but with exquisite iridescent shading.

"The fish." Mei Lu imagined how graceful it would look in flight.

Mr. Wu bowed. "I will connect the line-winder bobbins and roll the kites so they will fit in your car trunk."

"I'm walking today," Mei Lu informed him when she reached the counter. She pulled her debit card from her shoulder bag and her badge folder flew out and fell open on the counter. "Oops." She grabbed the shield and returned it to her purse. It wasn't until Mei had finished her transaction that she noticed the couple had shuffled close together. The Wus clung to each other, frozen. "It's okay," Mei said gently. "I am with the police force, but you've done nothing wrong," she assured them.

The man patted his wife's hand and pulled free of her in order to bend and retrieve a tray filled with kite bobbins. "Forgive us," he said, absently lapsing into Chinese. "My wife's family suffered much at the hands of authorities in old Peking. She was young, but she remembers. And recently we were questioned. A man, a countryman not known to us, died by the knife. This happened just up the street."

"Oh, I know," Mei Lu said, as she took her debit card from the still-shaken woman. "That's how I found your shop. I'm doing follow-up investigation on that case. A second man died on the docks. We think the deaths are connected." She sighed, watching the proprietor adroitly weave line from the spools onto the kite strings. "People in this community aren't talking. I believe someone knows more than he or she is telling."

"Not us," the old man said quickly.

"No. I didn't mean you," Mei Lu told him with a smile. "But if you hear anything, or see other strangers in the area who may have a tiger tattoo right here—" she pointed to the web between her thumb and forefinger "—I hope you'll trust me enough to notify me at once. For his sake, as well as the community's. I'd hate for anyone else to die." Mei slid her business card across the counter and under the man's gnarled hand. As she picked up her purchases, she added, "I carry a phone. You can call that number day or night."

Mei Lu left doubting she'd ever hear a word. The Wus had let her leave without the usual Chinese blessing for a first customer of the day—an almost unheard-of oversight.

Cullen's car rolled up seconds after she walked into her house. Still pink-cheeked from the exertion, she opened her door and saw the twins tumble from the back seat. Mei heard Cullen tell them to stay in the car.

"It's all right," she called. Although maybe not, considering the way Mei had the wind knocked out of her just seeing Cullen in his outdoorsy jeans and lumberjack shirt. His dark hair was ruffled by a stiff breeze, and that reminded Mei Lu of how rumpled it'd been during last night's tussle on her bed.

The twins and their father arrived on her steps at about the same time. Mei had shut Foo inside. But he leaped against the door, letting his displeasure be known.

"Can we see your dog?" Bobby asked excitedly.

"If your father doesn't object, I actually thought we might take him along."

Cullen didn't seem too sure, but when plied by wheedling kids, he capitulated. "Oh, all right. Why not? He won't bite rambunctious kids, will he? They're bouncing off the walls today. Neither of them has ever flown a kite before."

"Well, then you're all in for a treat."

Belinda jumped from step to step, and did a sort of hop-scotch with her feet when she landed on the small porch. "Can we see our kites?"

"Yeah," Bobby said, ascending more slowly than his sister. "Dad said they were Chinese kites and they look different from the kites we draw in pictures."

"The store wrapped them. It's probably best if we don't undo the wrapping until we get to the park. Hey," she said, noting their suddenly long faces. "The park isn't that far away. You kids can carry the kites to the car while I get Foo's leash and his traveling food and water."

The children were appeased enough to enter Mei's house at a more decorous pace. Bobby checked out the room, then remarked, "You sure have a squirty house."

Cullen prodded his shoulder. "Bobby, that was rude. You've got to learn to think before you blurt out remarks like that."

The boy frowned, and Mei smothered a laugh when he said, "*Squirty's* not a bad word, Dad. And her dog's great." As if to punctuate his statement, he dropped down and rolled around the floor with Foo.

Cullen, who had his gaze on Mei Lu, saw her indulgent smile. He gave up with a shrug. "Those are the kites, I presume," he said, pointing to the wrapped bundles.

"Yes, and each one already has a line-winder attached. The string," she explained as the three novices gaped at her. "The last thing we want to do is get the lines tangled up, either before or after we start flying the kites."

Bobby nodded, jumping up after he'd sent Foo chasing a ball. "Which kite's mine, Mei Lu?"

She sorted through the packages and gave the children theirs. "Cullen, can you carry ours?"

Foo, hearing the rattle of his leash, danced over to Mei. Though he was panting hard from his roughhousing with Bobby, the dog's eyes were bright with anticipation.

"Your dog acts like he knows he's going to go to the park," Belinda said. She'd hung back as Bobby played with Foo. Now she went down on her knees and stroked the dog's soft ears.

Mei Lu showed her how to scratch his back. "He loves to ride in the car, kids. But he has to behave. In my car I have a harness that's like your seat belts. Since you don't have one of those, he has to lie quietly between you in the back seat. He can't be up moving around. He could get hurt, or distract your dad. That could be dangerous."

The kids nodded solemnly. And once in the car, they took their responsibility seriously. As a result, they were quieter than usual.

"Hey, this is great," Cullen muttered half under his breath. "This dog idea may have benefits I've never explored."

Mei glanced into the back seat. Foo was thrilled with all the attention. His eyes were closed and he wore a blissful expression as both kids constantly petted him. "I can probably rent him out to you during the day. I'm not happy about having to leave him alone so much when I'm working."

"Speaking of work," Cullen said, "what's the word on your car?"

"The mechanic phoned this morning. After he told me I should take the car out and shoot it, he said I'd be lucky to have it back by Friday. Instead of flying kites today, I ought to just go and buy a new car."

"Not nearly as much fun," Cullen said.

"No, and I did want to mention this about my morning

buying trip." Mei went on to tell Cullen about the reticent kite-shop owners. "I'll bet someone who has a shop in the vicinity of the club has information on our courier. If not on him, then on the letter-writer's contact. I noticed a lot of little shops along the route I walked. I figure I can spend the rest of this week trying to pry information out of someone."

"I don't know, Mei Lu. I'm not keen on that idea. People haven't come forward for a reason. You said the waitress was scared, and now it sounds as if the kite-store owners are, too. You could shake the wrong tree out there."

"Isn't that what we want?" She directed Cullen into the park entrance, not giving him time to voice the objection she could see forming on his lips.

It turned out the park Mei had hoped they'd have to themselves was already crowded with kite-flyers. Bobby and Belinda had spotted them, too, and twisted around in their seat belts to see the sky.

"At the west end there's an empty hill. If we hurry," Cullen said, "I think we can lay claim to it."

Mei Lu had to leash Foo and grab the bag she'd loaded for him. As well as dishes and food, she had a stake and cable she used if she went to read or eat lunch in the park. She'd pretty much resigned herself to the idea of spending her time teaching the kids and maybe even Cullen to fly their kites. To her surprise, when she finally caught up to them, they were deep in discussion with an Asian family who had a boy and a girl near the ages of the twins. Those kids were showing Belinda and Bobby what to do. And the two men chatted like old friends.

Mei tended to Foo. The mother of the other pair came to introduce herself. "I'm Angela Yee. It's truly a small world, isn't it. Our husbands met on a job your husband did for Ron's insurance office. It seems they shared kid pictures and stories over several lunches. I decided to take a break from racing up and down the hills to meet you." She smiled. "The kids are on spring break, so Ron took the day off work."

Mei extended a hand. "Mei Lu Ling. Cullen's not my husband. But, as you said, Bobby and Belinda are his. The dog's mine. Meet Foo Manchu. I live in the area. Cullen lives across town."

"Oh, sorry I jumped to conclusions. I should've realized the children weren't yours."

"Don't apologize. I'm delighted to make your acquaintance—and to have your husband's help in teaching them how to keep their kite strings from tangling."

Angela turned and shaded her eyes. "I don't think you need to worry. They all have their kites up."

Mei unabashedly applauded them. Her attention lingered on Cullen's lithe, athletic form. She felt he didn't often relax. Well, he had seemed pretty relaxed last night, but that was relaxation of an altogether different sort. She found herself blushing at the memory.

"You two are dating, though, right? It's obvious that you care for him a lot."

Angela's comment brought Mei up short.

"I have an Asian friend who's engaged to a Caucasian," Angela went on. "She's having a hard time with his children and his parents. None of them accept her. Maybe you have some hints."

"Cullen and I aren't—we're co-workers, you could say. That's a shame about your friend."

"Well, he comes from a wealthy old family."

"Oh." Mei thought that description fit her and Cullen— except that they weren't engaged, of course."

"My friend is so sweet. Her parents objected at first,

but they've come around. Kim says they love and accept Roger now."

Mei filled Foo's water bowl from a bottle. "If anything were to develop between Cullen and me, I can see my parents having a fit. At least my mother. She thinks I should marry someone in China. Would you believe it? But…I'm probably never going to have to cross that bridge where Cullen and I are concerned," she added, capping the water and tucking it back in her bag.

"Hey," Cullen called just then. "The wind's fine, Mei Lu. Don't stand there talking all day." He moved closer so he could talk without shouting. "Ron says that according to the weather report, this gusty wind isn't going to last much past noon. Come and meet him. My last recovery was for his company."

Mei Lu went to be introduced to Ron Yee. "Cullen, you might want to take breaks now and then," she advised. "You fly that phoenix without one, and tomorrow your arms will feel like they're going to fall off."

He grinned like a schoolboy.

"Save your breath," Angela said, walking up behind her. "Men never listen to advice from a woman."

"And that doesn't bother you?"

"Used to. I've decided it's a defect built into the species."

The two women shared a good laugh as they returned to where they left their kites. "On that note, I think I'll go show Cullen what a born kite-flyer can do." Mei unrolled her three-tiered goldfish and prepared to carry it to the top of the hill.

Angela picked up her own kite. "Mei Lu," she said, "if we lose the wind around the time my know-it-all husband claims, would you guys be interested in going somewhere for lunch?"

"Cullen's driving. I'll ask if he has to get back to work. Otherwise it's fine with me."

"Great." Angela hefted her kite, a dragon head with at least a twenty-foot tail.

Ten minutes later she and Mei Lu began to show off their prowess by making the kites dip and dance and swoop. Cullen reined in his phoenix and sat down by Foo to observe. Ron Yee did the same and the men laughed together, freely admitting they'd been bested.

The kids were still going strong by the time Mei Lu and Angela called it quits.

Cullen thought he'd never seen Mei Lu more full of life or more beautiful. Her face glowed from the exercise. Her eyes sparkled, and he wished he'd brought a camera to record how she and his twins looked against a picturesque background of green grassy knolls and blue skies. He swallowed back an unnamed longing, and turned his attention to stroking the dog.

"That's the most fun I've had in—well, I can't recall when," Mei said, letting out a big, happy sigh as she sank to her heels. "Cullen, Angela's invited us to join them for lunch." She turned to the other woman, who'd flopped down, flat on her back, her head cradled in her husband's lap.

Ron grinned at Cullen. "Hey, that'd be great! Only don't expect gourmet. We told the kids we'd go someplace with an outdoor playground."

"Anything's okay by me, if Mei Lu's good with it."

"It'll be fun," she said. "Today's still cool enough to leave Foo in the car. So the only thing we have to do is ask the twins."

"They'll jump at the chance. They've only got a few more days left in Houston this trip, and we haven't done a lot in the way of social activities. Their mom gets home on

Saturday. On Sunday they're headed back to Austin. Until summer break," he added, a noticeable sadness stealing over him.

"Must be rough," Ron Yee said. "Oh sure, my kids get on my nerves sometimes. But I can't imagine not having them greet me every night."

"Yeah, well…you're lucky." Cullen got up off the grass and whistled for the twins. All four kids came running.

From the way the twins jumped up and down, flinging their arms around, Mei Lu suspected that they agreed wholeheartedly with the lunch plans.

Cullen returned, leaving the Yee children to show his two how to roll their kites. "Ronnie and Jennifer only had to mention the big slide at the restaurant playground. Our plan met with Bobby and Belinda's approval, can you tell?"

"It's not-bad food," Angela said, climbing to her feet. "The kids and I go there if Ron's out of town. The play area's fenced, but we can sit out at picnic tables under some nice shade trees. And, Mei Lu, I've seen people there with dogs."

"I'm ready. All I have to do is collect my kite and Foo. I skipped breakfast to buy kites, so I'm more than ready to eat."

"I thought yours looked new. They're fabulous," Angela exclaimed, walking over to inspect Mei Lu's goldfish. "Ours need to be replaced. Where did you get those?"

The two women led the way to the cars, Mei Lu telling Angela where to find the kite shop. Cullen remained behind with Ron to wait for the kids.

Bobby and Belinda Archer raced around their dad, keeping pace with their new friends. When they reached the cars, Bobby threw his arms around Mei Lu in a surprising gesture of affection. "Flying kites is so cool. Wait till I tell my friends at school."

Mei felt a burst of happiness as Belinda echoed her

brother's sentiment. "I'm glad you two had fun," she said. "Foo and I enjoyed ourselves, too."

"If you're gonna come to our house this afternoon to work with Dad, can you bring Foo?"

"What about Mopsy?" Mei Lu wasn't sure how Foo would react to a rabbit.

Belinda danced around in circles. "We're s'posed to keep Mopsy in her cage. And we will, we promise, if Foo comes."

"It's fine with me, if it's okay with your father."

Bobby Archer screwed up his face. "Dad's always gotta ask Mom anytime we wanna do new stuff."

"It's what all parents do," Jenny Yee chimed in, nodding sagely.

"Yeah, but Mei Lu's not our parent."

Belinda, who liked having the last word, tossed out her show-stopper. "She could be like our stepmom, couldn't she, Bobby?"

Mei Lu sensed Bobby gearing up to attack his sister, so she stepped between them and took their rolled-up kites. "Kids, a lot more goes into becoming a stepparent than just giving someone the title. Your father would have to get married again for you to have a stepmother. I'm positive he wouldn't do that without talking it over with you two first. So, Bobby, you're safe. And I'm famished. Will you take Foo and get settled in the back seat? I'll store your kites in the trunk."

Seemingly mollified, the children told their new friends they'd see them soon. Peace descended once more.

Cullen had missed the whole stepmother discussion because he and Ron lagged behind, once again talking about the case they'd worked on together.

But Bobby had planted an idea in Mei Lu's mind.

From the time they all climbed into Cullen's car, until after they'd ordered lunch and now sat like families did around a shared picnic table, she tried to imagine what it'd be like to be married. More than that—to be married to Cullen Archer.

Four lives would be altered. She didn't have to ask Foo if he wanted ketchup or mustard or both on his hamburger. Not that he got a hamburger. He never argued about which dog food she gave him. Mei had a distinct feeling that mealtime arguments were minor when you were dealing with children on a daily basis.

She munched quietly on her chicken sandwich and watched the Yees interact. Their reactions seemed to be choreographed, but as Angela had mentioned, they'd been married for ten years. Cullen had been divorced for six, and he had an ex-wife to placate when it came to his children.

Jana Archer hadn't been on his mind last night. And judging by the many times he'd casually touched Mei since they'd taken seats across from the Yees—idly running his fingers through her hair or stroking her back as he talked—Mei knew that in some ways she'd already replaced the former Mrs. Archer.

Mei's cell phone rang about the time all four kids took off for the playground. She found the phone in Foo's duffel and frowned at the readout.

"Problems?" Cullen asked at once. "Is it your mechanic? You know, Mei Lu, I can lend you a vehicle."

"It's Catherine," she said, dropping her sandwich.

"Who?" Cullen paused as if he were trying to recall the name.

"Chief Tanner." Mei Lu shook back her windblown hair and covered her other ear in order to hear better. "This is Lieutenant Ling," she said, all business because she fully expected to hear Annette, Catherine's personal assistant, at the other end of the line.

"Mei Lu? Where are you? What's all the background noise? Sounds like a schoolyard." It was Catherine herself. Mei scooted from her bench seat to walk a few paces away.

"I'm at lunch," she told the chief, seeing no reason to make up excuses.

"I guess it is that time of day. Damn, another morning down the tubes. Is your meal something you can eat on the way to the station? I've got a development on your case, and I'll be locked all afternoon in meetings I can't change or cancel."

Mei Lu dashed a confused frown at Cullen. "My car's in the shop. Cullen picked me up today. He has his twins here at lunch with us. I can ask him to drop me at the station and then later I can take a bus home."

"If Archer's there, bring him. He was going to be my next call."

"This is crucial, then?"

"I'll let you two determine that. Can you be here in, say, twenty minutes? I'll have Annette go next door and grab me a sandwich."

"Uh, let me ask Cullen." Mei hadn't told Catherine that she also had Foo to contend with. Putting down the phone, she laid out her concerns.

Angela Yee quickly offered an alternative to driving across town to Cullen's place, where his housekeeper was available to baby-sit. "I realize we've just met, but Cullen and Ron have apparently discussed getting the kids together. We live only a few blocks from here, and we'd be glad to have the twins and Foo come over this afternoon."

Mei Lu waited. This was Cullen's decision.

"I hate to impose. I know we talked about getting our

kids together." Cullen listened to Angela's protests that it really was no trouble. "Okay, on one condition. You let me return the favor tomorrow. Bring Ronnie and Jennifer to our house in the afternoon. Angela, you and Ron plan to stay for dinner when you pick them up. Mei Lu, you come, too. I realize Ron's working, but Angela, I'm sure you can use a half day to yourself."

"Depending on this new development, Cullen, I may be tied up tomorrow." Mei Lu scowled at him for arbitrarily making plans for her.

"Darn, I can't tomorrow," Angela lamented. "Both kids have appointments to get their teeth cleaned and checked. Friday would work for us, though. If it does for you guys," she added.

"Cullen, can you be quick with a yes or no? I can't keep the chief waiting."

"Saturday's even better. It might take the twins' minds off leaving the next day."

Mei Lu slid the phone back to her ear. "Catherine, we'll be there as soon as possible."

They collected the kids, who of course fussed until they learned about the change in plans. "Goody," Belinda squealed. "Jenny has a Barbie castle. The one I want for my birthday, Daddy."

Bobby plucked his father's sleeve. "Why do you hafta go to the police station?" he asked Cullen. "You're not a cop. She is." He pointed at Mei Lu.

"Bobby, you know we're working on the same case. If you're going to cause a problem for Mr. and Mrs. Yee, I'll phone Freda and have her meet us at the station."

Ronnie Yee offered an enticement. He said he had three remote-controlled airplanes.

Bobby nodded. "That's cool. Okay, I'll be good, Dad,

so you don't hafta lecture me on the way to their house or nothin'."

The adults all laughed at that. They loaded up, and Cullen said they'd follow Ron's car. On the drive he did phone Freda, who agreed to pick up the children and Foo in two hours. Cullen relayed that to Angela as they entered the Yees' large, beautiful home, and left all the necessary phone numbers to reach him or his housekeeper.

Cullen waited until he and Mei Lu were back in the BMW before he bombarded her with questions. "What happened? Why did we have to drop everything and rush to the station?"

"I don't know. Catherine didn't elaborate beyond calling it a 'development,'" Mei Lu said, amusement twitching her mouth.

"That's not very helpful. I wonder if another courier's shown up dead."

"Doubtful. Otherwise Homicide would've called. And frankly, I wouldn't expect the chief to use that term if someone had died."

"Well, what do you think this is about?"

Mei Lu gave an exasperated shrug. "I have no idea. I'm not in the habit of interrogating Houston's chief of police, Cullen. Maybe that's how you work with Interpol. But we have channels. Protocol."

Cullen reached out and wrapped his right hand around Mei Lu's left as she drummed her fingers nervously on her knee. "Don't get huffy with me. Whatever it is, let's hope it's the break we're looking for."

She stilled her fingers. "Sorry, Cullen. Catherine was really helpful to a group of us women during our academy phase. After she was made chief, there were many people who believed—and still believe—that she's moved us up the ladder. But she's very careful not to play favorites. I'm not used to having her call me in the middle of a workday unless it's something very serious. So, yes, I'm nervous."

"Your face has guilt written all over it."

"Because…cops don't take time out during work hours to play. I let you talk me into doing that this morning, and Catherine caught me. You're corrupting me, Cullen."

He brought her fingers to his lips. "Wrong, Lieutenant. If I had corruption in mind, I'd pull over somewhere private and make love to you right in the car."

Mei felt herself blushing furiously.

Cullen let go of her hand and laughed. "You've acted so cool and controlled all day, Mei Lu. I've been dying to shake you up. Have I told you I've never met any woman who blushes as beautifully as you? And may I remind you that we're both adults? Neither of us is encumbered. I want to spend more evenings the way we spent last night. Don't you?" When she didn't respond, he looked at her sharply. "You did say you had no regrets."

"I don't. Well, none before you made that parting shot about being a notch on my belt. As if you'd have to wade through a crowd of men all used to—well, you get my drift, Cullen. Nothing could be further from the truth."

"I know that, Mei Lu. It was a poor choice of words on my part." He clasped her hand again, and this time brought it to his chest, where she could feel his heart beating. "I was only trying to make a point about intentions—and my feelings. I guess I made a bad job of it. I should've said I mean to stick around, and that I don't think of last night as a one-night stand."

Mei pulled her hand loose. She chewed on her lip, watching the string of cars exiting the freeway. "The truth is, Cullen, you *are* encumbered."

He couldn't take his eyes off the road, but she could see his frown.

"The twins," she said. "Bobby sends out all kinds of messages warning me off."

"My kids have no say in who I date. Sure, if I went out with someone who didn't treat them right, then it'd be different. You like them, don't you?"

"Of course. That's hardly the point."

"What is, then? You're the one who brought it up."

"Yes. Oh, shoot. Cullen, up to now I've avoided relationships for this very reason. They're too complicated. Add things like stepparenting and they're more than I can deal with."

"Is that what you're worried about?" A wide smile replaced his concern. "You're a natural at handling kids, Mei Lu. Give Bobby time. From what I've seen, he's torn between thinking you're fantastic and feeling disloyal to Jana. I don't think that's uncommon for a boy his age."

"No. I'm sure it's not, Cullen." Mei might have confessed to more concerns that involved the absent Jana Archer. But they'd reached a parking lot near the station, and Cullen whipped in and immediately paid the lot attendant.

Mei Lu climbed out. She led the way into headquarters, and fidgeted while waiting for Cullen to pass through the visitors' scanner.

In the stairwell, amid the echoing clatter of footsteps, she heard someone call her name. Lifting her head, Mei found herself face to face with Risa Taylor.

"You look casual and relaxed for a change," Risa remarked. Because Cullen had stopped behind Mei Lu, Risa moved to the same side and motioned him to pass.

"He's with me," Mei Lu stated. "Risa, this is Cullen

Archer. Cullen, Risa Taylor. She works in our sex crime division."

"A new detective?" Risa grinned, stretching her right hand. Her left brushed back strands of dark, shoulder-length hair.

"No," Mei corrected. "Cullen's not on the force. He's a private insurance investigator involved in a case I'm on," she added, moving ahead. She knew how good Risa was at interrogation, and Mei didn't want Cullen to be too free with information about the case, considering Catherine had never released her from the promise to keep it quiet. She saw the warm way Cullen looked at Risa. Everyone did; she was just so tiny, cute and personable. No one ever believed she worked the tough job of investigating sex crimes.

"Hey," Risa demanded. "You're taking off when I haven't seen you in a month of Sundays?"

"Sorry. We got a summons from the chief." Mei climbed two more steps.

"I take it the visit isn't social. Problem?"

"We don't know," Cullen said, and that resulted in Mei prodding him in the back, and Risa shooting them a quizzical glance.

"Cullen," Mei said. "Chief Tanner's in a hurry. Sorry, Risa, but we really can't talk."

Risa drew back, clearly hurt. "Well, excuse me. I see not much has changed between us, Mei Lu. I ran into Crista and she said you'd heard from Abby. But you're obviously still too involved with your job to make time for old friends."

"No, it's not that, Risa." Trying to change the subject, she said, "Abby and Thomas are getting married. Isn't that great? She left another message, but I haven't had a chance to phone her again."

"Lucy, too. Gosh, it's a regular epidemic."

Mei Lu walked backward up another step. "You and Grady?"

Risa shook her head. "We're living in his house in the Heights, though. He loves his job as a full-time professor." She sighed audibly. "I know you've gotta run. Mr. Archer, nice meeting you. Good luck on your case."

As Risa turned away, Mei Lu said, "I wish things were still like they were when we got out of the academy. When we all got together for coffee and dinner and—"

Darting a half-surprised, half-irritated glance over her shoulder, Risa interrupted, "Sure you do, Mei Lu. You were usually the one who phoned everyone and set something up. But I notice you don't try anymore. Not since…well, never mind. It doesn't matter." Risa had reached the landing, and a stride later was through the door.

Mei's shock would be hard to miss. Cullen noticed that she wiped at the tears rimming her lower eyelids. He wanted to ask, and would another time. Not now, though, because she lowered her head and charged on up to the next level, yanking open the door, and Cullen had to jog to keep pace.

Two more right turns and she stopped at a desk where a woman noticed them and immediately picked up her phone.

"The chief said it's about time you showed up," Annette Hayworth whispered.

Mei put a hand to her head, feeling a headache waiting to catch hold. She ran her fingers through her hair in an attempt to look less frazzled, then wrenched open Catherine's office door.

Far more calmly than Cullen would have expected, Mei Lu introduced him to the police chief.

"Sit, please," Catherine requested, pausing only to wrap up the remains of a sandwich. "Can either of you explain this?" She tore two tissues from a box. Spinning in her chair, she used the tissues to lift an open carton and urged her guests to view its contents.

"Ding porcelain," Mei gasped, reaching out to touch the piece, only to have Catherine, still using the tissues as gloves, lift it cleanly out of her reach.

"Of course," Mei Lu murmured. "You have to preserve possible prints. That exquisite vase is called Ewer with Dragon Head. I believe it was found in the 1960s in an excavation of Jingzhi Pagoda."

"It's on the list of missing museum items," Cullen supplied. "How did you get the vase?" he asked Catherine.

"Good question. The box was delivered to my secretary's desk during a meeting we both attended. There's no letter. No explanation. Just a handwritten label with my name and the address here at the station. I'd hoped you might be able to shed some light. If someone's playing cat and mouse with Houston PD, I don't like it one bit."

"Nor do we," Cullen muttered. Gesturing with one hand, he included Mei Lu in his statement. She'd withdrawn to sit with pinched face and fingers laced tightly together. Of course, that could be a leftover reaction to the encounter on the stairs. Cullen found all her recent actions confusing.

Mei Lu didn't look at anyone. She wanted to grab the box and run. Or throw up. Because she recognized every straight, bold black stroke on that address label. *Her father.* She'd read too many of his handwritten memos in the past to have any doubt.

What was the meaning of this delivery? Had a courier gone to Michael Ling with this piece, or was he trying to throw her and Cullen off the real trail?

While she didn't for one minute assume that her father

had any direct involvement in this wretched case, one thing would lead him to circumvent her.

If her brother were guilty.

Right or wrong, Mei made a snap decision. She had to find a way to leave Cullen behind and confront her father alone.

CHAPTER TWELVE

"THE GOOD NEWS," Cullen said, "is that apparently no courier's been knocked off to correspond with this artifact turning up." He watched Mei Lu out of the corner of his eye, not sure what should happen next. He could use some help here and she offered none. If anything, she seemed lost in thought.

Getting to his feet, Cullen held out a hand to Mei Lu, and said to Catherine, "Let us know if you get any clear prints. A match in the criminal data bank would certainly make life easier," he said.

"Wait," Catherine exclaimed, also rising as she reached for her phone. "I'll call in a technician to dust for prints now. Then I'll sign the piece over to you, Mei Lu. Frankly I'd rather not store a Chinese national treasure in our evidence room."

Cullen noticed that Mei Lu still hadn't budged. "I heard that evidence crucial to the city's biggest extortion case is the latest to go missing from the police evidence storehouse. So it's true?"

Catherine viciously poked a series of numbers on her phone pad. "That evidence must have been misplaced. We record everyone entering or leaving the room. There's a camera trained on the door. We'll find the bag," she said, suddenly changing her tone as someone came on the line.

"Joe? Chief Tanner. I need a print kit brought to my office. ASAP," she stressed.

Mei Lu stirred at last. "Sign the vase over to Cullen." She barely acknowledged him with the flicker of an eye. "With all his personal art, I assume he has adequate safes. I'm not equipped to hold anything of such enormous value."

Catherine, who'd replaced her phone, studied her lieutenant. "I meant, take it to your father." Catherine turned her attention to the vase again. "He'd have vaults at his gallery. I realize he doesn't have security clearance, but I've been in the store and I know the value of what he sells."

"Cullen's home is a fortress. His perimeter security alone is daunting. And after all, this is more his case than ours."

Cullen was flattered at the trust Mei Lu had in him, especially as she'd never seen his safe setup. She had to be a hundred times more familiar with Michael Ling's security. It occurred to Cullen that maybe this wasn't about trust— or at least her trust of him. What the hell was going on?

Mei Lu continued. "In fact, print collection will take a while. I'll run downstairs to pick up my messages. I'd also like an update from Captain Murdock on another case." She jumped up and crossed to the door.

Catherine briskly waved her out. "Fine. No sense tying all of us up. I'm going to be late for my next meeting as it is. Ask Annette to buzz me. I'll need her to pass on my apologies to the mayor."

"The mayor? Oh, should you keep him waiting? I can stay for the print tech."

"No, no. Run along. The mayor and our city manager set up far too many of these useless meetings where we all sit around saying the same things over and over. Oh, crap," she exclaimed, her eyes shifting to Cullen. "You didn't hear that."

Grinning, he shook his head. "Not a word." He had some questions for Mei Lu—like when she planned to return and where they should meet. But she'd slipped out already, and the next thing Cullen knew, the chief's intercom beeped and a burly man in uniform marched into the office bearing a print kit.

Mei Lu raced down the first flight of stairs in a daze. She had no car and, again, not much cash. Not carrying much money was a habit she'd gotten into on street patrol. Pickpockets hit on everyone, cops being no exception. She'd been razzed by her partner after losing money twice, so she'd stopped carrying more than a few dollars at a time, enough for a sandwich and a cup of tea.

Mei spotted a former patrol partner working at his desk. "J.J., hi," she said, rushing up. "I know this won't come as any surprise. My car broke down, and I need to get out to my dad's gallery. Can you lend me ten bucks until tomorrow? I'll pay it back first thing."

His eyes crinkled at the corners. "Only you, kid. You oughta think about changing your ways, especially now that you're a lieutenant. Congratulations, by the way," he said, delving a gnarled hand into his pants pocket. "I can spare a twenty. Will that do?"

"Great! Thanks. Tell Leta hi. I'll bet you have new grandbaby pictures."

"The rascal's walking already. I know you're in a hurry, but stop by tomorrow, and let a proud ol' gramps drag out his wallet full of pictures."

"I will. And J.J., I appreciate this." She dashed out and down the hall, and at the street entrance, met Crista coming in.

"Whoa. Where are you going? Are you hitting the gym at a different time lately? Haven't seen you there in over a week."

Guilt and grief over their damaged friendship overwhelmed her. She didn't know it showed so plainly until Crista grabbed her hand and pulled her aside.

"What's wrong? I've got a few minutes. Want to talk?"

"I do. But not here." Mei Lu's teeth sank into her lower lip. "Cullen's upstairs in Catherine's office. You remember—he's the contact from Interpol she assigned me to work with? He or the chief could show up on their way out any minute. I'm headed for my father's gallery and I can't let either of them see me." She still clutched the wadded twenty from J.J. "My car's being repaired, Crista. Darn…I don't see a single cab and I need one fast."

Crista allowed Mei Lu to drag her back out the door she'd just come in. "That was a mouthful you just reeled off. I'm afraid I didn't follow a word. But I just passed the coffeehouse down the street. It's practically empty. We can, uh, grab a table at the back. If you want to, that is."

Mei Lu felt sympathy from a woman who'd once been her best friend and her fears seemed to lighten. She'd wanted to come clean with Catherine or Cullen about her suspicions regarding her brother—and her father. But their roles in her professional life made that difficult. Crista had never judged.

"Crista, I'm in trouble. Or at least I think I am."

"You're pregnant?" Crista gasped.

"No, silly." Mei almost laughed at her friend's shock. "Let's take a break," she said with a sigh. "It's worse than that."

"This I've gotta hear. Knowing how fastidious you are about reports and everything to do with work, I can't picture anything really bad."

"You'll see."

The two women hurried down the street. The coffee shop was half empty. They slid into a booth farthest from the other customers. The waitress knew them on sight. She brought Crista black coffee and Mei Lu green tea. Neither woman really wanted her drink.

Haltingly, Mei Lu brought Crista up to date on the artifact-smuggling case. Anything she tried to keep vague, such as her after-hours relationship with Cullen, Crista wormed out of her with well-placed questions.

If Crista guessed the extent of what had gone on between her and Cullen, she didn't press. Instead, she focused on the real issue. "Mei Lu. Your family isn't you, and you're not a chip off the old block. You're an excellent cop. I understand why you are torturing yourself, but you know the rules as well as I do."

Mei gazed morosely into her cup. Then she took a bracing sip. "You think I should go back and tell Catherine it's my father who wrote on that box? I should let her take me off the case and send another cop to investigate him? Why don't I just resign from the force?"

"You asked my advice, and I'm going to tell you exactly what I think and then I'm going to forget we ever had this conversation. For both our sakes. Any idiot could see that quitting the force is the last thing you want. And you're right—if you told Catherine, pfft…you're off the case. Somebody with no tact or sensitivity could be assigned. If Shel Murdock gets to pick the cop, your name and your family's is likely to get dragged through the mud. Are you with me?"

Mei cupped her hands around her tea. "I am, but I'm not sure where you're going, Crista."

"Just this. Who's the primary on the case? Houston PD or—"

"Interpol."

Sampling her cooling coffee, Crista downed about half, then slid out of the booth. She tossed down money for both drinks. "I have to run. I know you'll figure it out."

Gulping the last of her tea, Mei Lu also slid out of the booth. "I might as well walk you back to the station." She adjusted her watch to see the time. "Crista, I knew what to do all along—but I needed a good, swift kick to remind me. I'll just get Cullen and tell him what I told you." She shook her head. "How can I ever thank you?"

Crista Santiago shrugged. "For the tea? I think you bought last time. Advice to a friend is always free."

Mei Lu smiled her first smile since she'd entered Catherine's office.

Parting from Crista inside the station with a brief hug, Mei plowed past people in the stairwell in her haste to reach Catherine's office before Cullen gave up and left without her. She yanked open the fire door and barreled into him.

"Hey," he said, struggling to maintain his grip on the box holding the priceless vase. "The chief's assistant phoned your office. A clerk down there said she hadn't set eyes on you in three days. I was just standing here trying to figure out how to locate you. To tell you the truth, I'm a little leery about hauling this baby around town. Police protection would be welcome," he teased.

"I got waylaid and never made it to my office," Mei Lu admitted. "I'm free to go if you are."

Cullen stood aside, letting her open the heavy fire door again. "I spoke to Freda. She was just pulling out of the Yees' driveway with the kids and Foo. We'll probably beat them to my place."

"Probably. Cullen, there's another…side trip we need

to make after you secure the vase." Mei Lu sucked in a deep breath, then told him what she thought about the writing on the box.

He said nothing until he'd unlocked the car and they both got in. He set the box on Mei Lu's lap, his gray eyes stern. "This doesn't sound like a conclusion you arrived at just now. How long have you suspected Michael?"

"Never! I don't suspect him of the smuggling." She picked restlessly at the fabric of her jeans. "That's not quite the truth," she said with a catch in her voice. "You know I talked to him. He is, after all, a leader in the Asian art market. I told you his reaction—instant shock. A person can't fake that."

"In light of what you've admitted, about your dad writing the label, explain why I should believe you."

Mei felt Cullen's mistrust, and she flinched as if he'd physically struck her. In all her internal wrangling, it had never occurred to her that he'd continue to question her veracity after she spilled her guts. Not after everything they'd shared.

"Please, Mei Lu. Don't clam up now. Enlighten me."

"Why can't you believe I know my father, Cullen? He lives by a stricter code of honesty than any man I've ever met."

"You might not be such a good judge. You're definitely not an unbiased one," Cullen charged, barely containing the disappointment and anger roiling through him. *Why couldn't Mei Lu have trusted him all along?*

Neither occupant of the car spoke again until they arrived at the house and Cullen used his under-the-dash button to electronically open his front gate. "Wait here," he said.

Setting his brake, he practically ripped the box out of Mei's hands and his keys from the ignition. "As well as stowing this someplace safe, I'm going to phone Freda and let her know we won't be home when she gets here. And that we may be gone a while—in case you have to bring in someone from Houston PD to read your dad his rights."

Mei Lu watched his self-righteous stride through a thin sheen of tears.

Crista had given her good advice. What other choice had Mei Lu had but to share her concerns with Cullen? That didn't mean she was bound by either honor or duty to accept any more of his derogatory remarks.

Waiting only until the front door closed on his heels, Mei Lu left the BMW and sprinted toward the street. She didn't slow her blind rush until she found herself three blocks from Archer's estate. Using her cell phone, she punched out police dispatch with shaking hands. Relaying her badge number, she requested a cab. She didn't explain why she was stranded, nor was that necessary. She dug out the cab fare J.J. had lent her earlier. It seemed like a decade had passed before her cab arrived but in reality it'd been barely long enough for her to repair the damage from her tears.

Based on the time, Mei thought her father had probably left his office by now. In that case she'd find him at home.

CULLEN HANDLED HIS BUSINESS inside the house in short order, or so he thought. The very last thing he expected was to come out and find Mei Lu gone. "Dammit to hell!" He slapped a hand down on the hood so hard, shock waves ran up his arm. "Where would she go?" he muttered over and over as he backed swiftly into the street and checked both directions without detecting any sign of her.

However, he knew she wasn't a woman without resources. Add to that, a high degree of intelligence mixed with more street savvy than one might guess to look at her.

Pulling to the curb at the end of the block, he let his car idle. Cullen admitted she'd given him the slip, although he still had difficulty believing she could just vanish. Then he began to worry.

The truth was simple—she'd gotten under his skin. Way under.

Cullen had let his temper override his good sense. As well, he ought to be ashamed for lacing into her. *Was* ashamed, dammit.

As if that helped his situation. He had to find her. Before long it'd be dark. Propping his elbows on the steering wheel, he closed his eyes and willed his growing panic to recede. A chill walked up his spine as he realized where she'd gone. To face down her father.

Freda's Land Rover turned the corner just then. She passed the BMW, then stopped and backed up. "Are you all right?" she asked over the noise of the barking dog and excited twins. When he had trouble hearing, she left her vehicle and ran up to Cullen's BMW. He rolled down his window.

"Yes and no," he answered. "I blew up at Mei Lu a few minutes ago. Then while I was inside, she took off. Walking," he lamented, dragging his hands down his cheeks.

"Going where?" The housekeeper snapped her fingers suddenly. "She mentioned that her folks live off Bingle Road. It's not far. I don't know the name of the subdivision, but she did say the house stands out because the fence has Chinese lettering in wrought iron. If you know her dad's name and act like you have an appointment, you can probably get by the gate guard."

"Freda, you're a jewel. That's probably what she did— went home instead of to her dad's gallery."

"Well, I'd better get these hooligans home. Will you

and Mei Lu show up in time for dinner, or should I feed the kids?"

Cullen shrugged. "Let me call you, Freda. I feel terrible for having treated Mei Lu the way I did. It may take a while for me to straighten things with her."

"Flowers, Mr. Cullen. Might not make up for everything, but flowers are hard to resist. They say a man cares. If you care, that is."

He pursed his lips. "That's the heck of it, Freda. It was after I came out and found her gone that I figured out how much I do care," he said gruffly.

"Then I wish you luck. It's high time you stopped rattling around in that big house by yourself for half the year."

Cullen watched her climb back in the SUV. Freda knew him well. He'd hired her after his divorce because Jana and her parents were claiming a man couldn't take good care of year-old twins by himself. Cullen would always be grateful to the woman who had, at that time, recently lost her husband to cancer. Cullen never inquired as to what kinds of questions the family court judge asked Freda in his chambers. He only knew that when she emerged, the judge signed the joint custody petition. As far as Cullen was concerned, Freda had a home from then until forever if she wanted.

He drove past a market and happened to see buckets of colorful flowers sitting out front. He made a sweeping turn into the graveled parking lot. Hauling out his wallet, Cullen bought an armload of daffodils. "Thanks," he told the clerk, who sponged off the water and wrapped them in green florist's paper. If he didn't find Mei Lu, he'd take them home to Freda.

It was important to him that she seemed to like Mei Lu. He recalled two women he'd dated after his divorce who had big plans for him and his home. All dates were history the minute any of them complained about his housekeeper or his kids. If those were tests, Mei Lu had passed both.

Cullen drove up to the guard house at the gates leading to a swanky subdivision. "I have a meeting with Michael Ling," Cullen announced brashly, not even sure he had the right area. "He's expecting me."

"Huh. They having some do tonight he forgot to tell me about?" the guard asked, his gaze lighting on the bundle of daffodils. "I passed Ling's daughter's cab through just a few minutes ago."

Relief flowed through Cullen at the news. But a cab? That he hadn't expected. "Far as I know, there's no party. Just Mei Lu and me," Cullen said, almost guilty about lying, yet not wanting the guard to call the house, either.

"Residents are supposed to supply us with the names of expected visitors. They never do. And who gets yelled at if I question one of their important friends too closely? Sheesh! Go on in. Y'all might tell 'em the association rules say I'm not supposed to let in any Tom, Dick or Harry just because he drives a fancy car."

"I'll mention it," Cullen said, wondering if he dared ask which direction he needed to turn at the cross street he could see up ahead. Still, he hadn't become a successful investigator without learning a few tricks. "I've only been to Michael's home once, and it was daylight. Is it faster to get there if I turn right or left at that next cross street? Oh, never mind, I see Mei Lu's cab coming out. A right turn is what I thought, but jeez, it's easy to get mixed up in these crazy subdivisions."

"Ain't that the truth. Don't know what maniac lays 'em out. Bear to the right, then make a sharp left almost immediately. Can't miss the house if you've seen it before. Sits smack-dab at the end of the cul-de-sac. The roofline reminds me of a pagoda or something."

Cullen cut the talkative guard off with a wave. The gates had slid open as the cab exited on the other side.

Even through the gathering dusk, Cullen saw what the guard meant. The Ling home did look as if it'd been plucked straight out of *Flower Drum Song*. Mei Lu reminded him of Lea Salonga, the actress in the Broadway version. Same grace, same…beauty. Cullen's mind stalled there as he pulled up to the house.

Nervous about his uninvited visit to the traditional parents of a woman he'd not only slept with but wanted to sleep with again, Cullen felt his palms grow damp. He wiped them down his jeans before gathering up the huge bouquet of daffodils. He wondered if he'd be better off handing them to Mei's mom.

As he approached the Chinese-red door, light and sound spilled from an open window to his left. A disagreement, he guessed, based on the heightened voices. The occupants were speaking Chinese.

Cullen located the brass doorbell and pressed it. A loud *gong, gong, gong* echoed inside. It couldn't help but interrupt even the fiercest argument.

Expecting either a butler or housekeeper, Cullen was surprised to have the door opened by Michael Ling himself. Even if Cullen had never met the man at Chamber of Commerce functions, he'd have known him on sight. Mei Lu got her height, her rangy frame and fine features from her dad.

Shifting the armful of flowers, Cullen stretched a hand across the threshold. "Cullen Archer," he said. "We've met at Chamber meetings, but you may not remember me. I've been working with your daughter on a case. Is she here? Mei Lu?"

She was, although her father didn't give her away. Mei Lu revealed herself, appearing in the dimly lit foyer. "Cullen," she exclaimed, the color leaching out of her face. "How did you find me? And how did you get past the gate guard?"

A second woman moved in behind Mei Lu. She was older than Mei, yet she'd obviously been a great beauty herself. Cullen guessed it was Aun Ling. She wore a hip-length tunic of emerald brocade, elaborately stitched with gold embroidery. Emerald silk pants shimmered in the light from the next room as the woman glided between her husband and daughter. Her braided hair was twined in an elaborate knot. Something held it in place—two chopsticks, Cullen saw, with carved dragon heads set with emerald eyes. They formed an *X* in her dark hair. The woman's scowl almost negated her attractiveness.

After those quick observations, Cullen ignored her parents and focused his attention on Mei Lu, thrusting the wrapped daffodils into her arms.

Surprised, she licked her dry lips and her features softened appreciably. "For me? What's the occasion?"

"The beginnings of an apology," he said, moving close enough to run the backs of his fingers over the curve of her cheek.

She hugged the flowers. "Daffodils are my absolute most adored spring flower. How did you know? Cullen, as I've said before, you are the most thoughtful man."

"I wish I could take credit. I can't—it belongs to Freda. Although she didn't need to hit me upside the head with a two-by-four to make me see the error of my ways. I've never met your mother, Mei Lu. Are you going to introduce us?"

Flustered, Mei Lu stammered through introductions in English and then a repeat in Chinese.

Mei's mother either wasn't impressed or she was plain unhappy to have him show up at the door without an appointment. She began to wave her arms and rattle off a stream of things that didn't sound promising to Cullen.

Standing her ground, Mei answered in kind, until Michael shut the door and quelled the women's byplay with a soft-spoken reproach. Both women clammed up immediately.

"What's going on?" Cullen asked Mei.

"I'm afraid you arrived at an inconvenient time. Just as I introduced the subject of the Ding ware."

"The what?"

"The Ewer with Dragon Head vase that turned up on Catherine's desk. It's Ding ware."

"Oh, the vase. Speaking of vases, shouldn't you put the daffodils in water? Otherwise, I'm afraid there's not going to be anything left to enjoy. You're squeezing the life out of them, Mei Lu."

"Sorry. Arguing with my parents makes me tense."

"I grant you, family feuds aren't fun." Cullen grew tense, too, under the distasteful scrutiny meted out by Aun Ling.

Michael came to the rescue again. He pulled a bell cord just inside a room that brimmed with museum-quality Asian art that Cullen wanted to examine more closely. A diminutive woman appeared like magic, and after a few directions from Michael, relieved Mei Lu of her burden, then exited the room as silently as she'd entered.

Following an even briefer exchange between Michael and his wife, Aun also bowed her head and fell silent. She went directly to a serving cart Cullen hadn't noticed at first, where she poured pale brown liquid from a squat teapot. Aun returned bearing a tray of small round cups filled with fragrant tea.

Reacting adversely to her continued glare, Cullen

wasn't sure he wanted to taste the tea. For all he knew, Aun might have poisoned his drink. And he had yet to figure out why Mei's mother seemed to dislike him on sight. Unless it was something as simple as Aun not wanting her daughter to accept flowers from a man. Or just from a non-Chinese man, perhaps. Cullen supposed he could understand that.

Had he not spent some time in Asia, the long drawn-out silence that ensued after the passing around of tea might have caused him to bolt. He racked his brain, attempting to recall the protocol—like, how many cups of tea were a minimum before it was proper to begin discussing business?

When Cullen's nerves were stretched tight, Michael collected their empty cups and returned them to the cart himself. "You have placed the Ding ware in a safe spot?" he asked, abruptly fixing Cullen with stern eyes.

Cullen inclined his head. "Early tomorrow I plan to arrange for an envoy from Interpol to take possession of the vase. If it's not deemed necessary as evidence, I'm confident it will begin its journey back to Beijing. My role in this is merely to recover the goods for an insurance company that insures museum art for the Chinese government. Any ramifications beyond that fall into your daughter's capable hands."

For several seconds Cullen thought that getting Michael to open up would be hopeless. Then, for a man so broad and tall of stature, Mei Lu's father seemed to shrink.

"Come into my office. I'd hoped to avoid further involvement with this accursed abomination against the country of my family and my wife. I will tell you everything I know about the vase. Which is precious little. But it will be the complete and categorical truth, I swear."

Mei Lu reminded Cullen of a woman standing on the

brink of a crumbling cliff. He got up and moved to her, helped guide her resistant body into the room her father indicated. Cullen gently brushed his fingers up and down her stiff back. Since Mei's mother hadn't yet entered the room, Cullen politely held the door ajar.

"Close it, please," Michael said, motioning with his hand.

"Your wife?" Cullen let the question hang quietly in a room that could only be described as masculine. Dark wood walls. Sturdy leather chairs. Heavy ashtrays. Even an array of brass spittoons, which Cullen hoped were only props.

"I never involve my wife in business matters. It's a promise I made to Aun's father, Lee Wong. As a reward for taking her so far from home and family, I pledged that she'd always live like a royal Chinese lady. A pledge I've kept for many years."

Cullen did shut the door then and returned to stand beside Mei Lu. "Are you saying that to emphasize your honesty? If so, don't I hold evidence that probably bears your fingerprints?"

"You have nothing but suspicions," Michael stated. "Suspicions put in your head by my own daughter." He stabbed a finger at her.

Cullen saw Mei Lu grip a chair back. He slid an arm about her waist. "Beyond suspicions, Michael, we have the vase and two dead men. What about them?"

"I know nothing of them. Hush, and I'll tell you the sum of my knowledge about this unfortunate happenstance. Wednesday noon of this week, I attended a meeting of the local art dealers. Lunch at Commerce Towers. Our speaker came from Customs. He explained new forms they've devised. The meeting ran from noon until two o'clock. I lingered maybe ten minutes afterward. No more, as I had a two-thirty appointment with a new client. I left, headed to my car." As Ling strode to a fireplace set in one wall and back again he supplied the name of the garage. Cullen and Mei Lu were familiar with the parking high-rise for clientele who frequented the tower.

"I walked, and as it was a pleasant day I removed my jacket before I unlocked my car. The minute I turned to lay my jacket on the back seat, I saw the box. A box not there when I parked."

"You'd left a door unlocked?"

Michael shook his head. "I don't believe I did."

"Who else has a key to your vehicle?"

"No one. That I am sure of." He took a breath. "I made a cursory inspection of the box, which I feared might be rigged to explode. I almost wish it *had* been a bomb," he said, shaking his head. "Especially after I slit the seal and saw what lay inside. The box had no markings. The filler could have come from any importer. I drove straight to Ling's and shoved the vase, box and all, into my office safe. All afternoon I waited for someone to contact me. Nothing that day or since. But I feel it's only a matter of time. In the middle of the night, I remembered Mei Lu urging me to contact Chief Tanner if I received a letter or photograph. This was more than that. Today, I addressed the box, slipped into the police station and placed it on an empty desk outside the chief's office."

"Why didn't you call Mei Lu?" Cullen asked when it appeared that Michael had finished stating his case.

"I read the news. I see how police officers try to falsely discredit their own. I want her to return to Ling's, but I would not bring shame on her."

Cullen stared at him. "You expect us to believe this thousand-year-old vase crops up in the back seat of your locked car for no apparent reason?"

"I know how it sounds. Believe me, I've lived with the facts longer than you have. I'm telling the truth. That's all I know."

And this time, because Cullen saw the man's deep-seated anguish and felt his fear, he believed Mei's father.

Mei sensed his acceptance—her first sign of hope. "Cullen, is it possible someone's trying to frame my father? I mean, it happened while he was at a meeting of local art dealers."

Cullen rubbed his thumb along a deep crease down the center of his forehead. "Anything's possible in this case. The question would be, why him? Who stands to benefit?"

Father and daughter slowly shook their heads.

"Usually insurance investigators look first at disgruntled employees." Cullen's statement prompted a flurry of denials from Michael. "Does the description fit anyone?"

"I pay my staff well. They've all been with Ling's for many years. I'd stake my life on the honesty of each and every one."

Mei fought the bile sloshing around in her stomach. "Father, have you given any thought to, uh, Stephen?"

"My *son?* Your brother? Impossible! As you're aware, he's many miles away." Michael Ling sent his daughter a look that could only be described as scathing. She reacted with silence.

Cullen immediately slipped a protective arm around her waist. "Is your brother anxious to take over the company? If Michael dies or is otherwise out of the picture, does Stephen inherit the whole shebang?"

"No," Mei and Michael said together.

"Ling's is in a three-way trust split equally among Mother, Stephen and me," Mei Lu explained.

Cullen's cell phone rang, startling everyone in the room.

He frowned at the readout. "It's from my house," he said to no one in particular before he answered. "Freda? Are the kids all right? Foo? What? Jana left a message to call her *where?* Australia? What the hell? She's due in Houston on Saturday at six a.m. No, I hear Bobby wailing. Yes, I did—find Mei Lu. Can this wait, Freda, until I get home?" He sighed loudly. "It's anybody's guess what Jana's up to. I'll be home soon. Then I'll call her back and we'll find out."

Mei Lu clasped an anxious hand over his arm. "I'll go with you. There's no sense in you having to deal with your problems and my dog, too. Father, may I borrow a car? Mine's in the shop."

Michael pulled out a set of keys and handed them to her, but Cullen pressed them back into the older man's hand. "I still have fences to mend with Mei Lu. I'll see that she and Foo get home safely. And, for the record, sir, I believe you about the vase. We'll need to schedule a time to talk more about your son. Soon," Cullen emphasized, now in a rush to deal with his next problem.

Mei's mother was nowhere in sight when they left Michael's office.

"Wait, Cullen. I'll tell Mother goodbye. And I'm not leaving without my daffodils. Go ahead and start your car. I'll only be a minute."

Worried now about what Jana's call meant for the twins and why it would make Bobby cry, Cullen took Mei Lu at her word. He left after bowing briefly to his host. The bow was returned—although curtly, Cullen noted.

CHAPTER THIRTEEN

WHEN THEY WERE INSTALLED in the BMW, Cullen at the wheel and Mei Lu hugging a massive pale-green vase spilling over with bobbing daffodils, she asked, "Did you mean what you said back there, Cullen? You believe my father's telling the truth about how the vase came to be in his possession?"

"Don't tell me you've changed your opinion?" He looked sharply at her.

"Definitely not! I wasn't sure if you were lulling my dad into a false sense of security, all the while planning to have your friend at Interpol launch an investigation."

"I apologize for doubting. His outrage seemed genuine. When you're up to it, though, I'd like to discuss your brother."

Mei Lu's shoulders slumped. "Father is furious at me for bringing suspicion and dishonor down on Stephen's head. You will have a chance to meet him, Cullen. Right before I left the house, Father informed me he's called Stephen home from Hong Kong. You can be sure he'll learn the truth."

"You do know I have to put Stephen's name in the daily report I make to Brett Davis at Interpol? How much harm will come to Ling's overseas operation if Brett snoops into the company's business practices? Activities, records, that sort of thing?"

Mei shook her hair out of her face. "I've checked transactions and company banking records for the past six months. I still have computer access, since my father never removed me as an officer in Ling Limited."

"So, Stephen's been in your sights for how long? When were you going to mention him to me, Mei Lu?"

"Not until I had more than a vague suspicion. Don't you have information on this case that you haven't shared? You never said Ling's was on a list."

"They weren't, believe it or not. Not until you came to translate. The fact that you were related to an Asian art broker made me realize that Michael fit Interpol's profile better than most. But, later..." Cullen paused, sucking in a breath.

"Later?" Mei Lu prodded.

Stopping at a light, Cullen turned slightly, allowing his gaze to move slowly over her face. "Later...I admit to having developed this desire to shield you from anything hurtful. So, shoot me, Mei Lu."

A tentative smile nudged aside the tension that had stretched between them from the time they'd left the Ling home. "A feeling I return," she said. "Which probably places me at a disadvantage. Because it's the last thing I expected. Cullen..." Her eyes sought his. "I took an oath to uphold the law. I'd never ask you or anyone else to look the other way to protect me or my family."

Cullen turned the corner and stopped in front of his security gate. His finger hovered above the opener. "I'm thinking of telling Brett I want off this case. What if I have to call in people to bring Stephen down?"

"You won't have to," Mei Lu said, trailing her fingers down Cullen's leg to squeeze his knee reassuringly. "I want to know who the players are. Especially since they've dared to implicate my father. If I find any valid evidence pointing to Stephen, you won't have to call anyone. I will. Until then, he deserves the benefit of the doubt."

He wavered, but only for as long as it took him to part the daffodils and find her lips. "I'm glad we cleared the air," he said softly, opening the gate after their brief kiss. "God only knows what my ex has in store for me this time. Her manipulations and lies led to our divorce. You can't imagine what a relief it is to know I can trust you, Mei Lu. I hated doubting your dad, but what I hated even more was suspecting that you might cover for him. I thought—what if I have a tendency to fall for the wrong women? Although... Don't ask me how anybody can control love."

"Boy, do I know that feeling. I asked a friend how she knew she'd finally met Mr. Right. Crista. She'd gone through horrible, abusive relationships with her stepfather and her ex-husband. Now with Alex she's blissfully happy." Mei Lu fell quiet as Cullen glided to a stop in front of his home, which blazed with lights.

Even before he got out, the twins tore out the front door and charged down the steps. Freda stood framed in the doorway, having captured Foo before he dashed out after the kids, who threw themselves at their dad. Bobby unleashed the first battery of questions.

"Belinda said if Mom's in 'straylia, that means we can't go back to Austin. Why is she there? If we don't go back, we don't hafta go to school Monday, do we? Is that true?"

"Don't get your hopes up. I know Australia wasn't on your mother's itinerary, but maybe she made a change and plans to arrive here Sunday instead of Saturday. Give me a chance to phone her, okay?"

"O...kay," he said in a lackluster manner, then moped all the way inside.

Belinda hopscotched over to Mei Lu. "We had fun at the Yees'. So did Foo. If we don't go home on Sunday, can you bring Foo over again? Hey, where'd you get that big bunch of flowers?"

"I'm glad you enjoyed Foo, Belinda. I can't answer your second question until your father completes his call. And…he gave me the flowers. Aren't they pretty?"

"Uh-huh! But why did Dad give you flowers? Are you sick? That's when my gramma takes people flowers. Or she sends flowers if they're dead." Belinda did more hop-scotching. "You don't look dead." She giggled.

"Belinda, give Mei Lu a break." Cullen urged the girl up the steps, then he turned to assist Mei Lu. "Here, that vase is heavy. Let me carry it inside."

"I've got it. Go on in, Cullen. I know you're anxious to return Jana's call."

He made a face. "I'm *not* anxious," he muttered, taking the vase anyway. Stepping aside, he let Mei Lu precede him.

Once everyone had crossed the threshold, Freda shut the door and let Foo loose. The housekeeper then pried the vase out of Cullen's hands. "Good job," she exclaimed, beaming at him. "My suggestion got results, I see."

"No need to talk in riddles, Freda. I gave you credit for the idea of buying Mei Lu flowers. And she graciously gave me points for picking her favorite kind."

"Are you gonna tell Mom you bought *her* flowers?" Bobby demanded rudely.

Cullen, who'd led the way into the kitchen and had already ripped off the message stuck on the wall phone, glanced up from reading it. "Bobby, I can buy gifts for anyone I like without informing your mother. She and I lead separate lives, with one exception. That's where you kids are concerned."

The boy kicked the refrigerator with the toe of his sneaker. "How come Mom asks us all that stuff, then?" He whirled on his sister. "Doesn't she ask who Dad has over for dinner when we're here? She always wants to know who he dates and stuff."

Belinda nodded. "I'm not sure we're s'posed to tell him that, Bobby. Gramma said we're not s'posed to spill those beans—that's what she says—when we come to Houston."

"Good grief." Cullen put both hands on his hips, frowning first at one child, then the other. "Gramma Vaughn fishes for information about me, too?"

"Gramma doesn't fish, Daddy," Belinda hooted. "You know she hates getting her hands dirty."

"Okay, okay." Cullen raised one hand. "I've got the picture. I'll take this up with Gramma, and with your mom. Speaking of which, I need you all to be quiet while I make this call."

The children climbed up on stools by a breakfast bar that divided the kitchen from the dining nook. Not sure what Cullen expected of her, Mei Lu was grateful to Freda for providing an answer. The woman handed Mei a piping hot cup of oolong tea, then pulled out a third stool at the end of the counter.

As Cullen punched in a string of numbers, she noticed that the twins were fidgeting and spinning around on their stools. Bobby more than his sister. The wait seemed so long that Mei Lu began to catch their nervousness. At long last, Cullen's call connected.

"Jana Archer, please," he muttered. "No, I don't see why she'd be registered as Jana Sullivan. Maybe Vaughn. Vaughn's her maiden name." Cullen scowled at whatever he heard. "All right, try the Sullivan number."

"Jana? Is that you? It's Cullen. What in heaven's name

are you doing in Sydney?" He rubbed at his forehead with the knuckle of one thumb. "You *what?* Got married!" His eyes opened wide, and he nearly dropped the phone. "Slow down. Let me get this straight. You met an Australian in Singapore. Lorne Sullivan...and you flew home with him. Yesterday you got married? Jana, have you lost your mind?"

The children stopped spinning. Freckles stood out on each pale face. Freda stopped scraping carrots at the sink and turned to study Cullen's jerky movements.

He waved a hand wildly and said, "I don't give a damn if Lorne has two stations in the outback. Your home is in Austin. You have eight-year-old twins due back in school this coming Monday." Cullen smacked his forehead. "You've pulled some real stunts before, but this is the ultimate. No, I do *not* want you to phone your folks and have them come and get the kids. Our custody agreement is between us. You and me."

He stomped so far from the wall, he nearly detached the cord from the phone. "You know what? I'm handing the phone to the twins. You explain it to them, Jana. It's not up to me."

He gave his daughter the phone and stormed from the room. Foo slunk out of the way and ran to hide under the table in the breakfast nook.

Belinda greeted her mother hesitantly at first. She listened intently, nodding all the while.

Bobby jumped off his stool, rounded the counter and began to pummel Mei Lu with flying fists, catching her off guard. "You said Dad wouldn't never do nothin' like get married again unless he talked to Belinda and me first," the boy screamed, his face beet red. "That's a *lie.* 'Cause that's what Mom did. Liar, liar!" He started to cry.

Freda, small woman that she was, attempted to shackle Bobby from behind. "Mr. Archer, Mr. Archer!" she called.

Cullen, who'd probably only stepped around the corner to compose himself, rushed back into the room. "Robert Archer. Stop it! What's gotten into you?" A string of apologies tumbling from his lips, Cullen lifted the boy bodily. That was when Bobby broke down and sobbed in earnest. Wiggling around, he threw his arms around his father's neck so hard that Mei Lu thought he'd choke Cullen.

Her heart broke for father and son. Through it all, she couldn't help but be angry with the selfish woman who'd do such a thing without regard for her kids. Those beautiful children deserved better. Cullen deserved better. Mei's stomach heaved. How would Jana's latest actions affect Cullen's custody agreement? Mei wondered if he might not be forced to move to Austin. After all, he'd said his former in-laws wielded a lot of power. Cullen would never risk letting them take his children away.

No matter what happened, Mei Lu foresaw this turn of events having a negative effect not only on their work relationship, but also on their personal one. The relationship they'd barely begun to explore…

"Excuse us," Cullen said through gritted teeth. "Belinda, don't let Mom get off the phone before I can talk to her again. I have a few more things to say. I'll be upstairs."

"Cullen." Mei Lu gripped his arm. "I'm…I think I'll call a cab so Foo and I can make ourselves scarce. Phone me later, after things settle down, okay?" She pushed her teacup back and slid off the stool.

"Stay, please!" There was definitely a pleading quality to Cullen's request. "Freda's fixing dinner. Things will get calmer. We're going to eat a normal family meal."

Freda nodded and retrieved her half-scraped carrot.

Mei Lu hated confrontations. Still, she couldn't walk out

on Cullen if he needed her. "Take care of Bobby. I won't leave."

Obviously cheered by her promise, Cullen hauled Bobby from the room. They soon heard his heavy tread on the circular stairs.

"Freda, if I'm going to stay, I want to help. Assign me a job."

"Bless you," the woman said. She used her arm to shove a lock of red hair out of her eyes. "I'm almost done here. The kids asked for chicken-fried steak and biscuits. I'm making a carrot, raisin and apple salad to go with it. I'll let you set the table."

Mei Lu washed and dried her hands. She noticed that a teary-eyed Belinda had hung up and now sat staring at the wall. "You okay, muffet? I could use some help finding the dishes and silverware."

More listless than Mei had ever seen her, the child crossed her arms and hunched over. "I'd better go see how Bobby is. Daddy's on the phone with Mom again."

"No, you don't, missy," Freda said, blocking Belinda's exit. "Your daddy will take care of your brother. I know how it goes when one of you decides to get in the act because the other's in trouble."

"Why is Bobby in trouble? What's going to happen to us?" Copious tears tracked down the girl's pale cheeks.

"Honey, honey." Mei Lu skirted the counter and knelt to gather the child against her. "Things will work out. Do you believe your father would let anything bad happen to you or Bobby?"

Belinda shook her head. That got the front of Mei Lu's shirt wet. "I didn't hang up right away after Daddy got on the phone again. Mama said Lorne, the man she married, doesn't want kids around for two years at least. Mom said she's gonna sell our house in Austin so she and Lorne can take his boat someplace I never heard of." The tears fell faster, even though Belinda sniffed hard and tried to wipe them away. "Mama told Daddy she's happy for the first time ever, and said for him not to screw things up for her."

During her two years on street patrol, Mei had gained some experience consoling children affected by trauma. The rule books all said kids needed an assurance that their world would be okay. Mei heard Freda slamming pots and pans around in the background. She had to say she shared the housekeeper's sentiments. But for Belinda's sake, Mei Lu pasted on a small, steady smile. "I know all of this sounds awful. But trust your dad to figure things out. I know he loves you and Bobby more than anything in the world. Look, Foo's come to make you feel better. If you sit on the floor, Belinda, he'll climb in your lap."

"Okay," Belinda said, drawing in a shaky breath. "Mei Lu, will you bring Foo back…tomorrow?" The girl sank to her knees and hugged the animal. Foo licked her tear-stained face.

"I'll do better. I'll ask your father if Foo can spend the night. Everything he needs for a sleepover is in the bag you brought from the Yees'. And don't forget, they're coming for a visit on Saturday evening, too. Won't that be fun?"

"Uh-huh. Mei Lu, I love you." Belinda squeezed Mei Lu hard—a hug that gave her the time she needed to hide not only her surprise, but the tears rimming her eyes.

She'd risen, repaired her face and was just setting out the silverware when a much-subdued Bobby and a grim-faced Cullen entered the kitchen again.

"Freda, how close is dinner to being done? I have a couple of calls to make, but I can make them now or later on, after I take Mei Lu home."

"Ten minutes," Freda announced. "Enough time for Miss Belinda to wash the doggie smell off her hands and face."

Belinda rose, reluctantly releasing the dog. "Daddy, Mei Lu said maybe Foo could have a sleepover tonight. She said he could stay until she comes back or maybe even until Ronnie and Jennifer Yee come for a barbecue."

Seeing Cullen's shock, Mei Lu swiftly interjected. "I'm not trying to mess up your plans, Cullen. What I told Belinda is that I'd ask you first."

Surprisingly, he tunneled a hand under Mei Lu's hair and, in front of everyone, delivered a long and tender kiss. "Mess all you want," he said huskily, leaving her reeling as he pulled away by inches. "I'm beginning to think I need a keeper. I forgot to say a word to Freda about inviting company over Saturday night." He peered worriedly around Mei Lu, sending his housekeeper a sheepish look. "I hope it's not too late for you to get all the stuff we need for an old-fashioned barbecue for the family and five extra people, Freda."

"The freezer's full. Weather's probably perfect to eat out around the pool."

Even the children perked up at that prospect. They seemed in a better frame of mind as everyone found seats at the table. Mei Lu had taken a minute to show the twins how much kibble to give Foo. "It's important never to let his water bowl get empty. He gets dehydrated fast," she explained.

The boy and girl nodded solemnly. When Bobby slid into his chair, he wriggled a lot, finally blurting, "Dad, if we're going to stay here instead of going back and forth to Austin, we can have a dog of our own. Let Mei Lu take Foo home. We can get our own dog, Belinda."

Juggling a platter full of chicken-fried steak, Cullen threw Mei Lu a quick glance. "I don't know about that,

Bobby. Maybe I'm considering inviting Mei Lu and Foo to move in with us."

Bobby stopped wriggling. "Why?"

"Praise God," Freda muttered as she plunked a basket brimming with golden biscuits down in front of Cullen. She thrust a dish of carrot and apple salad into Mei's suddenly numb hands.

Cullen forked off a piece of breaded sirloin and cut it in half. He set one piece on each child's plate. "It's something to consider, since we're going to be making some big changes around here." He avoided Mei's stunned expression.

Belinda stirred excitedly. "I think that'd be *cool,* Dad. Foo likes us, and so does Mei Lu. Bobby, what's wrong?" Her brother's face left little doubt as to his feelings.

"Cullen," Mei Lu chided, reaching to kick him none too gently under the table. "Bobby doesn't know you're teasing."

"I'm not." Cullen grinned at her. "I tossed out the idea to start everybody getting used to it. Obviously we won't make a final decision tonight, but my feelings are on the table. Would you eat a whole piece of steak, Mei Lu?"

"After that bombshell, Cullen, I'll be lucky to eat one bite."

"Like I said, there's no rush." He shrugged casually. "Frankly, I don't know why you're surprised. I thought I'd made my intentions clear on the drive from your parents' house."

"If you did… No, no, I… Uh, can we discuss this later? Everyone needs to eat this great meal Freda fixed." She poked her fork into the tender meat and cast her eyes down, having seen how the twins' heads whipped back and forth between her and their dad.

"If anybody wants my opinion," Freda announced, dragging out an empty chair and plopping into it, "I say it's way past time. Your dad needs someone, darn it." She helped herself to the other part of Mei Lu's steak, still on the platter, and appeared not to notice Mei Lu's sputtered expulsion of breath.

Cullen noticed her fiery face. He figured he'd have a lot to answer for when he finally got down to driving her home. He hoped she might invite him in once they got there. Heaven knows they'd both had a rough day. They could benefit from a certain amount of up-close-and-personal attention.

Whether Mei Lu granted that part of his wish list remained to be seen. From the way she picked at her food, Cullen suspected they might have different opinions about making love tonight—or any other night. If so, he'd have to see about changing her mind.

"I always try to read the kids a story after our evening meal." Cullen pushed back his chair as his children polished off portions of strawberry shortcake. "Tonight, however, I should phone Jana's parents, then the three of us have some talking to do." He studied Mei Lu briefly. "Will you be all right entertaining yourself for another half hour or so?"

"Cullen, you look exhausted. Wouldn't you rather I called a cab?"

"No. I want to drive you home, Mei Lu. I insist."

The kids had run off, coaxing Foo to follow them upstairs. Freda moved toward the sink with a load of dishes.

Cullen bent nearer Mei Lu, teasing her lips apart with his. "If nothing else," he whispered, "I'm hoping to steal a few more good-night kisses. Maybe they'll wipe away that exhausted look I have."

"With a promise like that, I'll just go help Freda clear the table."

Uttering something resembling a sexy growl, Cullen hurried from the room.

Mei Lu stood on rubbery legs, needing a minute to recover. Then she found a small bowl for the leftover salad. The biscuits had all been eaten.

"Mr. Cullen's a fine man," Freda remarked out of the blue.

Mei Lu tried to restrain a sigh, but it slipped out anyway. "I know he is."

"You like the twins, don't you? I mean, they're not the problem?"

"Heavens, no. They're great kids."

"But something's holding you back."

"Yes, well, Cullen and I are working on this case together."

"Is getting married against the rules?" Freda asked, returning from the table with a second load of dishes.

"Marriage?" Mei squeaked. "Oh, no. I'm…well, you could say it has to do with family, though."

"You mean, because your folks are set on you marrying a Chinese man?"

"Who told you that?" Mei Lu frowned slightly.

Freda shrugged. "Nobody. I probably watch too many TV counselors. Just the other day, one said it's a common problem in ethnic communities. They specifically said in Asian communities."

"My concerns aren't about our cultural differences, although I suppose it'll upset my parents. My mother, for sure." Mei fluttered her hands helplessly. "It's complicated, Freda. For one thing, I'd never want to bring dishonor to Cullen."

"Huh? You're talking in riddles. Forget everyone else. Listen to your heart."

Mei Lu wished she could. Wished it were that simple. But until they were able to clear Stephen totally, the potential was there for him—and by extension, her—to bring shame on friends, colleagues and, of course, Cullen, should he and she become seriously involved.

Obviously not understanding Mei Lu's concern, Freda nattered on about Jana Archer's latest escapade. "She's done some screwy things. None quite this crazy. Mr. and Mrs. Vaughn, they're gonna throw a hissy. They haven't hesitated to use their clout to get their way and keep the twins in Austin. It kind of amuses me that Jana's handed Mr. Cullen the edge."

"For the children's sake, Cullen still needs to maintain an open dialogue with his ex and her family. Freda, I'm not in any position to comment one way or the other as I've never met any of them. Maybe we ought to talk instead about Saturday's barbecue. You'll like the Yees. How can I help you? Tell me, what can I bring?"

"Yourself. I like nothing better than fixing meals for a crowd. My husband was a navy man, and we always had a houseful of neighbors and friends. We moved to Houston after Don retired and needed bypass surgery. Great military hospital here. During the surgery, the doctor discovered that Don had inoperable cancer. His appetite got so poor I hardly cooked anything for the five years he hung on through sheer grit."

"Sounds horrible for you both, Freda."

"Not fun, or easy. But I wouldn't give up one single minute our heavenly Father saw fit to let us spend together. Don's been gone nearly nine years. I still miss him like it was yesterday. That's why I'm saying, honey, don't let the grass grow under your feet. The hours you get to be with the man you love can be precious few."

Mei Lu slowly turned over Freda's words in her mind. Her mention of the heavenly Father served to remind Mei Lu that it was the theft of the Heavenly King and the other museum pieces that had brought her and Cullen together. His entry into the kitchen now pulled her from her private thoughts. He still looked tired, but she gravitated toward his warm smile.

"They've fallen asleep, mostly because I let them roll out their sleeping bags on the floor so they could share Foo. That offer was sheer genius on your part. In case I forgot to thank you, Mei Lu, let me do it now."

She relaxed and let Cullen tug her into an embrace. "Come three a.m. when Foo needs to be let out, we'll see if you're still thanking me," she said, grinning.

"I hope you're making that up." Cullen stopped nuzzling her neck and moved her toward the door. "Freda," he called over one shoulder, "If I'm not back by three a.m., guess who's on doggie duty?"

The housekeeper laughed heartily even as Mei Lu whispered in Cullen's ear, "Why wouldn't you be back way before then? It's only ten."

Cullen dropped a sweet kiss on her upturned face. He stopped twice more on the way to the car to kiss her, each kiss more intense than the previous one.

Mei Lu felt a sense of pure contentment. In the car, she burrowed into the soft leather of the seat. It'd been a long day and she was unable to contain a yawn that overtook her as Cullen got into the driver's seat.

"Oh-oh. Is that fair warning that I'll be saying goodnight on your porch?"

She stretched like a cat and carefully hid a second yawn behind her hand. "What if I said that once I pass this phase, I generally get my second wind?"

"I'd say you're teasing me, and loving every minute of it."

Mei Lu laughed. "You're so transparent. That's one thing I love about you."

"Ah. You pick a fine time to toss out a statement like that. Compels a man to ask for a list of the *other* things you love about him."

"Hmm. If I named them all, I think it would go to your head. So, maybe I'll let you figure it out."

"I need to know something—is any part of this serious?"

The smile she wore faded a little, and Mei Lu flipped the collar of her jacket high up under her chin, as if to ward off a chill.

"My feelings for you are real, Cullen. You're in my thoughts day and night."

"I hear a *but* coming."

"Yes. Maybe we're going too fast. Three or so weeks ago, neither of us even knew the other existed. Until today, you thought I might be playing fast and loose with the law, even looking the other way for my father."

"We've already settled that you're not, and that Michael's above suspicion."

"I know, but we haven't cleared Stephen."

"So? He's far removed from you."

She studied her short, well-kept fingernails. "I'm an extension of my family and they're an extension of me. We call it the circle of life. All the members of a family are tied together by thought, word and deed. When the name Ling is cleared of all suspicion, I'll be free to offer you my love. Not before."

He parked the BMW outside her house. As they unbuckled their seat belts, they noticed her car had been returned. Shutting off the engine, Cullen clasped the hand Mei Lu had been studying so intently. He kissed her fingernails, then her knuckles, and afterward turned her palm over and pressed a kiss there.

"I don't ever want to make light of your beliefs, Mei Lu.

But I married one woman who put her family, her parents, ahead of me. Sue and Hal ruled Jana's life. Their wishes, advice and suggestions always counted for more than mine. Their money meant more. They formed a circle, all right, and left me on the outside. If you and I are going to act on the feelings between us, I've got to know that my love means more to you. The most. That you and I stand shoulder to shoulder, no matter what happens in the world around us."

Mei Lu felt as though she vacillated between the customs taught her from birth, and her friend Crista's contention that to find happiness, she needed to take a chance—see where it took her. As if happiness were lying around for the taking. Yet Crista had managed to find happiness in spite of her past. So had Risa. She hadn't let her family dictate her future. Neither had Abby, nor Lucy. Their backgrounds were all so different from hers, though. Mei Lu was still confused. But…deep down she couldn't imagine living like her parents. "I—I want everything you're offering, Cullen."

The troubled dark eyes she slowly fixed on him shone with love and hope. He took that shaky declaration as gospel, because he wanted to so badly. She looked so fragile that Cullen thought maybe he wanted too much. Because he needed her. Tonight he was running on empty. Watching his children's heartache, sharing their fears, had left him completely drained.

Reaching out blindly, he wrapped Mei Lu in a massive hug and literally lifted her across the console. The arms she twined around him spoke of her strength and conviction, not her fear or fragility.

Much later, cocooned in each other's embrace in Mei's soft bed, Cullen couldn't recall the steps that had landed them there. It was anyone's guess how they'd managed to make it from the car into the house without leaving a trail of clothing for the neighbors to see.

"Do you have to leave?" Mei Lu murmured as Cullen thrust a leg out of the bed. She didn't lift her head, but let her lips graze the fine hair on his chest. "I'm not sure I can move. And anyway, I love listening to your heart beat."

He laughed, then rained kisses on her hair.

Feeling his laughter, too, Mei Lu traced a string of tiny kisses to his heart. "The Chinese character for love, *ai,* is the sign for a person, under which is the sign for a heart. Surrounding that is an all-embracing hand." Mei ran light fingers up his chest and let her palm rest on his sternum. Earlier his heart had slowed to almost normal following their frantic coupling, but now it started thudding faster again.

"Is that your indirect way of saying you love me, Mei Lu?"

"Indirect?"

"I believe I said 'I love you' at least six times in the last hour, but what I get from you is more like a lesson in philosophy."

"True love, like the Tao itself, can be alluded to but never really captured. It can be described, but never fully explained."

"Is that where all this wisdom comes from? The Tao?"

She shrugged. "I certainly don't understand love." She pulled herself up until their heads rested side by side on the pillow. "Mother taught Stephen and me from the lessons of Tao until Father objected. Traditional Taoists are too rigid, he said. And they don't talk in terms of love. In fact, I remember Mother saying there's no such thing as star-crossed lovers, and there is no perfect mate." Mei flopped over on her stomach, resting her chin in her hand. "I know I'd rather be with you than not," she admitted.

Cullen smoothed her tangled hair. "I think that's a fair description of love," he said, letting his fingers absently stroke the gentle slope of her shoulder.

She latched onto his hand and caressed the length of his index finger. "I sensed great resistance in Bobby...to us."

"Their mother dealt both kids a huge blow today, Mei Lu."

"Even before. The very first day, Belinda invited me back to lunch. Bobby escorted me to the door and couldn't close it behind me fast enough. It was as if he knew I was already attracted to you."

"You were? Attracted to me then?" Cullen's patently satisfied grin complemented his tousled appearance.

Mei Lu jabbed him in the ribs, wiping the smile away fast. "I'm trying to have a serious conversation here. Quit giving out the mating call of a bull moose. I'm afraid Bobby's resistance may be minor compared to flak we'll get from my family. Well, my mother and probably my brother."

"I realize your mother was less than impressed with me. But your brother and I have never met. We might hit it off."

She rolled off the bed and slipped into a robe, sashing it at the waist. "Stephen won't take kindly to being investigated by Interpol. He'll like being summoned home by Father even less." She walked over to a corner desk and booted up a notebook computer sitting there. "I haven't found a single discrepancy in Stephen's books. Do you want to take a look, Cullen?"

"I'd rather have a second go at what we were doing, but..." He swung his legs over the bed's edge and picked up his pants. Once he'd donned jeans and boots, he threw on his shirt and joined Mei Lu. "I somehow doubt that the people involved in an operation of this magnitude would be stupid enough to let it show in their books."

"*Something* would show. Receipts that don't match legitimate purchases. Unexplained payouts. Or deposits not matching listed sales. Going through cooked books is part of my job, Cullen. The crook hasn't been born yet who doesn't slip up somewhere. Money trails simply don't lie. Those couriers were paid—maybe not handsomely by U.S. standards, but plane tickets from China aren't cheap."

He positioned his chin in the hollow between her neck and shoulder, and peered at frame after frame as she scrolled through Ling Limited's records. She talked so fast and pointed out so much that Cullen was prompted to say, "Hell, woman, I'm determined to marry you quick, if for no other reason than to hand over my budget." Laughing, Cullen ducked when Mei Lu slapped at him with the pages she'd just printed. In the midst of their fun-loving scuffle, her cell phone rang.

The caller's voice was so soft, Mei Lu had to press the phone tight to her ear and motion for Cullen to stop laughing so she could hear. "Oh, Mr. Wu. From the kite shop? Of course I remember you." Mei Lu's heart thumped so loudly she had to listen extra carefully. *This may be our break in the case,* she mouthed to Cullen. "Thank you for calling, sir," she said in Cantonese. "I promise I will not place you or Mrs. Wu in any danger, nor your friends, the Hsiaos, who confided in you. I'm glad you told them of my interest in learning if someone new arrived in the neighborhood—someone wearing the tattoo of a tiger."

The old man reminded Mei of her promise. "I understand. I'll keep you safe. Yes, I wrote down their address. Goodbye."

"What was that? Calling about kites this late at night?" Cullen asked after she clicked off. He could feel her excitement as well as see it.

"I'd told the Wus to phone me day or night if they saw or heard anything out of the ordinary. Another man with a tiger tattoo is in town. He's at the home of a neighbor of Mr. Wu, the kite maker. Got in earlier this evening."

"What are we waiting for? Let's go nab him," Cullen said, swiftly buttoning his shirt.

"Not tonight. The host family has gone to bed. We'll stake out their place at first light. I gave my word that I wouldn't put the couple he presented his *guanxi* letter to in harm's way. Their names are Mr. and Mrs. Hsiao."

"What if Tiger Man slips through our fingers?"

"He won't do any business until after breakfast. That's the Chinese way, Cullen. We'll meet early and follow him after he eats and leaves his host's home."

Cullen plainly didn't want to wait. He might have argued more, but this time his cell phone rang. "What now?" he grumbled. "Oh, Freda, hi." He listened briefly, frowning all the while before hanging up. "It never rains but it turns into a hurricane—for Bobby, anyway. He woke up with a hundred-and-four-degree fever. His stomach and back are covered in red spots. Freda thinks it's chicken pox. I've gotta go, Mei Lu." Cullen was clearly torn.

She trailed him to the front door without question. Only after he opened it and she was hit by a blast of night air did her brain begin to function. "Kids can get really sick with chicken pox. That means you won't be able to go with me tomorrow morning."

"Damn, you're right," Cullen muttered, brushing his lips across Mei's pleated brow. "Maybe I can work it out. Freda said the more pox that pop out, the better the chance that Bobby's fever will drop. In any event, Mei Lu, I don't want you going alone. Don't you have a partner on the force you can call? Some backup?"

"Cullen, I'm a cop. I can't just wait and let another courier go off to kill or be killed. And my biggest concern is warning him with too obvious a police presence."

All the emotions Cullen was feeling exposed themselves one by one in his anguished eyes. "Please don't go without calling me first. Give me a chance to see if I can make other arrangements for Bobby."

"You'll need to notify Ron Yee, too. Not only to cancel Saturday's barbecue, but to warn them of possible contagion. The day before kids actually break out is when they're most apt to pass the germ to others. I know. Stephen got them first and gave them to me."

Cullen groaned. "Our first break in the case, and this happens. But my kid has to come first."

Mei Lu nodded. "Of course."

"Mei Lu. I don't care if you are a cop. I love you, and I can't imagine letting you head into potential danger alone." He kissed her. Softly at first, then more possessively.

"I feel the same about you, Cullen," she said when they broke apart. "I suppose that's what philosophers mean when they say love transcends the best and the worst in a person's life. You drive carefully on the way home. Tell Bobby that as soon as his fever breaks and he feels a bit better, I'll bring him a Chinese paper-folding kit and teach him how to make animals. Doing paper art kept me from scratching when I had chicken pox. My mother taught me how. Funny, I'd forgotten that she sat beside my bed for hours. She had patience then."

"So do you, Mei Lu. Patience and a huge capacity for love." Cullen bent again and gave her a deep kiss. He paused a moment more to trail a hand over the curve of her cheek, then reluctantly dug his keys from his pants pockets.

She blew him kisses, because he kept glancing back at her on his way to the car. Clutching her robe tight, Mei Lu waved as he drove off, her heart frantically skipping beats. That, too, must be love, she supposed. That feeling of never wanting to be apart…

Bobby's fever would go away within days; she wasn't sure hers ever would.

CHAPTER FOURTEEN

MEI LU'S PHONE RANG AGAIN almost immediately after she went inside. She assumed it was Cullen, missing her already. That would have been nice. But instead of his voice, she heard Catherine Tanner's.

"I realize it's late but I've got some good news," the chief announced. "The heads-up you gave Shel Murdock the other night resulted in our rounding up a boatload of half-starved illegal immigrants, three flesh traffickers, and five high-level ringleaders. Three are already out on bail, though."

"Murdock gave me credit?" That astounded Mei Lu.

"Are you kidding? Of course not. He strutted like a rooster and hogged credit with the press as usual. But one of the perps, a guy by the name of Burgess, was so pissed at you he freely flung your name around. As a result, Sheldon had to back off. I hope you know that did my heart good. Except it won't do the department's image any good to make a flap over it that gets into the papers. I'm sorry to cheat you out of your fifteen minutes of fame, Mei Lu. I have stuck a commendation note in your file, which I hope to parlay into a raise."

"Hey, I'll take that over having my picture on the front page any day."

"Maybe next time you'll get both. How's the special case coming?"

"Chief, the smugglers have lain low since killing that last courier. Tonight, we've picked up a possible lead. Not that this case will be as simple to solve as sending a team to the port to meet a boat."

Catherine made sympathetic noises.

Mei thought she heard a fax chattering in the background. "Don't tell me you're still at the office?"

"This is the only time I can get any solid work done. Otherwise, there's a line a mile long waiting to dump new problems in my lap."

"I'm up checking computer reports, too. In fact, Cullen only just left, after his housekeeper phoned to say his son broke out with chicken pox."

The airwaves hummed vacantly for a moment. "You seem to have come a long way from calling him Mr. Archer in that disapproving voice." Catherine said pointedly.

Mei Lu swallowed, hesitated, then decided not to feel or sound guilty. "A very long way, Catherine. We've, uh, discovered mutual…feelings. Is that a problem? I swear it won't interfere with the outcome of our case."

"I trust you, Mei Lu. Personally, I'm pleased. I hope he's worthy of you and that things work out long-term. I'd like to meet him in a social setting sometime."

"I'd love it if you—well, everyone from our old group— get to know Cullen." Shyness edged into Mei Lu's voice. "Soon, maybe, if everything works out."

"Like marriage, you mean? I don't recall your ever mentioning marriage. And I can't imagine that you'd want a big, splashy wedding of the type Archer's social set is probably used to."

Mei Lu laughed. "I never wanted any wedding at all. But…I'm starting to give it serious thought. Definitely nothing splashy, though. Cullen's a real homebody. Come to think of it, his house has the perfect staircase for a bride to walk down…. Catherine, nothing's for sure, so I may be telling you all this for no reason."

"Huh, if Archer passes you up, he's a fool. If it's a matter of cold feet, I'll be happy to hold his to the fire. Blast, here comes another fax. I think somebody's figured out where I spend my nights. Good luck on your case. If you need resources, call. I expect a full report on it—and an invitation."

Warmed by the positive reaction from a woman Mei Lu admired so much, she said goodbye, crawled into bed and dreamed for the first time of what life would be like as Mrs. Cullen Archer.

MORNING ARRIVED before Mei Lu was ready to release her dreams. She discovered that her body ached pleasantly, which brought Cullen immediately to mind. Smiling in her half-asleep state, she gauged the time in North Carolina. Owing Abby a call, she found the number and punched it in. Abby's enthusiastic greeting lifted Mei Lu's spirits. As Mei Lu had suspected, her friend had called to say she and Thomas had tied the knot. But she'd never expected Abby's next piece of news to be that she was pregnant. The friends talked about that, and progressed to discussing Cullen. Too soon, Abby had to go. But she extracted a promise from Mei Lu to keep in touch and to keep her informed. Basking in a return to a closeness reminiscent of old times, Mei Lu felt a lot better.

With visions of Cullen refreshed, Mei suddenly recalled the new lead. That spurred her to quickly shower, dress, and then brew a cup of strong black tea. She carried it to the kitchen table where she could watch the sunrise. Ordinarily she'd sit in her back courtyard while Foo chased chipmunks. Mei wondered how he and Cullen's kids were getting along. It wasn't really a surprise when her cell phone started to vibrate. She'd already clipped it to her belt, along with her Taser. Both would be hidden by a hip-length khaki jacket she'd pulled from her closet.

Expecting Cullen to call early, her voice held a smile when she sang out, "Hel...lo."

"Miss Lieutenant, you please come quickly," a hushed voice said in broken English. "You know who this is, yes?"

"Mr. Wu?" Mei Lu's hold on the phone tightened. She panicked, thinking he was about to deliver bad news about their man with the tiger tattoo. Either that he'd been killed or that he'd vanished.

The caller lapsed into Cantonese. "Come soon," he urged. "Our friends, the Hsiaos, came to borrow rice ten minutes ago. Their houseguest is up, demanding breakfast. He claims to have an important early-morning appointment across town. I proposed that Mrs. Hsiao cook a big breakfast to delay his leaving, but she does not like him or his attitude. She and Mr. Hsiao will be most happy to say goodbye. They owe much *guanxi* for help with their passage to America, and are delighted some is paid back. But this man frightens them."

"I'll leave now, Mr. Wu. I have your address."

"Please do not come to our door. The man has a mean look about him."

"No, I said I won't put you in any danger. Do your friends, the Hsiaos, know the person who sent this man? It may be a key to stopping others like him from bringing their *guanxi* demands here."

Mr. Wu uttered a name. "He has become a most powerful man in the Kowloon Peninsula. Many people here owe him for making it possible to flee China."

"I'm truly in your debt, Mr. Wu." Mei could tell that the

kite maker was extremely nervous even mentioning the name of the money man. It was a name that meant nothing to Mei Lu.

"Mrs. Wu liked you very much, Miss Lieutenant. She begs you to take care of yourself this day. Now I must go."

Mei Lu shivered unexpectedly, even though the morning sun warmed her breakfast nook. "Yes, I understand. Go about your normal routine. If you see me cruising the street, don't pay me any attention, Mr. Wu. If necessary, I may stop to buy another kite."

"The ones you bought were well received by your friend's children?"

"Very. I've recommended your shop to a friend, Angela Yee. But we'll talk kites another time," Mei Lu said urgently. "I need to leave."

Her caller hung up without further comment.

Mei Lu threw on her jacket on the way to her car, all the while praying the mechanic had fixed her car properly. Thankfully, the engine turned over and caught with the first twist of the key.

Making a U-turn, she headed for the address she'd jotted down. Mei Lu debated phoning Cullen. He'd said he'd get in touch with her. Really, she had nothing more to add to the information they'd learned last evening. In case he'd been up all night with Bobby, she resisted disturbing him—no matter how much she'd like to hear his voice.

Mr. Wu had not described the Hsiaos' houseguest, and belatedly Mei Lu wished she'd asked what he looked like. She had to assume he'd be dressed similarly to the other couriers. But as she scanned the street and saw only two men, both dressed in regular suits, she worried that she'd made a mistake. Mr. Wu had indicated the courier's appointment was on the other side of Houston.

Mei Lu assumed he'd grab a cab. Only, she'd passed three bus stops in the space of four blocks. Her quarry might well take a city bus. After all, trolleys, trains and bicycles were the major modes of transportation in his part of the world.

Mei Lu slowed her car. Many area residents lived behind their shops. There were also a few single-family dwellings sandwiched between businesses. Mei realized there was a great deal she didn't know about the Hsiaos, the family being paid a visit by Tiger Man. Were the Hsiaos shopkeepers like the Wus?

Taking a long look at the men standing at bus stops, Mei turned the corner at the end of the block, deciding to drive down the alley behind the stores. The backyards were small but well-kept. Flowers spilled from pots on every back stoop.

Uh-oh! Mei Lu thought she'd spied her man standing on the bottom step of a porch. A couple near the Wus' age huddled together on the step above him. They appeared tense, especially the woman. The husky stranger wore nondescript black pants and a loose shirt or tunic. He spun around, most likely at the sound of her car.

She took care to drive straight past as quickly as possible, averting her face. When she peered in the rearview mirror, she saw him disappearing through a hedge near the front of the house. Wishing the blocks weren't so long, and that she hadn't been so impatient, she had no choice but to keep going. She eventually reached the end of the alley and pulled up at a corner some dozen homes from the Hsiao place. She spotted her guy melting into a crowd at a bus stop.

And darn if she didn't see a bus at the previous stop. Mei Lu backed up and parked the car under a live oak. She fumbled to lock her car while digging bus fare from her purse and arrived at the bus stop out of breath, just seconds before it would have taken off without her. The driver wasn't overjoyed with her, either. He scowled when she stuffed quarters into the change counter.

At first Mei Lu thought the man she wanted hadn't boarded this bus at all. Her breathing slowed to normal the minute she saw him sitting stiffly in a back row. She wanted to shout triumphantly when she noticed that he carried a cardboard box of similar size and shape to the one her father had found in his car.

She should probably phone Cullen. Or Catherine. Yet she couldn't very well talk openly in this crowd. And what would she say? She truly didn't know any more now than they'd known last night. Except that their suspect was on the move. So, why cause either of them needless worry? If she needed backup, it was only a phone call away.

Several stops later, people disembarked and more got on. A side seat with a better view of the back opened up. Mei Lu sank down, pretending to watch the passing scenery.

"Beautiful day." A woman seated beside Mei spoke in Mandarin. Mei answered in kind. Beaming, the grandmotherly woman touched Mei's arm. "It's good to see a young woman your age who still speaks our language. So many have forsaken it for English."

They chatted about the weather and about the woman's large family and her pets. All of a sudden, Mei Lu saw the courier stand. He shuffled off behind others who were leaving by the back door. It was then she noticed that he clutched a bus transfer as well as the cardboard box.

Excusing herself in English and in Mandarin, Mei swam upstream toward the driver. "I forgot to get a transfer," she panted.

"Which type?" he asked, again unhappy with her apparent ineptitude.

"Type? I'm a new bus-rider," she mumbled.

He explained that there were differently colored edges, depending on which bus she planned to transfer to.

She gave a helpless shrug, which made him ask, somewhat rudely, for her final destination. How could she explain she didn't *know* her final destination? Luck smiled on her then. Darting a glance out the side window as she went through the motions of digging for a nonexistent address, she saw the courier pass directly beneath. The transfer he held tight in one hand was trimmed in blue.

"Never mind, I remember," she said. "I need a blue transfer." She plucked the proper transfer from a fistful he held out to her, then streaked out the narrow door.

Afraid she'd lost her courier, she kept hopping up on tiptoe, trying to see over and around the milling throng of bus-riders. This, she discovered, was the big downtown transfer station. Mei would never have guessed that so many people rode the bus. All the times she'd been stuck in traffic, she would've sworn everyone in the city drove cars to work.

Ah, she identified the man's black cotton shirt amid a host of traditionally attired businessmen. Her cell phone sounded its melody just as she wedged her way into position less than ten yards from him.

"It's Cullen," a scratchy voice said when she answered. "Where are you? I thought you were going to call me first thing?"

"I thought you said you'd phone me. Listen, Cullen." Mei lowered her voice. "Don't ask about the case, okay? We can discuss Bobby. How is he?"

"Miserable." This was said around a yawn. "An on-call physician's assistant agreed to phone in a prescription for the itch. He's supposed to take it by mouth. She said they don't use creams these days. I called the kids' pediatrician in Austin, and he was rather worried about Bobby's fever. I'm glad to say it's dropped a few degrees. Why can't I ask about the case? You haven't left your house yet, have you?"

Frantically following the progress of the man with the box, Mei Lu let several people surge past her as another bus pulled in. Whispering now, she cupped a hand around the mouthpiece. "I've got him, Cullen. Our courier. Well, I don't *have* him. Not in custody. Not yet. Hey, I've gotta run. He's about to board a bus I need to catch. I'll call you later. As soon as I figure out where he's going—"

"Mei Lu, wait! I talked to Brett. Your brother left Hong Kong last night. Interpol already had a tail on him. Word on the street in that region says the smuggling operation's headed by someone with a well-placed family member in Houston. I'm sorry, sweetheart, but...what *will* you do if you're faced with arresting your brother?"

Mei couldn't describe the pain squeezing her heart. "Cullen, I really have to run. Literally...to catch a bus. To answer your question—I'll call for backup. It's what any good officer does."

"I'm just so sorry. Be careful," he stressed seconds before she cut him off.

The day seemed far less bright after Mei Lu boarded the bus. She took a seat near the front, worrying about Stephen. The stranger she was following suddenly looked more sinister. Maybe she ought to call for backup now. But Cullen's words didn't really make sense. They knew her father wasn't the contact. Wasn't it conceivable that the person responsible could be a private collector? In any case, if she brought the uniforms in too early, she risked blowing the entire case.

This bus held far fewer riders than most others pulling out ahead of it. Obviously her man wasn't headed into the city center.

Near-paralysis set in when it became apparent to Mei Lu that they were on a perimeter route circling around to some of the wealthiest subdivisions. One stop on the route would probably be near the Lings' place.

Forcing her brain to cooperate, Mei Lu still couldn't make head nor tail of Cullen's information from Interpol. They were aware that Stephen was going to be summoned home by his father. Therefore Cullen's friend, Brett, and Cullen were wrong in thinking that the courier she now had in her sights planned to meet up with her brother.

Mei Lu found it difficult to take any but shallow breaths. Did Cullen's repeated apologies mean he'd changed his mind about believing in her dad's innocence? She longed to phone him back and sort everything out, but she didn't dare. Tears burned her eyes. There had to be a missing link. Mei Lu would stake her very life on her father's sincerity. But she hadn't asked him again if he'd found anything out about the clients he no longer served.

Twenty minutes later, still trying to fit together the pieces, Mei Lu saw the courier disembark within walking distance of the back entry to her family's gated community. She wanted to vomit.

For moments, nothing worked. Not her legs, her brain or her lungs. She let the driver shut the bus doors and drive off. Suddenly, something clicked, prodding her to remember who and what she was. A proud, dedicated servant of the law who had graduated from the Police Academy with honors and with honor.

Yanking the cord, she managed to have the driver stop in the middle of the next block.

It was just as well, she decided, because otherwise the courier would surely have noticed that she'd been on each of the buses he'd ridden. Now, oblivious to being followed, he marched straight up to the gate guard and passed the guard a note of some kind. Presumably someone had authorized the man to enter the complex.

She kept within the long shadows cast by leafy trees. When the man with the box nervously glanced behind him, she darted behind a sprawling butterfly bush that needed trimming. Mei searched her own purse for identification that would allow her in the gate. If she'd ever doubted where her suspect was headed, her hopes were dashed when he casually hopped a fence that would place him in her parents' parklike backyard. A yard she could picture, landscaped with a stream, a pagoda designed for meditation and a pond filled with good-luck goldfish. Mei's heart skidded erratically. How could she have been so *wrong* about her father?

Mei approached the guard and flipped open her badge. He was new and didn't know her on sight. It took a moment to make him understand the urgency of the situation. "I need you to call 911 and request that a squad car be sent to this address." She hastily wrote her parents' house number on the shocked guard's clipboard. "Tell the dispatcher that you have an officer in need of assistance. This is my badge number," Mei said. Her fingers grew stronger and held the pen straighter as duty crowded past heartbreak. She had to follow the courier—now.

Though she wore slacks, she had no intention of climbing a fence. Besides, she needed the time it'd take to walk to the front door, needed it to brush the remaining cobwebs from her addled brain.

Two houses from the one where she'd spent her childhood, Mei Lu opened her cell phone and punched in Cullen's number. "You were right and I was wrong," she said brokenly the minute he answered. "I'm facing my father's house. Our courier's inside."

"God, Mei Lu! You can't—you're not going in alone?" Cullen's voice sounded raw, but that barely registered with Mei Lu.

"I have to," she said. "But don't worry. Police backup's on the way."

"Listen," he was saying. "I can be there in five minutes. I'm—"

She hung up, not wanting to hear yet another apology, or him ordering her to wait. Technically, she supposed he could, as this was originally his case. She stowed her phone and began what seemed an endless walk to the door.

She couldn't wait. Someone had to witness the transfer of the stolen goods. Besides, she needed to be the one to say to her father what burned inside her. She felt so horribly betrayed.

Unlocking the familiar front door, Mei slipped inside. The house seemed unnaturally still. Then she heard voices echoing down the hall. Cantonese. A man, whose voice she didn't recognize, sounded loud and argumentative. The voice that answered checked Mei Lu's forward motion. Not her father, as she'd braced herself for. *Her mother.*

Mei flew into a greater panic. The courier must have shown up on the wrong day. Her father would never leave her mother to deal with anything so unsavory.

Riddled now with fear, Mei Lu burst into the elegantly appointed summer room. It had long been her mother's favorite domain—a room Aun's children rarely entered because she'd filled it with delicate Chinese things. Silk wall tapestries and polished furnishings carved from a rare hardwood, *huanghuali.* A jade collection that surpassed any Mei had ever seen. In her haste, she bumped an intricate, lacquerware chest. The sudden noise startled the two people engaged in a shouting match.

Mei Lu skidded to a shaky stop. The man, of course, was the one she'd tailed here from her side of town. In another setting, Mei would never have recognized her mother. Aun Wong Ling's hair was slicked into its usual knot, but her face was powdered and slashed with dark paint. Neck to toe, she was attired in a crimson silk robe. Wide sleeves shimmered inside with ice-white lining. The same pristine hue was repeated in an exquisitely detailed, fearsome tiger stretching down the entire front of the robe.

Between the angry pair stood the open box the courier had brought. Mei recognized an ancient, painted earthenware figure known to museum-goers as The Female Servant, a piece purported to be the oldest ever excavated from the Tomb of Lou Rui in Shanxi province. It was near the top of the list of stolen artifacts in price and prominence.

"Mother!" Mei squeaked in a voice more quavery than knees that might not hold her for long. "What's the meaning of this?"

Aun first looked stunned. Then an expression Mei could only describe as cunning crossed her face. "Way Shen, this is my daughter. The very one who will become your wife. She will be more beautiful once you return with her to Beijing and manage to dress her properly."

"Wife? Mother, what nonsense! Who is this person? How do you even know him?"

"She is the woman who followed me," Way Shen shouted excitedly, switching from Cantonese to Mandarin. "This is not the docile wife you promised me, White Tiger Queen."

Mei's head exploded in pain as the couple continued to bicker as if she didn't exist. "Stop it!" she demanded, first in Cantonese, then in Mandarin. Surprisingly they both did, although her mother's lips thinned almost cruelly. "I am not going anywhere, especially not to Beijing. On the contrary, Mother. But *you* are going to explain why you're in possession of stolen Chinese art."

"I've helped my brother recover a good share of the former Wong fortunes," she said in a conversational voice. "He always told me that you, Daughter, would not go quietly. You will need to use something to calm her, Way Shen. I hope you came prepared."

"Are you deaf?" Mei Lu clenched both hands at her sides and advanced a step into the room. "Can't you hear the sirens? Mother, for heaven's sake, stop trying to ship me off with this awful man!" Mei knew that she sounded close to hysterical.

"Seize her!" Aun ordered. "The stupid girl has notified the police. I knew I should have ended my operation when your last messenger tried to extort more money than I agreed to pay. Or if not then, when my oh-so-honorable husband managed to convince the authorities he's too upstanding to have taken part in our very profitable triad. Mine! It's all *my* scheme." She pounded her breast. "I have restored the house of Wong, and I will implicate Michael. For daring to buy me. For daring to rip me away from everything I ever loved." Her laughter held an edge of madness. "Seize her! Take her away. That one's not worthy to be her mother's child."

Only Mei Lu's finely honed reflexes saved her from Way Shen's lunge. Crista's patient kung fu training helped her avoid his second attempt, too. She drew power from the earth. The moves were all automatic, because her mind, her heart and her body were far from centered.

She danced out of reach during his second grab and managed to jab him hard in the ribs. The unexpected attack brought the heavy man crashing to the carpet. Crista would've been proud of that move. Disconnected thoughts raced through Mei Lu's brain. She felt detached from everything around her.

In the distance she registered that not one police car but two had drawn up out front. Uniforms swarmed toward her down the hall. She saw Cullen in the middle of the pack. Mei Lu's heart rejoiced merely to see him, although she wished she could have saved him from witnessing this... the most terrible of dishonors.

Cullen immediately reached for her, and she landed against his chest. But she was given no time to take even small pleasure in his comforting touch. It all seemed to happen at once. An officer Mei recognized bent to snap cuffs on the still-writhing Way Shen, who'd had the wind knocked out of him by her blow.

Cullen swore succinctly and attempted to pull Mei Lu aside. Not soon enough. She saw her mother straighten, and for a heartbeat their eyes met. Aun sent Mei Lu a withering glare. Helpless, pinioned as she was in Cullen's grasp, Mei Lu watched in horror and disbelief as her mother removed a wicked-looking stiletto knife with a flowered cloisonné handle from the voluminous sleeve of her blood-red robe.

"Mei Lu, don't...look," Cullen shouted, his voice coming at her from afar. "Knife," he choked out to an officer, as Mei Lu struggled to get free.

A chubby sergeant blocking the exit reacted. He pulled his Smith & Wesson and aimed it at the woman holding the knife.

"No, no, no!" Mei Lu screamed, lashing out with a foot to knock his weapon aside.

"Mother, don't," she begged. "It's over. Put down the knife. Let me phone Father. We'll get you help. And Stephen. Stephen will be here soon. You won't want him to see you like this." Mei all but dangled lifelessly from Cullen's strong hands. She tried to spread her own in supplication.

"Bah! You're both too much your father's weak offspring," Aun snorted. "My brothers understand the difference between wisdom and foolishness," she added haughtily. Then, lightning fast, before anyone in the room could read her real intent, she turned the stiletto with both hands and jammed it hard through the snarling mouth of the white tiger that flowed along her robe.

"Nooo!" Mei heard her own cries.

Cullen's fingers went limp and he released her, allowing her to spring forward.

Mei caught Aun as she crumpled slowly to the floor, the red of her blood blossoming flower-like at first, then quickly seeping outward to soak the snowy silk tapestry of the tiger's head.

"Call the medics," Cullen yelled. "Get an ambulance! Mei, don't do this to yourself."

She cradled her mother's head on her knees. Aun's last words were all Mei Lu heard. "Remind Michael of his last promise to my father. I won't be buried in this land, but in China where my soul belongs."

The woman—the mother—Mei Lu didn't know at all slumped to the side, and Mei, who'd seen death in her early days as a street cop, knew it was too late for medics.

Inside she cried. Outside, she let nothing show. In that way she was her mother's daughter. She teetered on the verge of cracking, but she refused to break down before her peers. She saw the horror on their faces. Saw how everyone in the room stepped back—waiting for what? For her to follow her mother into madness?

Only Cullen acted. He came up behind her and tried to

loosen her hold on her mother's body. Poor Cullen, he must not be aware of how his name could be dragged through the mud with hers in tomorrow's paper.

Shaking off his soothing hands, Mei Lu pulled together the tattered edges of her pride. She could do this, separate herself from the scene—and from Cullen. It was for his own good, and for his children with whom she'd also fallen in love.

She rose and gave a toneless statement to the ranking lieutenant. A homicide team materialized out of nowhere. For their records, Mei Lu repeated everything that had occurred from the time she boarded the first bus. "This man is Way Shen," she said. "He and my mother were working together in an international smuggling ring, along with at least one of her brothers in Kowloon. She has three. Their goal seemed to be to restore the lost Wong fortunes."

Mei Lu paced the room, touching her mother's false treasures. Behind a silk trifold screen, she found the Heavenly King and various other museum pieces. "Interpol has a list of these." She waved a hand that shook. Clasping both hands in front of her again, she blurted everything she knew, keeping the Wu and Hsiao names out of her report.

Cullen watched from the other side of the room. Mei Lu seemed all right. *Too* all right. Any minute he expected her to collapse in tears. It wasn't a good thing to be so self-possessed. He ought to get her out of there, and certainly intended to keep an eye on her. But then a squad car brought Michael Ling. He didn't fare half so well as his daughter and broke down crying.

Over the next hour, as Homicide signed the scene off to another unit, who listed Aun's death as suicide, Brett Davis's envoy arrived with Stephen Ling in tow.

In the ensuing chaos, Cullen lost track of Mei Lu. After

another hour had passed, during which he brought Brett's partner up-to-date, Cullen discovered that one of the officers had authorized Mei Lu to leave the house. No one could tell him where she'd gone. Not the cops. Not her father nor her brother. She wasn't answering her phone at home or her cell.

She'd simply vanished.

CHAPTER FIFTEEN

FRANTIC, CULLEN plied Mei's father with questions about where she might be.

"She expressed a need to be busy," Michael said, sounding disconnected. "Perhaps she's gone to make funeral arrangements."

"I doubt that very much," Cullen responded. "Her mother's last words were that you'd promised your father-in-law you'd see Aun buried next to her family."

Michael flushed and wiped his eyes for about the thousandth time, then said haltingly, "I knew Aun had never fully adjusted to living here. I was blind as to how deep her hatred ran...of America...and of me. I loved her from the moment I set eyes on her photograph. She was so beautiful. Unspoiled." A tremor shook his body. His son, taller by a head, slung a bracing arm around his father. "All I ever wanted was to make life perfect for her."

"Let me take care of getting her back to China, Father. I've met two of her sisters, and I like them. Her brothers could well be involved in this evil triad. I've never trusted them. In their bitterness, I feared they'd turn Mother against me. And my sister, as well..."

Cullen stiffened. "That's not true. Mei Lu loves you. She's worried sick that you had a hand in this smuggling, Stephen."

"Me?" Stephen wore a shocked expression. "I've been working undercover with Hong Kong law enforcement, to try to trace the path of the stolen goods. The woman my family thinks is my fiancée is really a member of the Beijing police. They cleared me and our gallery weeks ago." He turned sheepish eyes on his father. "Father's name headed everyone's original lists as the number-one link. But I knew he couldn't be involved. The Hong Kong police cooked up the idea of my phony engagement, hoping to entice him to come and meet his prospective daughter-in-law. They wanted to judge, by Asian standards, his guilt or innocence." Stephen's laugh was off-key. "Who would ever have suspected Mother? While all of us were suspecting each other, Aun and her brothers were busy ruining us. One of them holds *guanxi* for many immigrant families— that's how the couriers operated. And it's how they must have been killed." He took a deep breath. "Father, we'll have to liquidate Ling Limited."

Cullen frowned. "The shame falls on only one."

"That's not how it works in the Asian community. Ask Mei Lu. She'll tell you the shame brought by one in the family taints us all. I don't envy you, Archer, trying to convince her differently. You love my sister, don't you? I can see you do. It's written all over your face."

"I do love her. Michael. Stephen." Cullen bowed. "I plan to marry her. I hope we have your blessing, even though I know this is a terrible time to ask for it."

Michael nodded dully.

Stephen clasped Cullen's hand. "You'll have your work cut out for you. If I know Mei Lu, she'll quit her job and fade from the life of everyone this might hurt. She hates disharmony. That's why she opted out of Ling Limited. Life is black and white for Mei Lu. Gray areas don't exist."

"I can't believe she'd quit the police force. She loves it. And she's good."

Stephen Ling merely arched a brow. "I'm a betting man, Archer. And I'm betting that's what Little Sister is doing right now. Saving everyone she knows from guilt by association."

Cullen didn't believe the arrogant man who thought he knew Mei Lu so well. But he wasn't willing to take the chance that Stephen might be right. "Like I said before, I love her with all my heart. Maybe Chinese marriage vows don't contain the words 'for better or for worse.' Ours do. I intend to make Mei Lu understand what those words mean."

Excusing himself, Cullen ran straight to his car and headed downtown to police headquarters.

It hurt him to learn that Mei Lu's brother did know her best. Cullen ran her to ground in Catherine Tanner's office. He burst in and saw Mei Lu's badge and her Taser already lying between her and the chief in the middle of Catherine's desk.

Both women glanced up with startled looks when Cullen barged in. Though Mei Lu appeared pale and drawn, Cullen saw only her substance. Her grit. Rushing forward, he knelt beside her chair and held her eyes with a look of love as he reached for her hands.

"Thank goodness the cavalry's arrived," Catherine exclaimed. "I hope you can help me talk some sense into her."

"That's my aim. Sweetheart," he said softly. "None of you—not your father, not your brother—need to take on the sins of your mother. She was sick. Even your dad admitted she's been unhappy for a very long time."

"Why did you come, Cullen? This doesn't concern you. You have the children. Think of them. Think how knowing what my mother is, what she did, will affect them."

"I love you. They love you. Well," he said, screwing up

his face, "Belinda loves you. Bobby's coming around. I told him about your promise to teach him Chinese paper art. He's interested. Please tell me you aren't planning to disappoint him."

Her lips turned down. "How horrified will he be when he finds out my mother's a thief and a…murderer? That's the legacy I'd bring to your family."

"Bobby's never met her. And at the moment he feels let down by his own mother."

"The two aren't comparable, Cullen. To make matters worse, rather than stand up and face her deeds, Mother committed the most cowardly act of all—suicide."

"Correct me if I'm wrong, but doesn't Chinese history say the way to wipe clean the family slate is to fall on one's sword, so to speak?"

"I suppose," she mumbled. "But that's ancient history, and the men written about were warriors. Anyway, this isn't China. I guarantee the news media won't paint her act as honorable. You have no idea what people will say behind my back. Other cops, even. Who'll trust me?" She sucked in her lower lip and turned to Catherine. "Tell him. We know how everyone avoided Risa. Me included, I'm ashamed to say."

The chief brought the tips of her fingers together. "Totally different circumstances. I'm not saying rumors won't fly. They will. For a while. Until the next disaster befalls our community. Mei Lu, I know who you are. I know the kind of officer you are. And with the mayor and city manager ready to fire me over false charges of missing evidence, witness tampering and the like, I need every good officer I can hang on to. You've done nothing wrong, Mei Lu. Nothing."

"But in spite of everything, I loved her." Tears flowed down Mei Lu's face.

"Of course you did. And Bobby and Belinda love Jana despite all her faults. That's okay." Cullen rose, bringing her with him. He rubbed her shoulders and her neck, feeling relief when her tears subsided and he felt her tension slowly began to dissipate. "How much time is she allowed for bereavement?" he asked Catherine, although he never took his eyes off the woman he held.

"Two weeks. I can swing more. I understand the funeral will be in China. That'll take some arranging." Catherine tapped the eraser end of a pencil on her desk calendar. "Take thirty days if you need it, Mei Lu. I'll justify it by digging up another reason."

"Is getting married a good reason?" This from Cullen. "A respectable two weeks after your mother's funeral," he rushed to assure Mei Lu.

"What about my brother's investigation?" Surfacing, Mei Lu wiped her eyes.

"Oh, that…" He quickly filled her in on how Stephen was helping the Hong Kong police. "Maybe he'll attend our wedding." Cullen let the statement hang in the air.

"Was that a proposal?" Catherine asked excitedly, snapping forward in her chair.

Mei Lu turned slightly. "Shouldn't that be my question, Catherine?"

Cullen smiled, feeling he was making progress. "I have your father's and brother's blessings. I spoke to the twins at length this morning. And it appears that your boss thinks marrying me is a good idea. You're the only holdout, Mei Lu."

"Oh, but to have a wedding on the heels of this…" She waved a hand vacantly. "I'd be too mortified to invite anyone. And what if I did and they were too embarrassed to show up?"

Cullen thought he saw a glimmer of hope edge out the

misery swimming in her eyes. "We could slip off somewhere. Just the two of us."

"Go away where? Elope, you mean?"

"Why not? Marriage mainly concerns two people. Hawaii's a nice stopover on the way home from China." Cullen rubbed the ends of her hair between his thumb and forefinger. "I love you, Mei Lu. You said you loved me. Who else do we need at our wedding?"

"The twins. I'd want them involved, Cullen. I grew up in a divided home. I'd want us to start out right, as a family."

"I think that can be arranged. I have a friend I'm sure will watch Foo. And Freda's due a vacation. I doubt she'd object to chaperoning the twins to Hawaii and herding them around a beach resort for a few days while I honeymoon with my bride."

Ever so slowly, hope erased the dramatic lines that had bracketed Mei Lu's mouth. "If you're sure…"

Cullen bent his head and unerringly found her lips.

Mei saw the sheen in his eyes, a sure indication of what he felt in his heart.

It wouldn't have been a short kiss, either, except that the chief leaped to her feet. Grabbing each by an arm, she ushered the couple to the door. "These matters are better finalized privately—away from the eyes of onlookers. Consider the paperwork for your leave under way, Lieutenant Ling. When I see you again, I'll expect you to be refreshed and ready to do justice to your next assignment. As a personal aside, I'm so very sorry for your tragic loss. But death is a part of life. You and I both know it. So is change. You're starting a new chapter in your life. Embrace it and enjoy every minute, Mei Lu."

Mei finally shared a secret smile with Cullen as she clasped Catherine's hands. "I can't thank you enough for your understanding. Will you do me a favor? Tell Risa, Lucy, Abby and Crista about this. Say that when I return to duty, I'm going to do everything in my power to make sure things get back to normal between us. I'll write them each a note, as well."

Catherine nodded.

"Chief, you've been there for me from the day I first broke with Ling tradition. You have my word that I'll do my best always to be worthy of your faith in me.

"And Cullen…" Mei Lu turned and lightly traced two fingers over his lips, then followed the outline of his solid jaw. "The same goes for you. Now and for always. I give you my love. And my word."

Turn the page for an excerpt from
A MOTHER'S VOW,
the final book in our series,
WOMEN IN BLUE.

This exciting conclusion by K. N. Casper tells
Catherine Tanner's story. The police chief is confronted by a case that might be connected to her
husband's death a year ago....

A MOTHER'S VOW is available in March 2005.

CHAPTER ONE

"MOTHER, I think this man was murdered."

Catherine Tanner's head snapped up from the police reports she'd been reviewing. She had been only half listening to her daughter rambling on about her preparations to teach second grade in the coming school year.

"What are you talking about, dear? Who?"

Kelsey held up the morning *Houston Sentinel* and pointed to an obituary. "This man, William Summers. I think he may have been murdered."

"William Summers," Catherine muttered as she accepted the newspaper. "Is the name supposed to mean something to me?" She scanned the death notice. The sixty-seven-year-old retired teamster had died after languishing in a coma for the past year, following a fall from his roof.

"He's the man who told Dad about the missing uranium."

Evoking the memory of Jordan had a predictable effect. Catherine felt herself pulling inward, withdrawing from the conversation.

"What missing uranium?" She felt like a straight man in a very bad knock-knock joke, parroting everything her daughter said.

"We were having lunch at the deli around the corner from his office when this guy came over and told Dad the numbers in that day's lead article were wrong. There should have been sixty barrels of yellowcake in the warehouse on the waterfront that the Superfund was cleaning up, not forty.

Yellowcake. The first step in enriching uranium for nuclear reactors—or weapons. Its potential, especially in the wrong hands, made it a commodity that needed very careful guarding and tracking.

"How did Summers know that?" Catherine asked.

"He said he was the warehouse foreman when the place closed in '77 and the last one out the door. He insisted there'd been sixty barrels of uranium stored there."

As editor of the city's largest newspaper, Jordan had been meticulous about ensuring the accuracy of his information.

"What was your father's reaction?"

"He asked him if he had any proof. Summers claimed he did, so Dad jotted his name, address and telephone number in his pad, thanked him and said he'd be in touch."

Catherine glanced at the picture on her desk, the one taken two years ago when the mayor swore her in as police chief of the country's fourth-largest city. The unmistakable pride in the smile on Jordan's face as he stood behind her threatened now to bring fresh tears. She blinked them back ruthlessly, ashamed of her momentary inability to cope with the loss of the man she'd loved so deeply.

"Why haven't you ever mentioned this before?" she asked.

Kelsey screwed up her mouth. "Because Dad died right after that and I had other things on my mind." She rushed on to add, "Besides, you know I rarely get to read the paper anymore. I wouldn't even have thought of it now if I hadn't noticed the obit on your desk and recognized the name."

Catherine cleared her throat. "I still don't understand why you think this man Summers was murdered."

Kelsey snorted. "Well, let's see. He blows the whistle

on a cache of uranium missing from an abandoned ware-house in front of a bunch of people, claims he can prove it, and that very night he falls off his roof. The timing doesn't strike you as a bit strange?"

"But that was a year ago—" Catherine picked up the newspaper and scanned the article again "—and he only died yesterday."

"Without ever regaining consciousness."

"A year-long murder? It's a stretch, Kel."

"Aren't you the one who's always telling me coincidences are in themselves suspect?"

"I'm a cop," Catherine reminded her daughter. "It's my job to be suspicious. But if I investigated every coincidence, I wouldn't have time for anything else." She slipped from behind her desk. "Let's get out of here before someone comes charging in with a reason for me to stay. We haven't had lunch together in ages—"

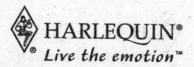

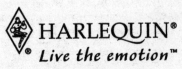

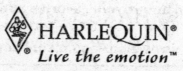

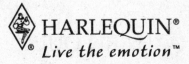

HARLEQUIN *Super***ROMANCE**

WELCOME TO *Crystal Creek*

If this is your first visit to the friendly ranching town located in the Texas Hill Country, get ready to meet some unforgettable people. If you've been here before, you'll recognize old friends...and make some new ones.

WILD HORSES
by Bethany Campbell
(Harlequin Superromance #1261)
On sale in March 2005
Wild horses might be the only things that could drag Mickey Nightingale into another disastrous relationship—especially one with Adam Duran. He has a secret that threatens the ranch of Carolyn Trent, a woman who happens to be Mickey's boss and the only mother she's ever really had.

MEET ME IN TEXAS
by Sandy Steen
(Harlequin Superromance #1271)
On sale in April 2005
When Del Rickman leaves the FBI, he can think of no better place to start his new life than Crystal Creek. Years ago he worked a kidnapping case here and never forgot the town or the people. He's surprised to learn that his new career has put him in opposition with his neighbors!

Available wherever Harlequin Superromance books are sold.

HARLEQUIN®
Live the emotion™